A BOLDER VIEW

CRISTOPHER MANN

First originally published by Parker Publishers 2026

ISBN 978-1-970751-68-0 (HB)
ISBN 978-1-970751-67-3 (PB)
ISBN 978-1-970751-66-6 (digital)

Printed in the United States of America

Series Reference Note (for readers)

Before you begin, note that this novel is part of an ongoing Cold War espionage thriller series. If you've not yet read it, start with *Simonson's Gambit* (Book One), where the first moves of this dangerous game were set in motion. The book you hold now continues that story. And keep your eyes on the horizon: *The Second Coming* (Book Three in the series) is coming soon. Expect betrayals to deepen, alliances to be tested, and the shadows of the Cold War to stretch into the present day.

DEDICATION

To all my friends, family and especially my wonderful wife. Buckets of thanks for going out and putting up with me and all my little bug-a-boos that irritate even the most patient of loved ones. You have championed me and my efforts all these many years, and I am forever grateful. Finally, a humungous shout-out to my 6th-grade teacher, Mrs Warren. You were the one to encourage me to read early on with all your little games and rewards. If I could locate you, I would thank you personally!

Table of Contents

PROLOGUE

It is 1950, and the world has changed. Only five years removed from the Second World War, the United States finds itself inching toward another conflict. The Cold War is in its infancy, and most countries, including the United States, seem to be playing nice but secretly vie for the riches and knowledge that remained of the spoils following the previous war.

The science of destructive and preventive measures, along with those who can understand and apply it, has been claimed and hidden by the largest and most powerful players. Everything is guarded carefully, intended to keep them ahead. Those who succeed in mastering it, gain a leg up in the fight for geopolitical world domination.

But it would not be the greater powers of an established but recovering Russia, or a secluded and strengthening China, who each had already strengthened considerably since the end of the war. It would ultimately be the North Korean war machine that would use a war-weary world as an opportunity to expand. The communist nation would ultimately take the first step forward in their attempt to dominate and reunite with their southern counterpart.

A move fully interpreted as a proxy for the much larger communist countries of Russia and China, the Korean nation has drawn the scrutiny of not just the United States, but the world in general. More importantly, those who hide behind their conglomerates and vast bank accounts, controlling the stealth group Otter One, have also turned their attention toward Korea. Unsanctioned, that outlier group and their covert operatives would be heavily involved in determining who wins.

Otter One's newest asset, Zachary Ransom, is now twenty— just twelve months after the Simonson affair and freshly through his essential training. He's in need of a well-deserved hiatus—it's not going to happen. His world will soon be extended across the Atlantic and to the shores of Spain, where he will start the real journey of being a covert agent. There, chaos will once again force its diabolical way into his life, and he must respond as only he can.

CHAPTER ONE

A CONTINUING JOURNEY

June 1, 1950 –

Western shore of Oahu, Hawaii

EVERY ROLL and ripple of the warm Pacific that gently ebbed its watery foam up to tickle his toes… made him smile. It was a genuine smile and one that had not come so easily just a few weeks before—but here it was. Warm sand, a bright sun shining, and a gentle trade wind caressing his face and sweeping away any recent calamities brought on by others.

Zach had already blown through nearly twelve months since the Simonson affair, with the whirlwind year going by so quickly that he could hardly remember the initial months of training. Jack Tanner had told him that he would definitely be going back to school, and with scholarship offers already from M.I.T. and Harvard, it had been difficult to delay that part of his life for a whole year, but there would have been no way to have navigated both. The Otter One training had to come first, and it did with a vengeance.

He joined Otter One alongside two other new recruits. Apart from two brief days of orientation, the training demands over the next ten months were nearly overwhelming. One woman and one man, both slightly older and given no names, had been recruited separately.

Zach guessed the man was about twenty-four or twenty-five. He nearly quit in the second week after passing out on a twenty-mile jog, only continuing after being helped and encouraged to finish the final two miles. But his determination to complete the program was firm, so only a little encouragement was needed.

The woman, however, was something else entirely—intense, silent, and unyielding. She wore loose-fitting clothes and a hat that hid her face, but even so, Zach could tell she was pretty.

Conversations, especially of a personal nature, were discouraged among the three candidates. However, from their little exchanges, Zach sensed he would like the guy and was certain that he would get it together to finish the program. If not, failure came with quiet but serious consequences: a long debriefing, a handshake to swear secrecy, and a check—five thousand dollars, nearly a third more than the average American earned in a year.

However, the check could, and would be confiscated, along with some form of unsanctioned punishment, if one chose not to follow the rules and divulge anything about the program. Zach wasn't sure exactly what the "unsanctioned" part meant, but it was delivered sternly and with no smile attached. The words "with prejudice" seemed ominous.

Along with the less-is-more mantra of Otter One, they each roomed and ate separately during the following ten months and, again, were only allowed to speak with each other while in training. The names allowed were "Texas" for the gal, which she quickly demanded to be shortened to Tex, and "Montana" for the man. Zach was "George," and he surmised this was short for Georgia, and he hated it— thinking he looked nothing like a George.

He was also required, even under the sweltering southern sun, to wear baggy clothes. Several times during training, the relentless pressure from instructors and fellow recruits had caused his muscles to tense and swell beyond what he could easily conceal—an exhibition of strength he had no intention of explaining. To everyone else, he already seemed well-built and formidable, but they had no inkling of the full power he could command.

The training had been rough, and a few weeks in, it had occurred to him that he had been challenged aggressively more than the other two recruits. At least that was how it had felt at the time. So much so that when the final day came with just a handshake and little fanfare, followed only by the acknowledgement that he appeared ready, he had been respectfully requested to move up the unseen ladder with only his handler, Jack Tanner as his conduit.

It was quickly accommodated by those who supported him, and off he went with a hastily thrown-together rucksack on the first commercial flight out. At no time did he ask, or was even allowed to ask, about the others. It was only mentioned that at some point, they may run into each other or possibly work together.

And at that time, all would be perceived to be seasoned agents, they could choose when, how, and how much, they would want to give away information about themselves. Protocol would not be strictly enforced, but it was strongly emphasized that their individual lives could be affected, and for that reason, it would be to each his own. They would be the ones at risk.

Zach closed his eyes and then let his head fall backward—giving way for the full force of the tropical noon sun to radiate his face. His bent elbows were propping him up while his legs sprawled forward and wide, as he let his mind wander over all the corner recesses that held his past and his current position. His life in the last few years had moved quickly, and unequivocally, more than he could have ever expected.

The summer had arrived on the island along with its humidity, and there had been rumblings amongst the locals about the Hawaiian island chain eventually becoming the next state of the union. Many thought it could still be years away, but the talk and debates had started.

It had been of little interest, though, to Zach because all that he was currently interested in was a much-needed vacation. Only two weeks removed from his arduous and extensive training, he had been due for a long time away from the rigors put on him. The Simonson mission that he had been unceremoniously thrown into had taken a toll on him and others, both physically and mentally.

When it was clear a break was deserved and necessary, his original hometown on Oahu, and much to the chagrin of his auntie Emma back in Savannah, had been his first and only choice. She had unsuccessfully argued with her need to see him; one, because she really just wanted to see her nephew, then also, and this was a more selfish reason, so she could enlighten the hens back home, who had always shown an interest in the handsome Zachary—*as if one of them would ever have a chance*, she would say. Ultimately, though, she had acquiesced to a visit after his downtime.

After arriving and settling in, he spent much of the first week sleeping, rarely rolling out of bed before noon. Only then, as he stretched and recalibrated his well-being, would his mind drain the previous drama away, clearing the way for taking stock. First thoughts always seemed to be of his once-steady girlfriend, Jenny Mathews. She—and everything she had endured for someone so young and naïve—had never truly recovered from the ordeal. And although she professed a love for him, at the insistence of her parents, and following her six months of intense therapy, she had made the difficult decision to move away to attend college at Penn State up in "Happy Valley"—a dubious name to be sure.

Not so far, he assumed, that her parents couldn't keep tabs on their precious daughter but also just far enough from him affording her. She had admitted that it gave her an opportunity to clear her head of the traumatic experience. Attending Penn State also gave her the understanding of not really understanding what Zach and all these other characters, that had suddenly come into the picture, had going on; kidnapping, torture, murder, and pure mayhem on the list.

No one had been forthcoming with answers, and that had been understandably unacceptable. Zach's Aunt Emma, on the opposite side and with an inner toughness that he had pegged her as having all along, compartmentalized and appeared relatively normal within days. While enjoying her renewed relationship with her recovering sister and Zach's mother, Abigail, she had consoled and mentored him until training started.

"You are still quite young with plenty of frolic in you coming," he remembered her saying in her strong southern accent. His mother had readily agreed, then added, "No one knows the timing of healing, Zachary. She may indeed return to your life at some point. Close no doors."

He remembered giving that scenario a lot of thought and wondering whether it could be true. Then, as the days turned into weeks of hardcore physical and weapons training, followed by midnight to dawn study of profiling and procedure, it had become much harder to focus on what he had lost. And with the process, Jenny had slowly faded away.

By the end of that first week, he had found solace in his thoughts. The early afternoons became Deja vu experiences as he found himself settling in the same location where he now lounged, giving much of his early meditation to the cove just five miles down the shore where it all started for him nine years before.

Instinctively, and his eyes still closed, he reached down and gently ran his fingers over the now tiny puncture scars on his left calf—it was still not fully understood but the miss-shaped pieces of the puzzle were continually forming. Someone had buried plutonium not so very far from this very beach, followed by another calamity that allowed its crated danger to escape which, in turn, created an odd domino effect that adversely changed the growth and strength of the local crustaceans for just a single generation.

Then, one such crab pierced him somehow. Something crabs just don't do—chaos again. For nearly a decade, this was where the trail for the past years had led him. This was the only logical reason for his strength and size. Doctor Rivera had put it together—he knew, but nobody would listen. Or they all knew and wanted it buried.

How it all worked, the metamorphosis wasn't clear or exacting—again, just chaos. The outcome had made him stronger, running faster and never tiring until others were miles behind and dropping from exhaustion. His mind, though, could not have been affected. He had always been sharp. He had always paid attention to people and his surroundings—he had always been smart.

Being kind and humble had come from his parents' teaching, but he sensed he had drifted away from that twelve-year-old person. Sudden confusion and death had had its affect. And he certainly had developed a smart-ass mentality since hanging around Jack Tanner, but somehow that had made it fun.

Zach sighed with the thought as he slowly opened his eyes. Squinting at first to adjust to the searing glare, he cupped his hand over to shield his eyes and gazed out over the deep-blue ocean to where a cloudless, light-blue line of the sky cut sharply into the horizon. Off to his left and a mile out, was a fishing trawler lazily bobbing up and down in the gentle chop, obviously settled on where the nets were to be thrown. To his closer-in-right, more action was happening.

A slew of both young and middle-aged men on what appeared to him to be nothing more than large makeshift wooden boards that resembled flattened hulls of canoes were attempting to stand and float atop small breaking waves—they were all in various levels of having a tough time with the balancing act.

He was thinking that they didn't seem to mind, though. In fact, they all, and with few exceptions appearing in their deep-tanned skins and being mostly a mix of full-blooded, traditional Hawaiians and a few mutts, were all smiling joyously amid the occasional raucous laughter with each canoe rider's feeble attempt. Zach sensed their beings were in tune with whatever gods they praised, and he somehow wished he could be like them—part of the "not a care in the world" family. *How wonderful to have that mindset*, he mused.

He took in a deep, refreshing lungful of the sweet ocean breeze and then slowly let it out. Then, looking away and back out to the trawler, he blindly reached for what was left of his beer. Taking a swig, he grimaced then poured out what remained when he realized he had left it exposed too long in the sun, then crushed the tin can with his powerful hand. *An easy, recovering morning*, he thought as he stood.

Cupping one hand over his eyes, he squinted back at the men with their boards and let out a laugh when one rider unceremoniously flipped over in the most hilariously awkward fashion, then got wiped out by the ferocious crashing wave he had been trying to ride. A few seconds later, the man regained his footing, appearing no worse for wear. He waved an "I'm okay" to his friends, retrieved his board, drove it through another incoming wave, and began paddling back out.

I wonder if I could do that? Zach said to himself through an involuntary chuckle. After giving himself a silent reassurance that he certainly could, if pressed to try, he turned and casually pushed through the soft sand, curling his toes deep to propel him back up to the purple and white, Plumeria-covered path that led to his little shanty.

The humble and traditional domicile with a thatched roof and open-sashed storm windows, had been a secluded gift provided by some never-to-be known facilitator from Otter One. It had been quietly leased for him for the previous effort made on the Simonson affair, and as a reward for joining up and going through the rigours of training.

Whoever made the arrangement had made sure the bungalow had been well appointed and stocked for his pleasure. A comfortable down-filled bed was welcomed and plenty of beer, wine, along with assorted alcoholic beverages filled the standalone bar. The bed was cherished, but for him, none of the various alcoholic beverages had reached an acquired taste yet. He had never touched wine, and when Coke-a-Cola was not within arm's length, then a beer had been his beverage of choice, when pressed.

It was safe to say, though, that someone wanted him to stay with the organization and were more than willing to show their collective thanks. He, though, was beginning to understand what a commodity he had become. A chess piece to be used, or possibly sacrificed, as required.

Learning just how much he was valued would be something to hang on to if it were ever divulged, but he had learned in his short time that his worth would never be a known quantity and that names would never be attached. Moreover, it was important never to ask.

As he entered through a narrow clearing, brushing away annoying prawns with his arms, he continued through a short canopy of Pygmy Date Palms. Up ahead was the small and private open patio, and a few feet beyond, his pad. He could just see the rattan fan slowly spinning the humidity of its designated airspace through the open slider, and he wondered; it had only been eighteen hours since Jack Tanner had sent the telegram that he was coming, but he hadn't said when, and most certainly didn't explain why. That had made Zach somewhat nervous and wondering if his friend had indeed made it to the island. Again, the slider was open, which was not uncommon for those who lived on the island, but he was fairly certain that he had closed it earlier.

Pushing clear one palm frond that needed pruning, he stepped through the final opening to the rear patio and up onto the teak landing and the bamboo mat used for knocking the sand off. Looking through the open slider where the exposed, small Formica-clad dinette set with chrome edging was positioned just inside, he could see the staging of a single leather briefcase and one manila folder.

A Schlitz beer can, still sweating its frothy coolness, was set nearby. Zach sighed and began wondering whether his downtime had been enough. Before the thought could be completed with an answer, Jack Tanner, twenty-four years Zach's senior, stepped out from an adjoining bedroom wearing knee-high, frayed-edge, denim cut-offs and a white tee-shirt, then, with both arms out to his side, palms up as if to say, "I'm here," he grinned. Then impatiently waiting for some response from his young protégé about his being there, and non-forthcoming, he asked sarcastically, "What? You haven't missed me yet?"

Zach managed an uneven smile back. "Not sure. I may need another day or two," he muttered before plopping down on a weather-beaten sofa.

Jack ignored the comment and walked past Zach and slapped him on the near shoulder on his way to the dinette. Then, sitting down at the table, he took a swig of his beer while reaching for the folder. "A day we don't have, Mr Ransom. Come, and sit."

CHAPTER TWO

THE KOREANS

"De mutatione mundi."

IT WOULD, on any occasion, appear out of place to watch Asian Americans traverse the lush open space between the centuries-old and hallowed halls of Brown University. Liberal and progressive-leaning Providence, Rhode Island, notwithstanding, the world had changed. The aftermath of the Cold War, following the Second World War, was certainly at play. This included the void left when the Japanese vacated their wartime occupation of the Korean territory and their spread of communism.

Tensions had long been rising between the Russian- and Chinese-backed North Korea and the US-backed South Korea. Not to mention, the wartime incarceration of any one of Japanese descent, nine years prior, had marked the beginning of a period during which Asians across the United States were watched closely by suspicious eyes.

Si-Woo Lee and her twin brother, Ji-Hoon, were innocently stuck in the middle of it all. Being born in the United States had not given them any relief, but it did force them to be more aware of their surroundings.

Now, as they walked to class, they kept their collective eyes cast downward while purposely moving along the open corridors, avoiding contact with anyone. Further across the campus, they stayed on the soft grass of Simmons Quadrangle while heading toward Sciences Park and the Biomed Gateway, Lincoln Field building. They only strayed onto any one of the interlinking cobblestone pathways when necessary and when fewer curious eyes stood mingling.

Their parents, already second-generation and much Americanized, were well established in the local high society. Jeoung and Nari Lee had both been graduates themselves. They were also substantial donors to the university, and both spoke perfect English with very little trailing accent. Even this, it seemed, had failed to provide enough clout to escape suspicion. If anything, their intelligence made them even more foreboding, suspicious, and obvious targets from those less inclined to consider consequences.

To that point, just recently, there were two incidents that had raised enough alarm with the family, but apparently weren't enough for the local and campus authorities to take action. The eggs could be cleaned from the front door, and the beheaded mailbox could be restored—college hijinks for sure, the police had said. It would pass. The parents were not convinced and had their own security precautions set in place.

The trip to Seville, Spain, had already been planned and remained important, as it combined vacation time with Jeoung's keynote on mathematics and its applications in the fledgling field of computer technology at the University. Recent suspicious activities, however, had raised safety concerns, leading to curfews and conversations with the children about staying aware of their surroundings.

Now, less than a week in on their one-month trip, the parents had gone missing. The twins had been notified the night before by a knock at the door and badges displaying FBI. Apparently, Jeoung had not shown up for his first lecture, and the bureau had wanted to know why.

Deducing that their parents had been on somebody's watch list, both Ji-Hoon and Si-Woo managed to appear convincingly surprised by the news and admitted that they had not spoken with their parents since first arriving in Madrid, where they had a layover, and again three hours later upon reaching their favorite stay, the Alfonso VIII Hotel in Seville's historic district.

The meeting with the black suits lasted only twenty minutes. The two adult children asked their own questions but received no acceptable answers from the agents. As the FBI men stood to leave, the one who had done most of the talking, Special Agent Robert Dowling, handed a card over with his desk phone number, then advised that the two should stay local and contact him immediately if they had any communication with their parents. As he walked out the door, Agent Dowling left the children one final salvo that there would certainly be more questions forthcoming.

Knowing the parents' wishes would be to muddle forward, the two had a silent breakfast together the next morning, then walked the five tree-lined blocks to the campus. Five minutes later, they had traversed half the distance across the grounds of the private university, and arrived just early enough for only a smattering of students to be found milling about. Ji-Hoon directed his eyes up just enough to catch what was ahead.

He pointed to Si-Woo to cut across and angle toward the Lincoln Field doorway—but it was too late. Three older classmen had already locked in on them and were closing rapidly in an obvious attempt to block the entrance. The smallest of the three, a stout, freckled-faced ginger with a short flat-top, wearing a lettermen's sweater and looking every bit an athlete, put his hand out. "Whoa there, folks! Aren't you heading in the wrong direction?" he said, smiling a less-than-friendly smile.

"Yeah. Didn't you hear? Schools closed today," the tallest of the three chimed in with a tone that indicated he was all in on any trouble coming.

Si-Woo tried to brush by while mumbling, "Going to class," but was immediately grabbed on the arm by the third man. "You weren't listening, *Miss Kimchi.* School's out for you two. You need to be heading in the other direction."

Ji-Hoon, in full protection mode, threw his slight frame forward, but before he could defend his sister, he was pushed hard to the ground. His books and papers went flying every which way and cluttered a ten-foot diameter, as if blown up by a land mine. He slowly brought himself to his knees, gathered his composure, and fixed the glasses that had been knocked loose from his head.

"You'll need to do better than that!" the taller of the three said with a laugh.

Ji-Hoon felt his face flush with anger, and uncharacteristically, he launched himself forward again and burrowed into the laugher's gut, which sent him crashing to the ground. Surprised at the willingness of their target to fight, the other two jumped in to pull Ji-Hoon off.

"Hey! What's going on there?" a man yelled as he neared the altercation, surprising all and causing quick over-the-shoulder looks.

Registering the voice as faculty, Shorty belted out, "Nothing, sir!" The three quickly retreated and dispersed. As they moved hurriedly to get away, Shorty yelled over his shoulder, "Boy tripped over the sidewalk. Guess he wasn't watching where he was going."

The man who conveniently interrupted the confrontation was Professor Patrick Dowd. He quickly pointed at the classman and said, "I know who you are, Stanton!" Then returned to the Koreans.

A staunch conservative teacher of analytics, known to only a few he allowed into his personal life, was also a fair-minded and kind-hearted soul. Knowing better than to attempt to call the men back, he instead focused on helping Ji-Hoon up. "You kids alright?" he asked.

"Thank you, Professor Dowd. We're fine," Ji-Hoon quietly responded. "Like he said. I tripped, that's all."

"Okay then," the professor replied while not buying any of it. "You know that I know your father and mother pretty well, and I won't tolerate any bullying here, or elsewhere, for that matter."

Si-Hoon managed a grateful smile back. "Thank you. Our parents would appreciate that. It has been difficult the past couple of months."

"Yes, I've heard. This business in Korea can't be helped, and people around here should remind themselves of the last time we went to war, and that not everyone with a different skin color is the enemy." Both Ji-Hoon and Si-Woo agreed with nods.

"Your father and I spoke before they left," the professor continued. "He had asked if I could check in on you two, but it turns out that I didn't need to. Were you coming to see me?"

Ji-Hoon nodded. "Yes. We had men from the FBI come to the house last night. They were asking questions."

"I see," Dowd said while giving a nod. "Speaking of which, there is a man here wanting to speak to both of you. He's not FBI, though."

Ji-Hoon and his sister became alert. "Who is he?" Ji-Hoon asked. "Do we have to speak with him?"

"A Mr Scarpino is all he said. Says he's a friend of your parents, but I don't believe him. Seems to know enough about them, though, to make me curious."

The two sibs gave each other a look, and the professor registered the trepidation in their collective eyes. "Look. You don't have to speak to him," he began. "He's given me no credentials, and I'm not inclined to bring you to him. He's in my office waiting right now. You could just go home, and I'll just say you haven't shown for class today."

"Now that wouldn't be a smart thing to do, Professor Dowd," said a voice from behind.

Everyone turned to look. At the doorway, leaning on a wooden cane, was no other than Johnny Scarpino. His disarming yet mischievous grin widened, and his penetrating eyes swept over them like a shroud. The cane had become a constant reminder of the chaos from twelve months earlier, sparked by what Simonson had brought to the table. "Now that we are all here," he said, narrowing his eyes, "let's find somewhere we can talk privately."

CHAPTER THREE

―∾―

BACK IN ACTION

¿A dónde se fueron?

THE LOCKHEED Constellation, or "Connie" as it was called, angled downward and then leveled off, signaling the grueling flight was nearing its merciful end. Ever since takeoff, the four Wright Duplex-Cyclone engines had been humming through the steel carcass like a swarm of pissed-off hornets, and now, seven hours later, Zach was trying to recall if he was actually ever to be able to nod off. He was thinking he may have dozed at one point, but partial dream states can be tricky.

The trip had been long and annoying, with the exception of multiple leg-stretching visits to the onboard latrine: a cubicle so tiny that while standing upright and relieving himself, his elbows touched both walls. Feeling unrested, Zach rubbed his eyes and gazed across the tubular gap, past the few service men that joined the ride, until his orbs rested on snoring Jack Tanner, who obviously had of an issue falling asleep in the hornet's nest.

Just as Zach started an unforced yawn that cleared his ears, he felt the building vibration along with the motorized sound of the landing gear dropping into position, indicating a final approach into the Seville airport. *Thankfully, we're there*, he thought.

Zach reached into his bomber jacket, the one Tanner had given him as a graduation present, and pulled out a small cardboard pack of raisins. Taking one in hand, he tossed it at Jack's head. Missing, the withered fruit bounced off the hull to the left. Recalibrating, he fired a second raisin that found its mark, bouncing off Tanner's exposed dome. Tanner stirred and muttered, "What the hell?" Then, seeing the grin on his assailant's face, he said, "Oh. I guess we're here, huh?"

"Yup," Zach replied while popping several raisins into his mouth. "Do we have a ride when we land, or are we walking?"

Jack couldn't hold back a yawn, postponing his answer. Then while stretching his extremities he came back with his typical deadpan of, "Always thinking ahead, that's good."

Again, the question not responded to, Zach shook his head. "Never a direct answer," he mumbled. Two minutes later, the wheels of the Connie screeched and then caught brief air again before settling on a smooth roll. *Nicely done*, Zach thought. A moment later, the plane came to a lunging brake, sending everyone aboard toppling hard against their shoulder harnesses and having to right themselves.

Moving in unison like a squad of well-choreographed dancers, everyone aboard, mostly men around Zach's age, began unstrapping, standing, and gathering their gear for debarkation. Finally, the cabin door clanked open, and one by one, the smattering of servicemen aboard made their way out and down the exterior roll-up stairway.

Jack Tanner was ahead of Zach and, being first off, started walking briskly and with purpose across the tarmac. As Zach quickly veered around the obstacle course of military personnel trying to catch up, he noticed that about fifty yards ahead at a service gate, a cardinal-red Adler Limousine had rolled up and parked.

Jack was making a beeline toward it. A moment later, the driver emerged, decked out in his driving blacks, complete with a traditional flat cap, he purposefully strode to the opposite side rear door, scanned his three-sixty surroundings, and opened it. The square-jawed man looked menacing enough to make Zach feel that he was more than just a driver.

The man further proved it by standing back and erect, his right hand sliding under his coat as if something lethal was hidden inside, and again, began scanning all around, squinty-eyed, until he rested his gaze directly on them. That caused Zach to momentarily stop and reach for his own shoulder-harnessed Walther P38k service pistol.

"I wouldn't do that if I were you," Jack quickly cautioned.

Zach relaxed, figuring that if his partner wasn't alarmed, why should he be. He still kept his eyes alert for anything, but focused on the driver's lips as he spoke to the occupant in Spanish. The words mouthed amounted to an "All clear, Sir. They're here."

The occupant, obviously in no hurry to emerge and expose himself, sat still as they approached. Finally, and just as Jack and Zach reached the gate and walked through, the gentleman from the limo's back seat slowly slid out and stood behind the door. *A cautionary hesitation. What was he afraid of,* Zach thought, while quickly calculating the fellow's height at six-foot plus.

A few more seconds passed while the gentleman glanced around one last time before stepping out from behind the door. He was dressed to the nines in a jet-black, obviously tailored suit that matched his substantial, wavy mane that was highlighted with just a hint of gray. *Late forties, early fifties*, Zach guessed. The eloquent and obviously thought-through lines made his portly frame somehow look not necessarily thin and athletic, but rather strong and durable.

His shoes of cracked leather, which Zach surmised could only be Italian, glimmered in the afternoon sun. A second later, the gentleman's concerned face exploded into a broad smile that could only have been reserved for an old friend. Closing the gap between them, he threw out his hand and proved Zach right.

"Jack Tanner!" he said in a heavy Spanish accent. "It has been six years, and the miles have worn well on you!"

Jack received the hand with his own and grinned back. "Six years too long, my friend. Glad that you are looking well. And how is Misses Number Four doing?"

The Spaniard's grin faded. "It *has* been too long, my friend. Number Four has retired, I'm afraid, to some

Greek Island at my ongoing expense. I believe Number Five will be joining her directly."

That registered, Jack let out a laugh. "How do you manage them all?" he said in dripping sarcasm.

The Spaniard leaned in. "I must admit that it helps, as you Americans would say, to be filthy rich!" Then, looking over Jack's shoulder, he asked, "And who have you brought with you, my friend? A strapping lad to be sure."

Reminded of his friend's requirement of etiquette whenever possible, Jack quickly responded, "Oh, my apologies. Mr Javier Rodríguez, may I introduce to you, Mr Zachary Ransom."

Zach confidently thrust his hand forward while trying out his Spanish. " Estoy encantado de conocerte, Señor Rodríguez."

" *¡Bien hecho, Señor Ransom! ¡El placer es mío!*" Javier said, impressed, while displaying a playful enthusiasm. Turning to a confounded Jack, "I like him already, Tanner. And at least he can actually speak the language. Which, I might add, you've had opportunities to learn."

Once again flummoxed by his protégé, Jack turned to Zach. "Well, I hope you didn't just start another war!

How come I didn't know you spoke the lingo?" he asked. "Is there anything else I should know about you that might help our cause?"

"Well, for one, you never asked the question," Zach said with the sarcasm typically reserved for someone his own age. "And, by the way, Scarp knows, which bodes the question of who is better at their job?"

This solicited a squinted glare from the senior Tanner, causing Zach to realize he had overstepped. Then, in a sheepish and less abrasive tone, he said, "Uh, actually, I can speak three languages, or, at the very least, get by. Spanish, French, and of course English. I'm now just starting to work on Russian and German."

Javier, realizing the young Ransom's faux pas, placed a warming hand on his friend's shoulder. "Well, he's young, isn't he?"

"Yes, he is," Jack responded while shooting a final intimidating glare Zach's way. "And by the way, I know *"buenos días"* and *"¿dónde está el baño?"*

"I stand corrected," Javier offered.

"And as far as you're concerned, we'll talk later," Jack pointedly said to his underling, while leaving no doubt that a scolding would be forthcoming. Tanner moved the ball forward. "Where to now?" he asked Javier.

"Have you eaten?"

Jack rolled his eyes over to the plane then to Zach again. "I had a raisin."

This delighted Javier and he exclaimed, "Not enough! Have I not told you that the key to life is to be always ready for a good meal?!"

"You may have mentioned something to that effect a lifetime ago," Jack admitted.

"Well then, I'm starving! I know just the place!"

"Nothing changes, mi amigo," Jack replied. Then, turning to Zach. "Do you like wine?"

"Never had any before."

"There's a first for everything," Jack returned with a grin. "Just like Leon's, remember?"

Zach did, but he was fairly certain they weren't going to a roadhouse, strip joint.

"But trust me on this," Jack continued under breath. "Just take it slow, or I'll be dragging you back to our hotel from some Seville gutter."

Zach registered with a nod, as they all piled into the limo while the driver stowed their small luggage and climbed behind the wheel.

"This is my companion, valet, driver, and the one I trust above all others." Javier offered proudly, as if speaking of his own child. "His name is Miguel."

Jack and Zach said a simultaneous *hello* as Miguel adjusted his rearview mirror to look them both in the eyes, then nodded and stuck his hand out. "Please," he said.

"What's he asking?" Zach questioned Jack.

"My apologies, Mr Ransom," the Spaniard interjected. "For the time being, you will be required to hand over your weapon. Only temporarily, of course."

Zach gave a questioning look over to Jack as if to say, *Is this right?,* but Jack was already handing over his own weapon.

"Thank you both for understanding. He doesn't say much, but he's the best at what he does," Javier added, then followed with a wave of his hand, "The El Rinconcillo, Miguel!"

"Oh shit!" Jack exclaimed, while remembering the last time the Spaniard had taken control of their activities. "Maybe something lighter, Javy?"

"Nonsense!" Javier bellowed with another wave of his hand. "You've had a long and boring trip. For tonight, *we ride!*" as he let out an infectious belly laugh.

The man was certainly jovial, making it difficult for Zach to contain his own smile. He took his grin and turned to gaze out the window as they drove the next six miles from San Pablo airport until they finally entered the old town portion of Seville called Casco Antiguo. As they rounded onto the main avenue, all around were regular people going about their everyday lives, meandering in and around what he assumed was the main street marketplace.

The thoroughfare itself was an old-world and charming setting with its ornamental and arched streetlamps, hovering like canopies over the cobblestone avenues of clay-potted bougainvillaea shrubs and seasonal flowers. Very few cars were about, as horses and buckboards were in full use as they carried fresh vegetables and fruit to those wanting produce.

"And what does Miguel do best?" Zach said in a low mumble that only he heard. Then turning forward, he locked his eyes again with Miguel's in the rearview mirror. The man apparently had good hearing and was not smiling, only observing until he was certain. *I feel the same, mi amigo*, Zack thought to himself.

Registering the moment as a toreador and bull stare down, Javier let the necessary mutual evaluation play out while keeping his own eyes forward. Another few seconds passed with his own thoughts not verbalized, he let out another laugh, and exclaimed, as only a man on the edge and loving it, could. "Ah, El Riconcillo," the Spaniard said in reverence. "The best tapas in town, I tell you. The very best!"

Nari Lee raised her eyes from her book on native bird species, a singular remnant and the only reading material allowed in their sequestration. Then rolling them left to right, she scanned the small, modest, and not entirely uncomfortable room and finally rested her gaze on her husband Jeoung.

He quietly stood lost in thought, with hands clasped behind his back staring into the distance through a chest-high, cased window. Setting her book down, Nari stood and took inventory. A few feet away, a small double bed, just enough to share for a couple of their ancestral size, centered the opposite wall with a generic, floral-scene mural just above. The artist had not been a master, but it appeared good enough for the room. A small, dark mahogany-stained nightstand was on the left with a Tiffany lamp centered upon it.

On the right side, a century-old cast-iron, wood-burning heater was positioned snug in the corner, with a short stack of forearm-sized logs next to it. Nari had been sitting in a years' worn, singular high-backed chair next to a round, Queen Anne side table. *Funny,* she thought. *Nothing seemed to match, yet the eclectic styling somehow worked.* She let out a tired sigh, then slowly stood and moved toward her husband. Close enough to hear each other's breath, she then placed a gentle hand on his back while resting her head on his upper arm.

Jeoung dropped his eyes downward and kissed her forehead. Turning back, he let his gaze sweep across the valley below. From several stories up, far too high to jump, he took in the rolling hills lined with grapevines on either side. In the distance, the town of Constantina rested peacefully on the horizon, its castle rising majestically from a hill just beyond. Jeoung exhaled a long, quiet sigh. "What do they expect from us?" he softly wondered aloud. "It's been nearly a week now and nothing but food."

Nari thought for a moment, then preferring the glass half full, said, "But good food. And the wine has been nice. At the very least they haven't hurt us, and we are not starving. Think of it as an adventure."

Jeoung pulled his loving wife in closer. "At the very least," he whispered in her ear, "You always seem to find a fraction of good in every situation."

"And that coming from a mathematician," she said with a warming smile. "Haven't you always said that a fraction sometimes can mean everything?"

Trying hard to minimize his concerns for their safety, Jeoung managed just a hint of a nod. Then, they held their warmth for a few seconds more before they were interrupted by the sound of the door latch being pulled back. Both turned to see who it would be this time. The amicable and seemingly harmless Salvador who brought them food and always smiled, or the menacing other who didn't speak at all and only scowled. The heavy wooden door creaked its ancient metal hinges open and two men, one carrying a satchel, the other attempting a stoic face, and neither of whom had been met before, walked through. The one who scowled followed but stopped at the door. He looked menacing enough that if they ever contemplated making a run for it, he would snap their heads off their shoulders.

The first man through was the shorter of the two, and definitely moved like a man in charge. He scanned the room, walked over to the side table as if strolling through a market without a care, and curiously picked up the book with a black and yellow striped Oriole on the cover. He flipped through the first few pages, then carefully set the book back exactly where he had found it.

"My favorite is the Hawk," he said, not looking up and with a heavy Eastern European accent. "Disciplined, ferocious and exacting. Something to aspire to, yes?" There was no answer from the captives, so he turned. His eyes met theirs, and they all took a moment to evaluate the other. Finally, Jeoung spoke.

"And who are we addressing, sir?" he asked politely.

"Ah, yes," the other responded. "Proper introductions are in order. My name is Ivanski Kalpakoff. And my friend here—" he added, while head nodding the more menacing figure behind him. "…well, his name is not really important, now, is it? You may call him, comrade."

"I see," Jeoung followed. "Mr Kalpakoff, was it not just five years ago when both our countries fought the Nazis? It is hard to fathom how the relationship chilled so quickly between then and now."

"You have spoken the truth, Doctor Lee. Maybe a thaw is in order among this small gathering?"

"I suppose, when one understands where they stand in the gathering," Jeoung replied.

"Agreed, and well said, Doctor Lee. But we must also all understand and agree that we each have our own jobs to do, do we not?"

"What could we possibly offer you?" Nari asked. "We are only teachers."

Ivanski shrugged, then gave her a brief glance before going back to her husband. "I guess there *are* secrets between husbands and wives," he offered with just a tinge of skepticism. "This will obviously be a topic for later between you two, but the short version is that the professor here has been working with those in your government on some very specific mathematical equations that would bring much interest from several countries."

"What's he talking about, Jeoung?" Nari asked, turning to her husband.

At first, Jeoung was at a loss for words. Rubbing his temples, he regrouped then looked directly into his wife's eyes. "It is true, my love. For over a year now. I am sorry that I never told you." Then turning back, he was quick to deliver the practiced lie. "But still, the theoretical portion has barely been addressed and what I have offered has never been responded to. My understanding is that those who had asked for help were no longer interested. I have not, as yet, developed any equation and certainly have no information worthy of being a captive."

"Oh, but you do, Professor Lee," Ivanski returned. "You are not taking into consideration that you have been watched for some time, and that we are very aware that more is there. But regardless, the mathematical equation, the theory as you put it, that you developed is exactly what we need for now. Nothing more. This is what you will provide."

Jeoung shook his head. "I can't provide that! All my notes are back in the States, and it would take months to put something together without them. Besides, and again, it's still all theory. No one knows what to do with it yet."

The Russian reached back with a palm up as if waiting for a baton. The silent one had already reached into the satchel he was carrying and was now handing a stack of papers over to the open hand. "*We know* what to do with it," Ivanski said convincingly while extending the notes over to Jeoung. "Here are your notes, Professor. You have one week."

"How did you get those?!" Jeoung cried out as he cautiously reached out for the papers.

Ivanski shrugged, "Really, Professor Lee. Does it matter?"

"And if I refuse?"

Ivanski turned toward the door to leave while motioning for the other two to do the same. "Make no mistakes, professor. These papers were found in the same house that your children live in. But to put your mind at ease, they were sleeping."

Nari gasped at the thought of her children alone in the home with these men and grabbed tight onto Jeoung's arm.

"It's okay, my love," he said to comfort. "These men are not here to harm our children."

"Your husband is correct," Ivanski said, then laughed before his face turned into a menacing scowl. "But make no mistake. We are serious people with a serious demand of you. Sometimes we are forced into things, ugly things, to get what we want. And no parent should ever have to attend their own child's funeral. One week."

The Russian pointed toward the door for the others to leave, then followed them out. The quiet one closed the door behind, followed by the latch being slid in place. Jeoung silently returned to the window while waiting for the onslaught of questions to follow. *How will I explain this deceit to my cherished life partner?* he thought. He waited while taking a deep breath, filling his lungs with the crisp mountain air—and then it started.

"My love…" was all Nari could get out before breaking down into tears.

Jeoung moved quickly to her side, but she brushed his arm away. "Nari, please understand. It was not necessary for you to know."

"Not necessary?" she managed defiantly through her sobs. "Our children now make it very necessary!"

"I know, I know," he comforted.

"When did this happen?" she asked, trying to control her sobbing.

Jeoung sighed. He dreaded admitting this deceit to his one and only love. "Nearly a year ago."

"A year?!"

"After I had submitted my calculations for review, I was approached by government officials. The work, they said, and I knew, was revolutionary, but there was more to be done."

"How much more?"

"I was able to complete everything in my head, but had been wary of putting it to script just yet. No one knew I had gone so far," then he let out another heavier sigh before continuing, "What I've discovered will ultimately change the way countries view war and aggression on every level. It must not get into the wrong hands."

CHAPTER FOUR

WATCH AND LISTEN

THE MEAL just completed had been otherworldly for Zach. With all the seemingly over-the-top hyperbole from Javier, it initially seemed impossible that the El Reconcillo would have lived up to the reputation preceding it—but it had.

Zach leaned back in the hope it would allow space for his bloated stomach. As he did, he took in the restaurant itself with its wall-to-wall terra cotta pavers that appeared centuries old, and the murals on every wall depicting medieval battles and the horsemen with their gold-leaf lancers that carried the day. The ceiling, composed of heavy wooden beams, warmed the space and matched seamlessly with the floor-to-ceiling, wrapped around a dark, dark stained bar and detailed wainscoting behind.

The word "*comforting*" came to mind as his eyes circled, finally resting on three empty plates. All appeared like they had been licked clean, and the explosion of demolished dishes that cluttered the table, with not an inch of linen visible, was a testament to a job well done. He stifled a belch and muttered a quiet *"excuse me."* After giving a final glance at the three empty bottles of the restaurant's finest Rioja red, he reached for his water and took a sip.

He had managed to be on his game, as instructed by Jack, with the wine, but even the paced glass-and-a-half had brought on a mild fog. The whole experience had forced him to realize just how much he hated losing any sense of control, and that he needed to stay sharp.

Javier had intermittently encouraged him to have more, but under Jack's squinting and watchful eyes, he had managed several respectful declines. The clam dish had been a new experience and was attempted with great trepidation, but finished with a "not so bad" nod. He really enjoyed the *espinicas con garbanzos* and special risotto, but the *Pavía de pescado* and *Croquetas de jamón* were amazing. He had acknowledged this to both Jack and their host that he had never had a meal so wonderful, which in turn, satisfied the ever-gleeful Javier.

"This was my wish for you, young Mr Ransom!" the Spaniard had exclaimed in delight. "It is my gift to you!"

Zach barely knew the man known just as "the Spaniard" but liked him already. And the man definitely knew his food and wine. He placed a grateful hand over his heart. "I accept with full gratitude," he said sincerely.

Seeing Javier's satisfied facial expression, he then watched as the portly and charismatic Señor Rodríguez pushed himself from the table, then fumbled to unbuckle his belt and the first button on his trousers. Zach had to stifle a laugh. Something on his face must have registered with Javier as a comical question, and it elicited an easy, bellowed guffaw, reminiscent of a singular *ho* from Santa.

"Yes, yes, I know. But it is better for gestation to be able to breathe, yes?" he said unapologetically.

At that moment, Jack and Zach gave each other a "When in Rome" look, then proceeded to follow suit with their own push back and loosening of their belts.

"Well done!" Javier exclaimed, just as the maître d', a heavy-set man with a pencil-thin mustache and a get-up of a starched white shirt with a black bowtie, stealthily sidled up to him and handed him a note. Javier thanked the man as if they had been friends for years, and they most likely had, then read the parchment. Nodding his understanding to the maître d', he sent him away.

Leaning forward, he abruptly returned to a more serious tone. "Now that we have been satisfied at the table, it is time to speak," his eyes narrowed, and his brows furrowed as if angered from an inconvenience. "I am watched all the time, my friend. You coming here will certainly have consequences for me."

"You've been interrogated before. I'm not worried," Jack calmly replied. "What do we know?"

"The Policía do not worry me," then Javier let out a sigh and continued. "My sources say that they are local."

"Local?" Jack questioned. "As *in* Seville?"

"Not the city but the mountains nearby."

"Fortified?"

"I'm told the estimate is eight to ten. Small arms. And it's been confirmed."

"Let me guess. The Russians?"

"This you know," Javier said with a shrug.

Zach listened intently. The nuances of a succinct and informative conversation between two professionals, both of whom have witnessed and endured the challenges of their profession, was a worldly insight you did not get from a classroom. Zach fidgeted in his chair, wanting to ask his own questions. He decided it was best to let the more experienced Jack Tanner complete the interview.

"How soon can we move, and what help can we expect from your side?" Jack asked.

"A move would be at your discretion, but any help would be very little, I'm afraid," Javier said with a frown. "It now appears that you have competition from others. And those others would bring conflict that would affect certain people. And those people kill with extreme prejudice."

Jack turned to Zach and shook his head. "Shit!"

"What?"

Jack turned back to Javier. "Let me guess. China is also in on the hunt?"

Javier nodded his confirmation. "And they have dealings with one side of a very delicate fence that I balance this considerable frame on."

Zach leaned in. "But I thought that the Russians and the Chinese were working as proxies for North Korea. Why would they compete when their goals are essentially the same?"

"You have much to learn, young Ransom," Javier admitted. "Nothing is what it seems, especially where governments are concerned."

"That's right," Jack was quick to concur. "Nobody really trusts anyone to any lasting degree. It all comes down to how much territory you end up with, and the control of population, commerce and currency. Rockefeller, Rothschild, Getty, and their eastern counterparts are making all the moves behind the scenes. Dictators, presidents, and kings all have the utmost control and are in their pockets. Only the big boys win.”

“Only the big boys,” Javier repeated.

Zach had already more or less understood, but sitting on foreign soil and hearing it laid out plainly like this made it feel more real. “Well,” he said, while standing and fumbling to buckle his belt, followed by adjusting his shirt, “I need to use the men’s room.”

Javier pointed to the rear hallway, then he and Jack followed suit and stood while getting their trousers and belts reacquainted. “Back, and to the left. We will meet you out front.”

It was already nearing eleven-thirty as Zach made his way past the few remaining close-out patrons, who were finishing their desserts and paying their bills. He readily admitted to himself that he was tired and just wanted to flop on whatever bed Tanner pointed him to, and was hoping it would be sooner rather than later.

Reaching the hallway, he bumped into a man who had just exited the men’s restroom and seemed anxious, as if on a mission. Maybe to get back to his date so he could consummate a more intimate evening. Or worse, he could be worried he left his girlfriend alone long enough that she'd already be in the arms of another wolf.

"*Perdóneme.*" Zach apologized, which the rushing man ignored. He entered the small restroom while giving one last glance back, thinking, *How rude.* A few seconds later, he was standing over the porcelain catch-all and starting to unzip, when his mind began to digest his last encounter with the rude man. His height appeared much taller than average, about six feet two and lanky. An Errol Flynn trimmed mustache, with dark wavy hair, and a deep and purposeful scowl wrapped in a tailored suit. One hand braced for the minor impact, but where was the other hand? Then it came to him—reaching inside his coat!

Did he rob me! Zach thought, then frantically started checking his pockets. Found! Zach relaxed with relief when he located his wallet, right where he left it in his rear pocket. *So what were his instincts telling him?* Then it hit like a thunderbolt. Zach quickly zipped up and bolted for the door. Just as he burst into the short hall, he heard the first pops of gunfire, followed simultaneously by a slightly different pop sound in return. A battle was on!

He instinctively reached for the weapon he was no longer carrying while racing past several screaming and ducking patrons. Cursing the handover to Miguel, he caught part of the mayhem just up ahead. At the door was the man from the hall, turned possible assassin of his friends. He was crouched, his pistol raised, looking for angles.

As Zach cautiously approached, his muscles began to expand, and he sensed what was coming. He hadn't been able to control it when the rage in him took over, and this moment qualified. He felt heat rising through his shoulders and up his neck, and his shirt started to rip as the bulky mass inside was becoming too much to contain. He didn't care to even try to control what metamorphosis he was enduring—his friends were in trouble. He grabbed an empty wine bottle off the nearest table and quickened his pace. He had an angle, and his mark was distracted.

The assassin was a pro and suddenly had a sense of an approaching attacker. He quickly turned, just as Zach launched the bottle from ten feet away. Not quick enough to aim, the shooter fired a bullet that cleared his head by inches. Zach charged forward and dropped down into a slide that DiMaggio would have appreciated.

A split second before, the bottle had met the assailant's head, causing blood to immediately spurt from the gash it had caused. He grimaced while bracing for the impact as Zach slid, feet first, into him.

Before connecting, Zach could hear a continuous exchange of gunfire from outside. He had raised one recoiled foot just before impact, and enough to catch the man's chin while both hands stretched forward for the wrist that held the gun. The force of the collision sent the pistol flying. Once in control, Zach quickly realized his strength and abilities were too much for his opponent and that his weapon had been the assassin's only chance.

He grabbed a handful of the man's hair and pounded his head down into the red paver several times until he went limp. On his knees, he quickly located the assassin's pistol and began searching the battle scene. The firing had momentarily paused for either movement, reloading, or recalibrating options. The limo was to the left, about twenty yards away, with Miguel nowhere in sight.

Zach noticed two black shoes on the curb just behind the limo with a crumpled body attached and hidden just behind. Suddenly, Jack Tanner's face popped out, and he exchanged eyes with him—the man down was Javier. Jack pointed across the street at a parked Mercedes, holding up one finger, then gestured toward a window just above the car. Two more assassins, he indicated, were positioned there.

Zach crept forward to a small Fiat sedan at the curb just in front of the entrance and positioned himself low at the front bumper. A rain of bullets began flying everywhere. The remaining assassins didn't seem aware that they had one more to deal with. He peeked around and could just make out a darkened figure with a gun raised and hiding in the shadows of an alley across the narrow street.

With only his head exposed, the figure fired a single round at Jack, who ducked down again, just in time. The bullet caught the top of the rear trunk of the limo and caromed into the brick veneer of the building behind them. Zach raised his weapon but couldn't get the angle he needed. If he fired, then the figure would know he had another opponent. At that point, he would either flee, thinking the odds had changed, or attack. Just then, two more pops were heard from the window above, and the figure behind the car looked up.

The advantage happened quickly for Zach. Calculating in milliseconds the possible consequences, he bolted across the street and toward the distracted assassin. The man turned quickly back and saw him. Zach had gotten close enough to expose the man and dove to the right while firing several rounds. The figure had only enough time to spin and catch a fleeting glimpse of the man who would end his life—he never fired another round. Both bullets found their marks.

The first bullet hit the man directly in his chest, followed simultaneously by the single shot that exploded his head. Zach dropped to one knee and quickly pointed, scanning a full three-sixty for anyone else who might be lurking in the shadows before returning his gaze to the window. There came a flash from inside. He was startled when a head popped out, but didn't fire. The rest of the body followed as if pushed, and it plummeted into a lifeless and crumpled mass on the ground just a few yards away. Zach squinted at the man's face just long enough to make sure there hadn't been anything of a threat left, then back up to the window.

A second later, Miguel's expressionless face popped out and gave a thumb-up, indicating he was good at his end. Zach gave one last glance around to make sure, stood while still on alert, and trotted back across the street where Jack Tanner was kneeling over Javier Rodríguez.

"Is he dead?" Zach anxiously asked, his adrenaline still peaked.

"Not yet," Javier surprisingly managed through gritted teeth and a mounting degree of pain.

"They clipped his shoulder, but he'll live," Jack followed. "It turns out that our friend Miguel is as advertised and pretty good at what he does. He saw it coming and shoved old Javier here, to the ground just in time. There was a fourth, but he drove away. It was like we were in a turkey shoot from the get-go." Jack got a closer look at his partner's shredded shirt. "What the hell happened to you?"

"It was a meat grinder in there," Zach responded as he sensed his muscles beginning to recede. He knelt down next to Javier and placed his hand on the injured shoulder of the Spaniard. It was the second time in his life that he had experienced a violent encounter where someone had been killed or injured up close and personal. He thought for a moment longer about that and how he didn't seem to have any feelings either way.

He was certain that, at first, some would attribute his apparent lack of empathy to the horrific loss of his father, assuming that all his emotions had been drained over the ensuing months and years. To him, the dead left in the wake of his fledgling activities were either deserving, or their deaths had been a matter of life or death—his life or death. And he wasn't ready for that. The injured, including the Spaniard, had been close enough to elicit at least a flicker of concern. Zach noticed the thought, acknowledging that a trace of empathy still lingered somewhere within him.

"How does this get handled?" he asked.

Jack and Javier looked at each other, with Javier breaking into a pained grin. "I know a man," he managed through a grunted cough.

Zach stood back up and gave another look around. People were starting to gather on both sides to see what the commotion was about. "I guess that's supposed to mean no hospital?" he said while thinking he already knew the answer. Startled, he raised his weapon in search when more shots were fired nearby. It was Miguel, and the effect was getting the throng of lookie-loos to rapidly disperse—they did. Then he nodded over that everything was fine.

Jack briefly registered the concern, then turned back. "Our friend here obviously has added a few more enemies to his list of undesirables," Jack added. "And the local hospital would just make getting to him a tad easier."

Zach thought about it for a moment. *Who was this man? What had been his history and his value for those who might need his services?* There was obviously more to Javier Rodríguez than was known to him, and maybe a bit of Jack Tanner too.

"I know I'm to catch up at some point," he said while processing. "But a little more info might get me closer to putting the puzzle together."

This was his friend sprawled on the ground in a pool of blood, and Jack wasn't taking kindly to Zach's lack of compassion. Jack began to stand, determined to give a what-for to Zach, but was held back by Javier's firm grip on his elbow.

"In due time, young Ransom," Javier offered. "Should I ultimately survive this next chapter, I…we, will answer all your questions."

Jack could feel his shoulders relax a bit, realizing that his protégé still had much to learn about fieldwork and the liaisons acquired over years of duty. He took in a deep sigh, motioned to Javier that he was back in control, then stood up. Over Zach's shoulder, Miguel was slowly closing while he dragged the unconscious assassin from the El Reconcillo's doorway across the street. Now, at the rear bumper of the limo, he unceremoniously let go, and the man collapsed next to the curb. Miguel's concerned face relaxed when he could get his eyes on his boss, managing to sit up.

"Help me get him in the car," he commanded.

Zach and Jack did as they were told and muscled Javier up as Miguel hurried to open the back door of the limo. After placing him in the rear seat, Jack closed the door.

"We'll follow you," he said in a deadly serious tone.

Miguel put his hand up to make it clear on his next statement. "No one follows. Mr Rodríguez will contact you when he is ready."

"It's okay, Miguel," Javier interrupted. "I'm not dying. But, in the best interest of all, and seeing as we are not quite sure that I was the intended target, I think it would be best if you go straight to whatever safe house you have lined up during your stay," he locked eyes with Jack. "I'll send a message in the same way as our last game together. Do you remember?"

Jack smiled at his friend. "And how could I forget?" he replied. "Be well, my friend."

"And you, as well."

"What about him?" Zach asked while head-pointing to the crumpled mass behind the limo.

Miguel said nothing while giving a sideways nod to Jack.

"Right," Jack said while giving his own up-and-down nod. Then turning to Zach, "Trunk."

Zach quickly followed Jack to the back of the limo and popped the lid open. While Miguel kept a watchful eye, Zach helped Jack muscle the injured man inside. Zach double-palmed the lid back down and verified it was secure, then watched as Miguel made his way around to the driver's side, noticing that his trousers and his shirt, when his jacket fell open, had several large blotches of blood on them. He had obviously taken his own hits, but it hadn't seemed to slow the man. Miguel reached under his seat and retrieved both their weapons and handed them over.

"Are you okay to drive?" Jack asked him.

"Fine." That was all Miguel said. Then he got behind the wheel and sped off.

"Is he going to be alright?" Zach mumbled over to Jack.

"Miguel? Yeah, I saw that too. He's a tough son-of-a-bitch, that one," he said, as the growing sound of

Policía cars and their blaring sirens neared. "Looks like we need to hoof it. Don't want to be around to try and answer questions we can't answer."

"What about the other two?" Zach questioned.

"Those two?" Jack said with a shrug. "They won't be answering any questions either. C'mon, let's go!"

And with that, Jack and Zach took off jogging, then ducked down the nearest alley just as the first whirring lights turned the corner behind them with their red and green images flashing like strobes on the alley's walls. After a few minutes, and now, more safe than they were a few streets away, Jack, who clearly did not have Zach's endurance, slowed the pace to a hands-on-knees halt.

Zach, not breaking a sweat yet, just stood while looking back over his shoulder. "What did Javier mean when he said that he couldn't be sure if he was the intended target?" he asked.

Jack let his eyes roll up while slowing to deep inhales. "Javier and I have history, is all," he offered between deep breaths. "And there are those still out there that weren't too happy about that history."

"And?" Zach asked, still searching for more.

The pause seemed interminable as Jack was still trying to catch his breath. "I'm afraid all that I can give you is this…"

"You have my attention," Zach pushed impatiently.

"There was a girl involved, and it wasn't business," Jack admitted through a grin. "Right out of a movie, so that's all I'll say for now."

Zach stayed silent for a moment, then said, "Okay." Then, both men quickly braced against a shadowed wall, just as the first of two Policía cars, their lights pulsating in full three-sixty rotations, sped past the alley's entrance.

Jack gave a squinted eye-nod to Zach. "We're about a mile away. Let's move."

It was late April, and there was still a chilling, bitter cold, lingering in the air. Sitting in his car, waiting for anything for the past two hours, had left the FBI agent Robert Dowling feeling a little stiff. Between what body heat he generated and the cold outside, the windows had fogged, and he couldn't make out the front entry of the brownstone walk-up across the street. Reaching up, he hand-wiped the front windshield just enough, settled back and pulled his coat up tight around his neck, and turned the wool lapels inward.

Seconds later, the passenger side door creaked open and his partner, Jeffrey Pimpleton—an unfortunate name that had already provided more than its share of comical shenanigans at the department—plopped down on the seat next to him.

With his cold breath streaming from his mouth, he asked, "Anything?" while handing a fresh cup of coffee to his partner.

Dowling glanced at his watch. "No. But it's only seven, and if the pattern hasn't changed—" He cut his words short as he caught Ji Hoon Lee exiting the doorway. "There he is. Earlier by thirty minutes."

Keeping his eyes forward, he reached for the ignition and cranked. The louder-than-hoped-for initial rumble caused Ji Hoon, who was nearing an opposite corner a good several hundred feet away, to glance back over his shoulder. The occupants froze for only a moment; then realizing the distraction was not enough to blow their cover, they let out their collectively held breaths. Ji Hoon had not given it a second thought and was already disappearing around the corner.

Dowling reached up and pulled the column shifter down into the drive position and slowly pulled away from the curb. Keeping a safe distance for several blocks, he rolled the vehicle to a stop just across from the mom-and-pop pastry shop that had been one of two meeting places they had previously staked out.

They could see Ji Hoon approaching the counter and ordering something from a high-school-aged barista through the window. Two minutes later, he was handed what appeared to be a hot beverage, and then he moved to a window table and sat down. While performing an up-and-down dipping motion over his cup, he kept a constant watch around the shop and out the window.

"It's tea," Pimpleton deduced under his breath.

Dowling gave his partner a "No shit" look, then turned back. The two sat for nearly ten minutes more when finally the man they were expecting suddenly emerged from a car that had been parked just a few cars in front of them. He walked across the street toward the shop. Both men quickly locked eyes while thinking to themselves, *Did he notice us?* Then both simultaneously shrugged and returned to watch the man. Pimpleton was first to speak.

"That's him, right?" he asked.

Dowling nodded confirmation. "Yeah. It's been the same guy the last two meetings."

Up until now, they had not seen a vehicle and had lost their man several other times while trying to follow. Apparently, their quarry had been well trained in covert counter-surveillance, which made it seem all the stranger that he would now drive and approach so openly.

"He must know we're here," Pimpleton offered.

"Maybe," Dowling said while making sure their mark was far enough away. Taking another sip of his coffee, and one last look at the man entering the door of the shop, he said, "Okay. Go now."

Pimpleton opened the glove box and retrieved a small, palm-sized tracker with a toggle switch. He flipped the switch, and a red light began to blink. A corresponding red light, centered on the receiving counterpart set on the middle bench seat, began to blink in sync.

"I've never used one of these before. I guess it's working."

"Yeah. Not standard issue," Dowling added. "I've got a friend, ex-bureau, who's working private surveillance. Trust me, it's working."

Pimpleton nodded, then quickly exited the vehicle. Keeping one eye on the shop across the street, he walked briskly but stayed in the shadows not to attract attention down the fifty or so feet to the mark's car. Once there, he knelt down and placed the magnetic tracker under the rear curbside wheel well, then with a quickened pace, he retreated back to Dowling. Climbing in, he said just loudly enough, "That's done."

Dowling gave a nod, and after giving one final squint to the shop window and noticing the man sitting down at the table across from Ji Hoon, he pulled the column shifter down into drive, and pulled the car away from the curb with the intent of parking around the next corner to lie in wait. He never noticed the quick glance at them by the man inside, or the other one watching from a second-floor window just above.

CHAPTER FIVE

THE PLAN

"No budet li eto rabotat?"

THE SAFE HOUSE was set deep within the bowels of Los Pajaritos in the Tres Barrios-Amate district, a neighborhood whispered about as one of Seville's poorest, perhaps even its poorest of all. The building itself had been little more than a tiny third-floor walkup with a single window view of the rear alley.

Initially, when they had entered the one-notch above flophouse lobby in the wee morning, just five hours before, no one had been at the small lobby kiosk. The counter itself had been barely more than a section, no more than five feet in length, of a decades-old and severely worn bar, with just a singular barstool where someone could sit perched behind.

Jack had quickly moved to the unmanned counter and had double-tapped the equally aged, unpolished bronze bell with a years-old dried wad of chewing gum stuck on one side. A weak cough, followed by several mumbled curse words, could be heard from another room that was only just a few feet behind the counter.

A lengthy moment later, a diminutive gentleman wearing a nightgown and a sleeping cap suddenly appeared. Only his cap was initially noticed as he moved behind the counter, then he hopped up on the stool, presumably to reach the height necessary to grab a room key from a locked wall box, then gave a scrutinizing glare back at them.

The owner of the establishment, who also doubled as the night attendant, and could only be described as a cross between dwarf and hobbit, deftly opened the box and retrieved a key attached to a red ribbon. He eyeballed Ransom and Tanner standing on the other side and waited. Jack then tapped the wood counter three times, bringing a wry yet tired grin from the man, who then gently slid the key over.

No words were ever spoken, no money changed hands, and the diminutive one who offered no instruction, let out an uncontrolled yawn then hopped back down off the stool and disappeared to the back room where he'd come from.

"Let's go," Jack had said with exhaustion.

Zach remembered responding with a, "That's it? A grin and we've got a room?" and Jack's reply of, "The little guy just made two hundred American, so yeah. That's it."

A few minutes later, the two had been at the door of their room where Jack had fumbled the key to unlock, and they were in. Zach remembered that Jack had taken just one scan of the room and said, "This is it. Home sweet home," then he kicked his shoes off and made a two-step, beeline to the only bed in the room, then performed his best face plant.

Zach, as tired as he was, could have easily followed suit, but his training had kicked in and he wanted to inspect his surroundings a bit more. That, and the thought of not being in such a hurry to cuddle up with his boss, had also come to mind. Still, a tad anxious for a pillow, he had fought back the urge and willed himself to what had been taught by others: a quick once-over three-sixty-degree scan of the room, then a peek into the tiny closet, then a final eyeball out the rear sashed window.

At the time, Zach had noticed that the unit, oddly enough, did not have any exterior fire escape stairwell, unusual for a building of that age. Although, he had noted, that there had been a fire escape on the apartment just across the narrow alley. He remembered that he had had just enough energy in him to calculate to a reasonable certainty that if need be, he could make the leap.

Why, at the time, it had seemed important to know that detail hadn't registered, but he figured it had been good practice to be aware of it. The room itself, he remembered thinking, had been barely a modest accommodation at best, and not designed for more than a couple. So, he and Jack, being a couple, and after tossing his shredded shirt in the lone wastebasket, had flopped down and had shared the double bed with Jack, actually managing to strip down to his skivvies before crashing asleep.

Now, in the morning, Zach was blinking into a mirror, cracked and clouded from grime, and running his hand over a two-day stubble. *Not a bad look, but a clean shave would be better*, he thought. Grabbing a noticed razor from a leather travel bag that had been left on the sink by who knows who, he soaped up his face with the lavender scented bar that came with the room and started the shave. As he swiped away, he thought back to what had happened in the past sixteen hours.

The night before had been both enlightening and thrilling, and exactly what he had signed up for, minus the possibility of taking one in the head, of course. To his personal credit and satisfaction, he survived the onslaught of food and wine that could have, had he not had the will power, required a frequent need of a toilet or the popping of several aspirin—and that made him smile. Especially knowing that the man who had cautioned him, his partner, had apparently not fared as well.

In the other room sat Jack Tanner, on the edge of the bed, with all the bedding cleared and piled on the floor. His head down, resting on both palms, he was assuredly in worse shape for taking the overindulgence hit, courtesy of the Spaniard. Jack, looking the part after having just spent the last two hours near or on the toilet, was still working on recovery while preparing what would be their next move between toilet runs.

Relying on past history experience, Tanner had made full use of the provided hotplate, water pot, and one-pound bag of very stout coffee grounds, and was two aspirin and three cups of black coffee into his morning after. Regardless of his weathered appearance, he was not only dressed and ready to go, but had already poured over several white pages of a scribbled plan of action.

The pages were strewn on the floor below his downed noggin.

"We need to leave in fifteen," Jack announced loud enough from eight feet away.

"Roger that," Zach returned, while towel-wiping away the remnant soap from his face. Pulling on one of several extra shirts he had packed, which had been hanging on the doorknob, he stepped over to the bed and buttoned up.

"Are you good to go?" he gently asked his mentor.

"Don't worry about me," Jack said, seemingly annoyed with the question. "I've been worse."

Zach found that hard to believe, but wasn't about to ask when that had been. "What's the plan and where are we going?" he said. Not waiting for Jack to look up or answer, "Forget I asked."

"Already forgotten," Jack responded, managing a pained grin. Downing the last drop from his cup, he stood and brushed past Zach to the bathroom. "One last cleaning of the pipes, and we're off."

Thirty minutes later, they were several blocks away, sitting at a bistro table outside a corner stand, devouring egg-frittata sandwiches and going over Jack's plan. They had spoken only in brief, one-sentence, generic dialog as they walked along several streets to the café. But the underlying theme had always been that they were still hoping to hear from Javier at some point, and both were wishing for sooner rather than later. They had mutually agreed, though, that the idea of just going somewhere outside the city and sitting tight near the base of some mountain was not a plan to get them any closer to finding Professor Jeoung and his wife.

Jack wiped his mouth with his napkin, threw it down on his plate, and then stood up. "I'm going to hit the head one more time."

"You going to be okay when we get on the road?"

"Yeah. I'll be fine. It's already starting to tighten up. Be back in a few."

Zach watched his partner head for the back of the café, then returned to another scan of the nearest people on the streets and café patrons. All appeared normal, and so he went back to his meal. Another quiet five minutes passed before he took a final bite of his Jamón con queso bocadillos sandwich, and washed it down with what was left of his coffee, all the while keeping an alert eye on his immediate surroundings but trying not to look so.

He was still contemplating last night's words from Javier about the target not necessarily being him, and this, in turn, made him wonder how Jack would even consider sitting in the open and having his head buried in a Spanish paper he certainly could not read, seemingly without a care for being shot at.

Jack returned a few minutes later. "All good," he offered with a grin, sat down, picked up his paper again and pretended to read.

"How long are we going to sit here?" Zach asked while noticeably fidgeting.

Jack sighed to his impatient pupil, then squinted down both sides of the Cobblestone Street bustling with the morning crowds of shopkeepers and their hoped-for clientele. He glanced at his watch and let out a shallow belch before answering. "Nine-fifty-five."

"Okay?" Zach said quizzically. "Nine-fifty-five. And what does that mean to me?"

Jack went back to his paper, and as usual, left an answer in limbo while Zach, now used to the wait like some Chinese torture that he learned to endure, bit his tongue. A few more minutes passed, then quietly from behind the printed pulp, Jack spoke. "Can you see the bookstore behind me?"

Zach scanned over Jack's shoulder and locked in on the La Pequeña Librería across the street. "I have it," he said alertly.

"At ten o'clock, a man will open the store wearing either a black or avocado green hat. If it's green, we go. There will be a message waiting for us."

"And if it's black?"

"If it's black, we run like hell."

"What?!" Zach said, alarmed.

Jack slowly set his paper down while sporting a wry grin. "It just means that there is no new information yet. Relax, Ransom."

Zach shook his head. "You're an asshole, you know."

"This, I know," Jack said, losing the grin. Casually turning around to give a quick peek, he saw his man. "There he is, and on time, just like clockwork."

Zach followed Jack's eyes to the left of the establishment and marked the man nearing the door, fumbling for his keys. From a distance, the shopkeeper's face appeared gaunt, and he was unusually tall, which left the impression of a cadaver. His bony thin frame also contributed to the conclusion as his olive suit hung on him as several sizes too large. A dark-green fedora adorned his head.

"I guess we go," Zach said.

"Not so fast," Jack cautioned.

Zach was already standing when he caught himself. "Oh. Right. Spook works one-on-one. Never assume at any time that you're not being watched."

Jack furrowed his brow, "Now you're thinking," he said with dripping sarcasm. Then he gave a quick glance down the street in both directions, searching for any change in the landscape from thirty seconds before. Satisfied for the moment, he stood and motioned to Zach. "Okay. I want you to go back inside and get me one of those cute little pastries with the chocolate swirl on top."

Not trying to look dumbfounded, just on board, Zach responded, "Okay?"

"When you come out, go directly across the street at a normal pace and enter the store. You got that?"

"Sure," Zach obliged, "And then what?"

"Just browse for a while until the tall guy comes back out front. He will be in the back getting his coffee pot going. It's a ritual. You got it?"

Zach was thinking there should be more, but he didn't ask. He assumed if there was more, it would have been given—so he nodded. Two minutes later, he had his little bag with the requested pastry and was briskly crossing the street toward the bookstore.

Not that he had looked very hard, but Jack Tanner was nowhere to be seen. As he stepped up onto the walk just outside the shop, he gave a quick peek into the window and pushed open the swing door. Two little bells attached let out their weak *ding-a-lings*, letting anyone who wanted to know that someone had entered. Zach kept himself alert, then he tapped his chest to remind himself that he hadn't left his service weapon behind. It had been uncomfortable to travel in the plane with it strapped on, but it had been a huge mistake not retrieving it from Miguel before the restaurant encounter. He had made sure to wear the shoulder harness this time.

A quick survey of the shop let him know that he was alone and that the man in the fedora was probably in the back, as Jack had said, getting his coffee going. So, he went about browsing through books from the science section, which became funny to him because he was unconsciously drawn there. Oddly, his mind briefly wandered to his high-school chemistry teacher, and he began to wonder if Miss Veronica and her white lab coat still remembered him, as he had her. He awkwardly felt himself starting to get aroused with the thought and quickly shook the memory of his first sexual encounter and refocused.

A few minutes later, trying to be inconspicuous for no one while keeping his head on a swivel, he heard a cough from the back room. *Was that a signal of some sort*? he wondered. He gave a distracted glance back toward the rear counter when the familiar *ding-a-ling* sounded behind him, and his eyes rotated back to the door. It was a false alarm. An elderly woman, certainly pushing eighty, if anything, shuffled in and to the rear of the store with an obvious purpose. Zach kept his head tilted downward as if reading while his eyes followed her.

Her hair was less gray and more white like cotton, and she was carrying a small paper bag in one hand and her handbag in the other. When she made the rear counter, she reached into the bag and pulled out what appeared to be a worn leather-bound book and gently set it down. Distracted by the woman, he didn't notice another figure slipping in behind her before the door had closed—but thankfully, not quick enough to avoid the *ding-a-ling,* signaling the new patron's arrival. Zach gave a quick, over-the-bookshelf glance in that direction.

A rather large, bulky man in an overcoat who resembled a rhinoceros had made his way in. *What was under that overcoat?* Zach suspiciously thought. The new patron seemed out of place somehow and kept his own head down as he moved through the aisles, occasionally picking up a book from the modest inventory. At the same time, the proprietor finally emerged from the rear holding the expected cup of coffee, the steam rising to verify that it was indeed very hot. His coat and hat now removed, the presumed owner of the shop was revealed to be exactly what was thought, gaunt and bony.

Just like his coat had been, his clothes hung on him like some hand-me-down from the giant in Jack and the Beanstalk. His smile, though, to the lady at his counter, was warm and genuine. They greeted each other in a way that made Zach think that he and the woman had done business before.

"*¿Es esto?*" the man eagerly asked in Spanish.

The woman nodded, then slid the book across the counter. They then exchanged a few words, smiled their goodbyes, and ended the niceties with the owner saying in Spanish that it would be ready early next week. The elderly woman then slowly shuffled out, as she had when she arrived, never looking up but seemingly concentrating on not tripping over the floor's uneven tile.

Zach gave another glance toward the other patron who quickly buried his nose in a Zane Grey novel. When he did, Zach gave another follow-up back to the proprietor, who, to Zach's puzzlement, gave him a quick shrug and then fluttered a hand motion for him to leave before turning away and disappearing again into the back room. Consumed with appearing uninterested, none of this was seen by the rhino.

Now fully confused, Zach didn't know what to do other than what the man suggested, and that was to leave—so he did. Stepping back out onto the street, he quickly looked around to see if Tanner had been lurking about. Not finding him, he instinctively began moving and reacting like he had been taught during his training. Swiftly and inconspicuously, he quietly strode through several blocks of pedestrians, weaving in and around as if working an obstacle course.

At one point, he arm-halted a man moving in the opposite direction and used the gentlemen's momentum to spin the man while politely asking the time. "*¿Qué hora es, por favor?*" he requested. The gentleman, a suited professional of some sort, was not as annoyed from being so abruptly stopped as one would have thought.

Checking his watch to oblige, it gave Zach the opportunity to allow his eyes to survey the street over the man's shoulder. The rhino from the shop was there, a few hundred feet back. He had turned to make it seem like he was window shopping, but Zach knew he was indeed being tailed. He thanked the man for the time, then quickening his pace, he rushed across the street and cut down an alley.

Turning left at the end, he almost tripped over two cooks who were sitting at the rear entrance of a restaurant, taking a smoking break. There was a short flower barrel set on end between them, and they were playing cards. He quickly brushed past the two and jumped inside the open rear door with not even the slightest disruption from the men, then rushed through the unattended kitchen, down a short hall, and past the main dining room's tables and chairs toward the front entrance.

There had been only one other worker there, a young boy, no more than ten or twelve, who was busying himself setting linen and place settings. Zach halted at the front window and was there just in time to glimpse the rhino who had been following him, approaching, then disappearing down the same alley.

He and the boy locked their eyes, with Zach giving a silent finger to his lips. The boy nodded back, and Zach slipped out the front door and crossed back over to the other side of the street and headed back east. Two blocks further, he cut down another alley, pulled his pistol out, and quickly spun his silencer barrel on, and hid behind a large bin.

He reminded himself that usually it would be a two-man team following him, but he hadn't noticed or picked up on a second person. *Maybe Jack was working on that*, he thought. He waited while counting down two minutes exactly; then he bolted deeper down the alley and out the other side. Turning right again, he could see a small park a few hundred feet ahead and made a beeline for it.

It was still early, and the park wasn't crowded, so he leaned against a tree and kept an eye down the two closest tributaries to the park while waiting for the man who had been following him to reappear. Again, two minutes passed and nothing. Thinking he had eluded the man from the bookstore, he scanned the park while calculating his next move. *What had Jack said? If you've been followed, you need to assume that your follower already knows where you started from, so don't go back there.*

The dilemma of his next move was where the chess sense kicked in—and Zach loved chess. That made him oddly think back to the miscreant Fredrick Simonson being a chess master and what it might have been like to play against someone who may have wanted him dead. *And why would he think of that now, of all times?* Suddenly, he had a reason to get off the current thought as he noticed, then locked in on, a familiar face sitting on the nearest park bench. The man was laughing at him— it was Jack Tanner. Zach sighed, somewhat relieved, then walked over.

"You did well, Ransom," Tanner said, amused. "Do you think you lost him?"

"I think so," Zach said, walking up. "What happened back there?"

"Basically, I used you as a decoy."

"That much I figured?" Zach lied while trying to appear as if he knew all along. "But how did it go down?"

"There were two. One followed me, and the big one, you. My little guy got a tad close and is lying in an alley gutter a few blocks away, and probably waking up to a very painful headache, courtesy of our friend Miguel.

Who, by the way, would have had no qualms in putting a bullet in the man's head, had I not stopped him."

"That was very considerate of you."

"I try. Anyway, once he was out of the way, I circled around to the back of the store where our friend from the bookstore delivered a note to me."

Zach was puzzled. "Seems like a lot of work. Why was Miguel here, and more importantly, why didn't Miguel just give you the note himself?"

"You would think it should be that easy. Miguel doesn't deal with information unless absolutely called upon. He is too closely associated with the Spaniard, and should not be seen anywhere near action that would raise suspicion on his employer. That would make things worse than they already are for our friend. He was only sent to make sure we got what was intended. Besides, I'm guessing that the info never got to Mr Rodríguez and just came directly from those he had asked to get it. Plausible deniability."

Zach felt he understood. "But who delivered—"

"The old woman."

Now Zach understood. The octogenarian didn't arouse any suspicion in him, so why would the tail man suspect anything? "Does this gal get used a lot?" he asked.

"Never seen her before. Javier likes to have a rotation, and it's never the same person twice in a row."

Of course, this all made sense to Zach, and he recognized that he had learned much on the mission. *Assassins hide in bathrooms, keep your head down, trust absolutely no one, don't drink too much, little old ladies can carry out chores, and just listen to Jack. Oh, and don't go anywhere without your weapon.* "What did the note say?" he asked.

"Constantina, in the Sierra Norte. About fifty clicks from here. They are being held in an older estate overlooking the valley. It's going to be a difficult approach."

"Has it been confirmed that the Lees are there?"

"The gardener-slash-caretaker of the grounds is a family member of someone our friend Miguel knows. When the word was passed around, it was acknowledged that an Asian couple was brought into the home and had never stepped outside since. The gardener said that he had caught glimpses of the couple at a third-floor window. They're there. At least, as of yesterday."

"When do we go?"

A rumble came toward them and both Zach and Jack turned to witness the Spaniard's cardinal red Adler roll up. The now familiar and ever stoic Miguel was behind the wheel.

Jack looked away toward the morning sun and squinted into the distant hills. "Apparently, we go now."

CHAPTER SIX

IT HURTS UNTIL IT DOESN'T

Savannah, Georgia – 1942

THE PAIN came like a searing heat that spread slowly from his skeletal frame from toe to shoulders. A few months shy of thirteen, Zachary winced for ten excruciating seconds while waiting for what he knew would come next. Tears began forming in both eyes as the radiant heat started to push through toward his outer skin. This had been the second time this week he had had to endure the onslaught of suffering pain and the twelfth or twentieth time since the event on Oahu on that fateful day.

There had been so many episodes that he had lost track of just how many. Days, sometimes even a week would come between each similar event, but he had learned that it would come. And his fear had been that it may never stop,   that no relief, prescribed or natural, would ever solve what he perceived as his body's crisis. The only other human who had known, the only one who had cared, and he had felt could be trusted, had been Doctor Rivera. And he had somehow suspiciously disappeared and was nowhere to be found.

Zach had often wondered about that, and attempting to acclimate to his new Georgian home, it had been difficult to dwell on much of anything else. He had been hesitant to share the scary unknown with his only remaining relative in this world because he had only known and had been around, his aunt for just a few months, and he hadn't reached a point of trust with her yet. He knew the time would come… he knew. It just had to, because anything short of someone to be able to communicate with would create a desolate and unbearable existence.

Zach dragged his cotton shirt sleeve across his damp eyes and let out a low whimper as the heat intensified, spreading through every muscle in his body in a throbbing wave. Nausea followed, and he felt the urge to vomit, just as he had during all the previous episodes. Desperately, he summoned warm memories of happy childhood moments, trusting, as he always had, that they would help him push the feeling back.

The next phase was coming, he knew, but he held hope that it would end as before, a few seconds after. Then it hit—a sharp dagger piercing his muscles. As it struck, they swelled like balloons being filled with warm air, and the pain was excruciating. He let out a louder cry, trying to stifle it so as not to alert Aunt Emma in the other room, but he couldn't. All he could do was wait for her response.

No one came. At one point, the ordeal came close to him passing out. The greyness rose with his body's temperature, up his neck to his face and nearing his eyes to where the grey would darken for the expected blackout, which had happened six times before. Then, just as suddenly, it would disappear like a magician's trick, and it would be over. The whole episode would only last three minutes—but it felt like an eternity.

Zachary pulled his T-shirt up, exposing his belly and used it to wipe the sweat from his face. The throbbing in his muscles had gone away but the swelling and the now obvious bulging muscles would remain for several more minutes, then, as before, they would finally lessen, as if the balloons were punctured by a straight pin so tiny that they would slowly lower rather than burst.

But they never went back to where they had started. His muscle mass would always gain just a little and his strength would equal in unison. He had taken to using his aunt's garment measuring tape that he had found located in a thread-spool case next to her sewing machine, to gauge the increase. An eighth inch here, a quarter inch there, but always more than the previous.

He sat down on the edge of his bed, fell back onto his pillow and stared at the ceiling. He started taking slow and methodical breaths in an attempt to follow a regimen that Doctor Rivera had laid out when the event started happening back at the Pearl Harbor Naval Hospital. It helped calm him. Then, as always, he would slide his hand over his calf and upper leg muscles to feel the growth then follow with a slide up to his stomach where twelve defined ridges formed, and again to his pectoral muscles before concluding with a gauge of his bi and triceps.

As concerned as he had been with the cause and then the unusual transformation—he smiled. He *was* strong… he *was* powerful, and that wasn't half bad—but was it worth the agony? And if there was to be this pain, would it grow to be worse? Could he endure more? Or the most traumatic of thought…*could he die from it?*

Zach took in another breath just as his Auntie Emma's voice bellowed from the kitchen. "Zachary?" she yelled out. "Dinner is ready! Come and sit!"

He laid there for a minute longer, wondering if his aunt had noticed anything strange in him. *Hadn't she at least noticed his growth,* he questioned? By his calculations, he had grown three inches in height alone in the last six months. Never having a child of her own, she may be thinking it was just a normal growth spurt— but this was nothing even close to normal.

She hadn't said anything, and he hadn't invited much of a conversation since the move, but she had to, *right?* They were still learning to trust each other, and perhaps she was keeping a respectful distance as he had also. This dilemma continued to rattle in Zach's head, then Emma called again to remind. He quickly responded by sitting up and cocking his head left, then right in an attempt to stretch and loosen what had just tightened.

Tomorrow, his skin will have stretched enough to relieve the tightness; this he knew from twelve or possibly twenty times before—he couldn't remember. One thing would be a certainty… he would need bigger clothes.

CHAPTER SEVEN

BE ON THE OFFENSIVE

"Atacar o ser atacado."

FORTY MINUTES later, the Adler was slowing to make a sharp turn on the winding but gentle-sloped incline of the hilly pass. Zach placed a two-page leaflet on the back seat that he had been reading about the historic area, and he stared back out over the vast, lush countryside that surrounded the Andalusian village of Constantina.

Avoiding the back seat, Jack had claimed elderly privilege and opted to sit up front. Their driver, Miguel, had given Tanner a short-lived fight with a glare and sneer; hopeful of deference for what he perceived as an invitation of his space. An under-breath growl followed, but with Jack's posterior already engaged with the leather, he ultimately decided to let it go.

Just below the two-lane road and nestled in the gentle and sleepy valley, the village of Constantina was everything a touring visitor searching for old-world charm would hope for. The gothic tower of the Iglesia Parroquial de Santa María de la Encarnación, *more words than the name of any church should rightfully have*, Zach mused, stood majestically, with the equally impressive and Moorish-inspired, Castillo de Constantina's expanded ruins, just beyond the Barrio La Moreira's cobblestone streets.

The village, he had read, had been founded by Celtic ancestors mining for copper and silver. The Celts had settled there only to endure Roman occupation and again, centuries later, a brief two-year period of French rule. And now, there had been another, albeit secretive, occupation just outside of town. The question that remained was whether or not they could gain access, unseat the current occupants without loss of life, and in the process, recover the two captives unharmed.

The conversation on the drive had been lean at most, with Jack trying to subtly pry from Miguel any nuances he may have missed in the past few years since his last escapade with the Spaniard. Miguel gave grunts and askance looks, and even one stealthy fart for good measure. Eventually, he offered that his boss was now up and about and healing well. Jack managed a "That's great!" and "We wish him well," while ending with a "We couldn't do much of anything without his help."

This last statement elicited a quick and dismissive scoff as if to say, "No shit!" from Miguel. Jack just nodded. After that, it was just silence and the warm breeze of the rolling hills, caroming through the open windows for miles.

FBI agent Pimpleton emerged from the station bathroom and made his way through the maze of desks and other agents that cluttered the tiny Providence, Rhode Island, field office. Looking ahead, he could see an animated agent Dowling mouthing what appeared to be a series of expletives into his phone, then slamming the receiver down on its cradle. A few nearing and pensive steps closer, his boss was embedding his elbows deep into his desktop and rubbing his temples in frustration.

"What's up?" the underling asked, hoping he wouldn't need to duck from a thrown stapler.

Dowling shook his head in disbelief, stood up, and circled the desk muttering. "How could this have fucking happened!?" casting death stares at the oblivious others working on their own leads. He grabbed his coat off a nearby coatrack and pulled his arms through. "Let's go!"

After checking in with the section chief to fill him in while Pimpleton waited patiently on the other side of the door, they made their way outside, crossed over the blacktop, past several rows of mostly empty car stalls, and soon were at their government-issued Ford and climbing in. Pimpleton got behind the wheel and slid the key in, then waited a few seconds in hope of some enlightenment from his superior. It wasn't coming freely.

"You seem a little stressed, boss," he finally said. "Are you going to fill me in or should I just guess?"

Dowling let out a heavy sigh. "The Lees are missing."

Pimpleton was confused. "They've been missing. I don't understand."

"Not the parents, the kids. Start the car."

"Oh shit! Where are we heading?"

"To the Lees' apartment, where I will quite possibly have a violent ass-chewing to give to two agents that fell asleep!"

From his fetal position, Ji-Hoon managed to roll over on his side. His head was covered by a burlap sack cloth, and his mouth was taped while both his arms and legs were tightly bound with duct tape. He didn't know for how long, but he realized that he had been unconscious for a period and that some ground had been covered. He took in a deep but difficult nose breath while the grogginess he was experiencing was fading into an anxiety-filled *what the fuck!*

A few more stress-filled moments passed, then, with his head nearly cleared and not really sure yet if he was alone, he managed to maneuver just enough to rest his kneecaps on what he was relieved to find, his sister Si-Woo's back. Coming around herself, she was startled at first, then muttered through her own gag something unrecognizable. Ji-Hoon returned his own unintelligible, muffled response. It was enough for her to recognize that it was him. Neither understood what the other offered, but it had helped to calm things, knowing they were, at the very least, together on whatever trial that lay ahead.

Ji-Hoon rolled over onto his back, where his knees were up and just clearing the bottom side of the trunk lid, all the while feverishly trying to start putting things together. He knew that there were, or so he had thought, at least three men who had grabbed him and his sister. The abductors never spoke a word in the moments before unconsciousness, so narrowing down who was involved, or their ethnicity, would be difficult.

He recalled the two men had sprung from either side of the front door when they entered, then also a third who had palmed his mouth and nose from behind with a pungent cloth. After that—blackness. As he came around, his initial thought had been that this was just another ultimately harmless attempt at ethnic intimidation from school peers. That thought quickly faded with the acknowledgement that the men who muscled him and his sister into the trunk were older and definitely rougher than college-age pranksters. He recalled, that within seconds, he had been overwhelmed and put under.

Struggling to draw a breath through his gag and sensing his anxiety piquing, Ji-Hoon forced himself to relax. That lasted only a few seconds more before he harshly convulsed and thrashed around to see if maybe, just maybe, he could loosen his bind, but it was futile. Frustrated, he let out a primordial scream that no one would hear. Then, once again, forcing calm, Ji-Hoon stretched his fingers out and was able to intertwine them with Si-Woo's noticeably trembling digits. Back-to-back, he could hear his sister sobbing, and he squeezed her hand in solidarity. They never let go the rest of the way.

As the stillness enveloped them, the horns and rush of the city faded as their rolling coffin traveled further away. Another twenty anxious and uncomfortable minutes passed, and Ji-Hoon and his sister could sense the car slowing down. A few seconds followed before they could hear and feel the gravel kicking up into the wheel wells of the car. They were off the paved road, then a minute later, they had come to a full halt. A vibration of the car doors opening rattled the trunk and its occupants. The kidnappers were exiting the vehicle, with their car doors being slammed shut behind them. Ji-Hoon and Si-Woo waited, but no one came for them. The sound of their captors' collective feet just fading into the distance. *Would they just leave us here to die?* Ji-Hoon silently questioned.

What seemed like an eternity, passed with both captives sensing that this could be the end of their young lives. Whatever trouble their parents were in, it had migrated to Rhode Island and to them. To exasperate their situation, even though their Northeastern summer's sweltering heat was still months away, the sun was radiating, and with the combination of steel, their own body heat and no real airflow, the cramped trunk space was beginning to heat up like a toaster oven. Beads of sweat began to build and roll down the side of his face, and Ji-Hoon let his tongue reach out to catch their salty presence one by one, when suddenly he froze to listen. He could hear the approaching footfall of several people closing in. Abruptly, the movement stopped, and the rustle of keys was heard. A moment later, the hood popped open, and the bright sun suddenly burst through, and even with their heads covered, the light was enough to cause them both to blink their eyes until their pupils adjusted. The air, though, had been sweet and appreciated.

"You fight, you die," one man said calmly. Then, two other men muscled the captives out of the trunk and untied their leg binds, then marched them forward. A few clumsy strides further, "Steps ahead," the same man said, then he gently pressed down on Ji-Hoon's head and said, "You will need to duck a little." Ji-Hoon, who was taller by six inches than Si-Woo, did as told, then the man grabbed his arm, before carefully leading both of them down the two separate flights of wooden steps.

Si-Woo clenched the back of her brother's shirt as they descended into the lair. When they finally settled on the last landing, Ji-Hoon and Si-Woo both took breaths of the heavy, musty smell, leading both to feel that they were being taken down into some medieval dungeon. A few more steps, and they were halted and shoved down to their knees. The hard ground was slick and mossy, wet from the thick humidity of the space.

"Please!" Si-Woo pleaded. "We know nothing!"

Suddenly, the burlap sacks that were covering their heads were yanked off, the cloth gags removed from their mouths, and their wrist binds were cut away. Four men, two in front and two behind, were standing menacingly in the bowels of what appeared to be a wine cellar. Large oak casts were stacked on both sides of a narrow hallway, where cables connected to dim lighting hung from the center and stretched far into an otherwise darkened space. One of the men stepped forward and leaned over the two while pulling out a revolver and pointing it at Si-Woo's head.

"Now would be the time for silence," he said in a monotone, reminding one of a man who had no qualms about ending another's life. "This will be your new home. If you try and escape, you die," he added, then, "Your parents are still alive."

This brought immediate tears from Si-Woo and a comforting arm wrap from Ji-Hoon.

"But for how long, we do not know," the man continued. "Hopefully, they will cooperate," then the man pulled out a Polaroid camera and snapped a photo of the two hostages. Following, he began to turn to lead two of the three men up the stairs and away, then stopped to give a final instruction. "If you need to urinate, go behind those casks there," he said, pointing behind them.

Ji-Hoon and Si-Woo looked at each other with the same anxiety-filled expression.

"What if we need to do the other?" Ji-Hoon asked sheepishly.

Their captor sighed, then looked around the open space, but apparently didn't find what he was looking for. Then he said something in his language to his underling before turning back to the two hostages. "He will provide you with a bucket and paper."

Miguel slowed and pulled off onto the gravel shoulder of the road, then cut to the right at its widest point and buried the hood of the limo between a narrow span of two ash saplings. The maneuver did not completely hide the vehicle, but anyone traveling in the opposite direction would be hard-pressed to see it. The three, confident in their position of approach and concealment, emerged and started walking.

A hundred yards further, the point man, Miguel, stopped behind one large holm oak trunk, and silently cautioned Jack and Zach to follow suit. Miguel quietly pointed forward, and their eyes followed in that direction. Up ahead, they could see through a gap of tall conifers, a large clearing, and the home in question on the far side.

Miguel stepped out and led the trio closer in a stealth approach, then at the edge of the clearing, he stopped again. All scanned the grounds and quietly acknowledged to each other with shrugs that no vehicles or lookouts appeared anywhere. Miguel motioned that he was going around to the back, and for them to approach from the front. All agreed, pulled their weapons out, and took off.

Zach crossed the open space and crept up the two steps onto the porch landing, and was first to the door. While motioning to Jack to follow, he noticed that the door was oddly already ajar. He leaned forward to briefly listen for any movement or sound. Convinced that a possible confrontation was unlikely, he signaled to Jack, then nudged the door fully open with his toe and slid in.

There were no sounds, as his eyes quickly ran right to left, giving a first impression that the house was empty. Jack was now in and wagging his weapon around in serpentine movement while quickly giving his own scan in the opposite direction of anywhere Zach was looking. They both gave each other a nod, then bound upstairs. Halfway up, they heard glass breaking from the downstairs rear of the home—Miguel had taken a more dramatic approach to his entrance.

Jack continued going through all the second-floor rooms while Zach moved on up to the third floor to do the same. Hitting the landing, Zach was feeling more and more confident that whoever had been there was no longer around, but he was always reminded during training to always assume that someone was always hiding in wait, so he kept his weapon up and alert. He checked each room systematically all the way down, approaching the last one, he reached a door that had a bolted latch that none of the others had.

Bolts and latches were usually on the inside to keep people from walking in, he thought. *This was a cell.* He slid the bolt back, stepped inside and gave a quick once-over as he had the others. Curiously, the room had felt different, triggering the idea that there had been something off. The bed was rumpled and unmade, and there was a partially empty water glass sitting on the open windowsill. He moved over to the bed, lifted one pillow and picked a short, coarse black hair off of it.

Next, he went to the window and gazed out to the expanse where Constantina sat in the distance, and the large church steeple rose above the rooftops of the village. Something crept over him, bringing a sense that the Korean couple had been there. He turned and stepped over to a small table and high-backed chair that reminded him of one from his Aunt Emma's parlor. A book about bird species was on the table. He picked it up and opened it to the first page, where there was a rough smear of words, apparently written in someone's blood. The word was *Ivanski*.

CHAPTER EIGHT

THE PLOT THICKENS

"No hay tiempo para relajarse"

BACK AT the safe house, it was Jack Tanner's turn to stare down the alley, while Zach sat on the edge of the bed doing the wondering: *Why hadn't there been, at the very least, a chair in the room?* he wondered. He was still considered a rookie, and all this waiting around had him feeling anxious to do something, anything, other than being in that room. His body felt stagnant and was needing to be in movement, but he didn't want to overstep Jack's authority. The last time he did, it didn't go so well.

The bed, specifically the mattress, had been uncomfortable from the get-go, and certainly not much better sitting up; it was as if a rusted bedspring was awaiting to pierce his left butt cheek at any moment. There also came the thought of how many vagrants had flopped their   collective sweaty and inebriated bodies on it. None of this helped him catch the shuteye he desperately needed to be sharp.

As he sat there pondering, his thoughts also ran to what Jack was thinking and what the next move would be. From his position on the bed, he watched his mentor with his hands behind his back, standing rigid and silent, seemingly without a care in the world.

Zach took a cautious breath. "What's next?" he asked, while feeling he was intruding on whatever thoughts Tanner had been deep in.

Lost in his thoughts, Jack's head barely moved to acknowledge. "What?"

"What's our next move?" Zach continued. "We obviously weren't quick enough. Or at the very least, someone knew we were coming."

Jack let out a held breath, then turned around. "*That* would be Ivanski Kalpakoff," he answered in almost a submissive voice. "He has contacts everywhere and almost certainly was tipped off that we, or someone, was getting close," then trailing softer, "But who…?"

"That was the name in the book. Who is this Ivanski Kalpakoff, and how would he know about us?" Zach questioned.

“Well, that’s the rub now, isn’t it?” Jack returned while staring down at his shoes and thinking Zach was deep enough in and deserved the full scoop. Quiet seconds passed, then he continued. “I, and specifically our Spaniard friend, had a run-in with Kalpakoff a few years back when he was an arms dealer and working with Turkoff. You remember him?”

Zach nodded. “A lake, a cabin and lots of blood. Yeah. Hard to forget the man who almost ended me.”

“Well, there’s that. Anyway, one down and one to go, thing there,” Jack acknowledged before continuing. “Kalpakoff disappeared off the face of the earth a few years ago, when this deal Javier and I had cooking went sideways and got bloody. Then, he reappeared briefly with our deal a year ago, only to disappear again. I suppose now, as the word got out about Turkoff, he’s decided to crawl out from whatever rock he was under.”

“Why are you just now telling me this?”

“To be honest? I’m as surprised as anybody. We were hoping he was dead already; that maybe Turkoff or the Russian syndicate had taken him out for getting in the way. Vladimir Turkoff had more cachet at the time, so it just made sense. Maybe it turns out that Kalpakoff ended up being the smarter one, since he's the last man standing between the two."

"Okay. So, you mentioned a run-in."

"That's right. Javier had been helping Scarpino, and I set up a sting operation to net the two—separate locations, but at the same time. We missed on both. Now it seems he's back up and running," Jack took a swig.

"I don't understand. You're leaving something out."

Jack's voice trailed as he peered again into the alley below, then upward to the lines of shared manila rope stretching across the narrow span from one window to another, and finally to the laundry billowing gently in the warm breeze. He tugged at his uncomfortable collar. "Anyway, he had help," he finally added.

"C'mon, Tanner. Don't leave me hanging, here," Zach pressed.

Jack nodded that he was right to ask, then continued. "As we closed in on them, both had been tipped, and they managed to elude us, but for Kalpakoff's part, not without a singular and cryptic message to get even."

"To get even?"

Jack turned, and his voice was back. "Yeah. You get the picture when one of your informants has his throat slashed and the blood was used to write on the wall that you're next."

"Whoa!" was all Zach could manage.

Already halfway through a bottle of gin and just a little wobbly, Jack crossed the room, squeezing past Zach to reach the other half bottle and the glass, which still held just enough for him to knock backbefore he poured another two fingers.

Zach was worried about his partner and friend. He had known Jack Tanner longer than anyone else still alive in his world, with the lone exception of his aunt, but he had been only three at the time, and when they had been reunited, he hadn't remembered her at all.

So, it was safe to say that he cared for Jack and didn't like the dark side he was displaying. Finally, he built the courage to address it. "A little early for the booze, don't you think?" he cautioned.

Jack forced a smile. "Son," he said with the meaning behind it. "It's five o'clock somewhere."

Zach knew he had overstepped with the man, who was a solid twenty-five-plus years older than he. "Sorry. It's just that…"

Jack quickly waved him off. "The bottom line is that the trail went cold," he continued, his speech starting to reveal the ravages of alcohol. "But we managed to recover several hundred caches of small arms and rifles destined for a North Korean dealer. It ended up being a win for the good guys."

Zach wasn't understanding. "That seems like a 'you win some, you lose some' scenario for him. There should be no hard feelings there; he got away."

Jack shook his head and smiled, thinking it must be nice to not have all that crazy shit in your head yet. "Yeah. You'd think, right?" he said, turning back again. "It turns out that it never had been about the deal going bad. Although it did piss off some of the oligarchs back home, along with dipping into Kalpakoff's petty cash to the tune of a few million. No. It was all about Javier and Ivanski, both ending up having a thing for this gal"

"A girl?" Zach interrupted.

"…and he apparently viewed me as being part of getting in the way of that," Jack finished the sentence.

"A girl," Zach repeated, still not reasoning it all out.

"Yeah. A nightclub Flamenco dancer, and a pretty good singer too. She liked to play the field, and boy, did she have the goods to do it, if you know what I mean. Curves in all the right places and a smile that would have launched an armada that would have dwarfed that Helen gal."

"Of Troy."

Jack slogged the fingers down. "That's the one," then he poured another. "Turned out that our Spaniard friend and Kalpakoff were both putting moves on her at the same time, hoping to get whatever info she knew about the other, but in the process, they both fell to her considerable charms. She played them both," then he chuckled. The kind of chuckle you wouldn't be able to manage if you weren't drunk and one that would induce an involuntary laugh of your own. He continued slogging away, "The funny thing was that neither one had figured out she was head over heels for this other guy."

"What other guy?"

Jack let out a stifled belch. "Get this…her guitar player. A real goof, too."

"Okay, but what's her deal, then?"

"Her Deal? She likes guitar players. Would even kill for them, him." Jack laughed at himself. "Turns out she was actually a killer in more ways than one—not just her looks."

"What? Do you mean, *actually*-actually?" Zach questioned, intrigued but also aware of something else.

"Rumor had it, then later confirmed, that she had put at least two known spooks to eternal sleep, and possibly one Spanish aristocrat who was getting too handsy. Word finally got out that she was working the back end for people who mattered." Jack slammed down the two fingers. "Poison's her deal."

Zach moved over to Jack, and casually reached for the bottle to remove it from his friend's hand, while not appearing like he was the adult blocking the child from going sideways.

Jack begrudgingly understood and scoffed. "Yeah, okay," then he plopped down onto the bed, fell backwards, and stared up at the ceiling. "You'd better go down to that corner café and get me some coffee."

"Yeah. Sure," Zach replied, relieved while moving to take his own peek out the window and wondering if he would be able to get Tanner back together for the day. Suddenly, he froze and focused; his eyes steady and glued to a point beyond. Down at the south-eastern corner, near Java café, where he was to get the coffee, two sedans rolled to a nearby curb. Six men emerged and were moving quickly toward their building. Two of them reached under their coats and exposed Sten guns. *We have to go!* he barked as he instantly began feeling the heat rise in him, then followed almost simultaneously with the swelling of his muscles.

Jack sobered in a millisecond. He leapt off the bed, then momentarily braced when becoming unsteady. "How many?" he managed.

"Six with two staying back to monitor," Zach said while feeling woozy from the oncoming change. "Maybe forty-five, sixty seconds tops." he momentarily reached out to the wall to steady and attempt to control.

"Arms?"

"PPS-43 subs."

"Shit! That would be the Russians."

Zach could feel his upper body mass pressing and stretching his shirt to the breaking point. "Forty seconds! What's the plan?" he yelled as the first tear over his left bicep ripped open.

"Get out of here and meet them at the top of the stairs! We'll have the advantage!"

"What if we jump?" Zach said while checking his sidearm and its readiness while trying to force the beast within down.

Jack was already at the door. "What?!" he fired back, more interested in getting out the door and down the hall. One step out, he glanced back. Zach was squeezing through the window and balancing on the ledge. What are you doing?!" he yelled. But as the words left his mouth Zach jumped. Jack managed a "Holy shit!" as he stumbled over to the window. When he focused across, Zach was on the other side of the alley, climbing over a third-story balcony rail.

"Fuck!" Jack muttered, not in any frame of mind to notice Zach's torn shirt. He quickly glanced over his shoulder and heard boots coming from the hallway. His resolve faltering but unnerved by the thought that he didn't have the spring for the leap, he pushed his body through the window and found himself momentarily balanced on a four-inch-wide brick ledge, barely wide enough for a pigeon.

"No time, jump! Now!" Zach yelled over.

Jack attempted a gulp, but his mouth was drier than a bucket full of sand, so he steeled himself, then with a primordial yell, he leapt as far as his fairly athletic and sodden frame would allow—he was two feet short.

Zach reached out over the rail in time to grasp the outstretched, flailing hands of his friend. They connected like professional trapeze performers, and the anguished and near-death expression on Jack's face turned to frantic relief until Zach suddenly let go of one arm.

"What are you doing?!" Jack yelled, then peered down three floors below with bulging eyes. "Don't freaking let go!" he yelled, while flailing his free hand to join the other on Zach's one arm.

Zach's grip was powerful and tight as he kept both eyes on the apartment window just ten feet away, his right hand already reaching for his weapon. "Climb!" he encouraged.

Jack didn't need convincing and did as told, but in managing the process of trying not to be dead, he couldn't help but notice Zach's arm muscles swollen to a ridiculous size, to where his shirt couldn't hold them and was torn in several places. He barely let out a "What the…?" before the two short bursts were heard across the road, and the door fifteen feet beyond the window was kicked in.

The first man stepped in and sprayed the room, his Sten machine gun rotating side to side with sparks flying in all directions. One of the rounds went through the open window and exploded the mortar a few feet above Zach's head. He had no time to consider anything more than the focus necessary to defend himself, while simultaneously feeling the full weight of Jack's one hundred and eighty pounds on his arm and shoulder, trying to claw his way up to reach the rail.

No sooner had Jack's first hand grabbed hold of the bottom post anchor that Zach aimed through the window and sent two perfect shots into the first gunman's chest. He crumbled instantly to the ground. Undeterred, the second man stepped into view and over his fallen comrade, then started spraying the window opening as he walked like a machine toward it.

"Swing to the right!" Zach commanded as he fired off another two rounds while the incoming pitted the building on either side of him and Jack—the two-hundred-year-old mortar splintering and cascading down over them. The new gunman had jumped to the side just in time, and Zach missed on both. A second later, Jack pulled himself over the rail as several bullets whizzed by from below. He quickly dropped down and leapt through the window of the attached apartment and pulled his weapon. Zach followed by diving through, and they both knelt, fully ready, while catching their collective breaths.

Jack couldn't believe Zach's leaping ability and strength. "I don't know of any man short of possibly Hercules who could have pulled that off!" he managed, almost reverent of his protégé.

"Hercules was a myth," Zach mumbled just loud enough, then followed with a grin.

"We'll have this conversation later," Jack quipped, then both turned to check their new surroundings and suddenly realized that they were not alone. The two occupants of the apartment, both aged and in their underclothes sans robes, were sitting at a dinette set, having their breakfast and sporting mouth-open faces that were locked in stunned disbelief. A second later, several more rounds caromed into the ceiling, sending the two septuagenarians shrieking and scrambling as fast as their aged frames could for the rear bedroom.

"They weren't expecting company," Zach quipped.

"Not very hospitable of them," Jack followed. "Leaving us like this."

The moment was over, and Zach was back to quickly peek out the window, but was immediately met with two more lead volleys. "Better move," he said, while glancing down and noticing that Jack's pants were turning dark, indicating he had taken a stray. A master of the obvious, he said, "You've been hit."

Jack winced while struggling to stand. "Barely nicked. I'll follow you. Let's go!"

They crawled away from the window, then Zach reached out to help his friend to his feet then pulled him to the door. As they moved, Jack's gait was smoother as if his will, mixed with the alcohol he had imbibed earlier, had overpowered whatever pain he was enduring. Zach let go and glanced down the hallway. He knew that they had time before whoever was on the hunt could reach them. "This way!" he commanded, and they were off.

Moments later, they were down the three flights of stairs at the opposite end of the hallway and exiting out into the back alley. Their weapons raised in anticipation of others waiting in ambush—luckily, none were there. The two that had held back must have chased the sounds of gunfire into the building.

Shouting could be heard from above, letting them know that they still had a few seconds more to elude the attack. The assassins wouldn't dare jump and would have to trek down the way they came in—even more seconds, and they all counted. A lone transient sat disheveled with his back against the wall, his inebriated snores meant that those following would not get a definitive direction from him as to where the pursuit should go.

They ran to the end of the alley, where the attacker's vehicles had parked, when a car, a late model Peugeot, turned the corner and was heading towards them. Zach stood in the vehicle's way, leaving no room to maneuver, then pointed his weapon at the head of the woman attempting to drive through. Her mouth agape and realizing her predicament, she panicked and slammed on her brakes, then reached to lock the door.

Zach waved his gun like a forefinger as if to say, "Don't do that," and opened her door, apologized for the inconvenience, while using gentle but ample force to pull her from the car and sit her down on the curb. Jack was already dropping his rear onto the copilot's side. Two seconds later, Zach was behind the wheel and throwing the shifter into first.

"That was very gallant of you," Jack replied flatly through whatever pain he was enduring.

Zach scanned up to the windows and balconies on both sides for any threat, then down the alley to its entrance. "Once Chivalry dies, the world dies, my auntie would say," then turning to Jack, he deadpanned, "One must have manners," then he pressed hard on the gas pedal and bolted forward.

He had the address of a second safehouse and was racking his brain as to how to get there. Thankfully, at a quick stop at a local park, he was able to get some help from a young couple pushing a stroller that got him going in the right direction. Once he found the street, he knew he would be okay. He thanked them profusely and apologized for how he looked, since both had been staring at his torso, which looked like he'd been attacked by a chainsaw.

An hour later, and after stopping into a local Farmacia for supplies for the injured Tanner, followed by a check-in phone call to an unnamed handler, they were pulling into an underground garage on the seedy, east-end of town and parking. Jack had already applied some disinfectants and did a field wrap on his leg and was feeling none the worse.

Of course, that included a half tablet of some opiate, which meant he was feeling no pain. Zach made a point not to ask where it had come from, assuming that any back room, or bottom shelf of any of the local stores could provide such drugs for a price.

Once Zach threw the shifter into park, the two exited the car with the injured Jack being more than a tad slower, appearing more drunk than drugged. Zach dropped down behind a Fiat a couple of stalls over, and immediately went to work on exchanging the license plate. The task completed and no one encountered, the hobbled Tanner and Zach made their way to a nearby stairwell. It was still early, not even noon yet, and Jack felt like he needed a bed and a few hours of shuteye before cycling through their next steps.

"Nothing like the drugs abroad, my man. They're starting to kick in," Jack said while numbing up and slurring his words. "Think I'm gonna need a few drinks…I mean winks," then he laughed at himself. "Man, I'm gassed!"

Zach had to laugh at his mentor and the idea that he was so vulnerable right now. He was certain that the drugs and Jack's already inebriated state may have had something more to do with his unguarded condition than anything else, and just hoped he could make it to the room. He was starting to feel the weight of his friend as Jack's body increasingly began to sag like a plastic bag full of Jello, and holding him up was starting to feel like a job. "I think the booze you downed already, and those painkillers are kicking each other. We had better get you inside," he encouraged.

Zach's instincts were still in full-throttle mode, though, and he didn't want to slow the thinking down just yet. "Do you mind me taking a swing at the locals while you rest up?" he asked, hoping Jack was still with him enough to answer.

"Sure," Jack slurred, just as they reached the apartment door at the end of the darker-than-necessary hall. The opiate had taken over, and he was sensing that some form of hallucination was in his future. He fumbled the keys over to Zach. "You'd better do this. I'm starting to see double."

Zach took the key and gently pushed Jack up against the wall, holding him steadily with his open hand as he slid the key in and twisted the handle. He toe-nudged the door open, then helped his partner to the closer of two double beds and gave him a gentle push toward it. Jack made no attempt at holding on and fell back on the bed into a blurry fog. Zach chuckled to himself, then wondered what it would feel like to be so out of it. He looked around the room and quickly assessed that it was worse than the one before. He couldn't help but think that the company must get a special rate for dingy. He turned back to Tanner, who was almost out but still able to mutter, "What time is it?"

Zach glanced at his wristwatch, "Twelve fifteen."

Jack coughed up an "a.m. or p.m.?"

Zach smiled and pulled the bedspread over his friend. "Better sleep for a bit, pal. I'll be back after a little recon."

Jack hugged his pillow and went into a more comfortable fetal position. "Take your mother's car. Curfews at ten."

Zach allowed for the charade. "You got it," he said softly. After giving another final scan of the room and the required eyeball out to the street below, he headed out. Just as he stepped into the hallway, he could hear the first of many deep strains of Jack's snoring. He made sure the door was locked properly, then a minute later, he was down on the street, figuring out which way to go. A row of dilapidated apartments was to his right, and as before, the common sight of laundry hanging on communal cords draped to mirroring apartments across the street.

To him, all the vibrant colors of fabric reminded him of the flags of countries. To his left and further away, there was a string of small commercial retail and service shops. Clothing, pastry, carniceria, tailor and barber. Zach reached up and ran his fingers over a day's stubble and thought, *I could use a shave.*

Three years in the Spanish "Blue Division" fighting against the Russians on the Eastern Front made Miguel one tough bastard. The Franco regime had claimed neutrality on behalf of Spain in 1939 but had petitioned Hitler to join the Axis of Germany, Italy, and Japan in 1940, in exchange for later help in expanding Spain's colonial empire.

When word of this had gotten out, the United States, a major importer of goods to Spain, made Franco understand that heavy sanctions would be applied if he joined forces with Nazi Germany. Franco correctly calculated that, having just completed their own civil war, those sanctions would have been too great for Spain to endure.

Franco relented, but did covertly put together the "Blue Division" with the caveat that the men of his army of mercenaries would only fight on the Eastern Front. Those three years of hardship had made Miguel the tough hombre he had become. Besides the acquired hands-on training of stealth, weaponry, and the skill to kill, he also walked away understanding that he hated the Germans as much as the Russians. In his eyes, they were all pigs.

Miguel leaned against a tree, keeping his frame in the shadowed side. Off in the distance was the sleepy little village of Cazalla de la Sierra, just nine miles northwest of Constantina in southern Spain. It had taken several hours using various tools of torture before their captive, who also proved himself to be a tough bastard, finally succumbed to the pain and gave up the town where the Koreans were to be moved to. Unfortunately, he did not have the exact location, or if he did have it, he died before he could spill the beans. Miguel took a drag of his cigarette while thinking that he somehow had admired the man.

What *was* gleaned, though, was that the location was someone's home and not a building of commerce. The other last tidbit muttered before the man faded into permanent oblivion was that the home sat on a small hill just a few blocks above the town's main thoroughfare; typical of the small towns and villages of the Sierra Norte de Sevilla, it was essentially just a cobbled road wide enough for two vehicles to pass each other without scraping fenders.

Miguel glanced at his watch. It read twelve forty-eight, *la hora de la siesta*, he acknowledged. Perfect timing to take advantage of the daily ritual prevalent in these parts. He took another drag of nicotine as he continued to cast his eyes in study of the midday on-goings of the town and the scattered hillside homes perched just above on the rolling hills that surrounded the enclave.

From a distance, a few men appeared like ants, and like clockwork, emerged their family-run shops and made their way to a small tavern near the centre of town. Miguel took one last drag and tossed the butt away, then, reaching behind his back to make sure his weapon had not dislodged from the hike, he started down the hill toward the tavern. In fifteen minutes, he would be buying rounds and commiserating with the locals about the hardships encountered following the war. Then, with all the charm of a friendly visitor, he would hopefully get the answers the Spaniard was looking for.

The clock on the wall was one of those black-and-white Kit-Kat numbers with a wagging tail. Not so uncommon back in the States, but appearing rather odd to Zach to find one so far from home. The perpetually smiling feline's abdomen showed it to be six-thirty and a full five hours since he dumped Jack Tanner back into the room to recover and sleep his drunk off. The Spaniard had already left word several hours before the interrogation was over, had been fruitful, and Miguel was already on his way to scope out a possible location in the nearby mountains that the goon had given up. He had some time.

Zach stood and rummaged his pocket for a single peseta and placed it under his cup. Giving one more glance about, including a left-right out the front open window, he turned back to catch the young Barista smiling back at him. The woman was near Zach's age and quite pretty in a natural way. She had long brunette hair that cascaded down to the small of her back, which she held in a ponytail, and it seemed to him that her watching him had been longer than that moment.

Not so curvaceous up top, but her tiny waist and wide, rounded hips overcame any other perceived deficiencies, making it easy for Zach to return the smile. They held each other's eyes for comfortable seconds, enough to make him feel that something more could be made of it. *Maybe even something that could make him forget Jenny for a few hours.* Then the thought of using Jenny's name brought him back, and he moved to the door, but not before giving the Barista a last gentle wave. The woman was generous with her hand wave back and as he opened the door to step out, she gave a cute head-tilt and offered in Spanish that she was looking forward to his coming back. He had to get out of there—and now!

Letting the door swing shut behind him, he walked briskly across the front of the café, but not before giving one last glance in the window. There she was, still watching and smiling. He had to move faster because this distraction could easily happen.

Zach crossed the street, feeling that other than an unexpected attraction to this woman and a nice shave, he hadn't really accomplished much. Most of the casual conversations with locals and the barber came up empty of any substantial or useful information. He now knew that the humidity they had been experiencing was quite normal for the time of year, and also the locations of the best tapas joints nearby. Of course, the very best ones were nearly always owned by one of their relatives, if not themselves. The truth was that they were all suspicious of him and anyone else who would come in and butcher the language.

Zach glanced at his watch again, then calculated that he had time to make an important call. A telephone booth was up ahead, and he ducked in to grab it ahead of an annoyed man holding the day's ABC paper. Zach managed an apology, then thought that if the man had just been a tad quicker, he would have been on the other side of the glass, searching for the next booth, which there may have been two in town.

When at the café earlier, he had made change for just this case, and he plunked a few of the appropriate coins in the slot. A moment later, an operator with a gravelly smoker's voice came on, and he gave her the number. The call would require more change, and he obliged. A few seconds later, he could hear the ring, not much different from back home, drone several times, and it immediately brought back the sights, sounds and smells of his home in Savannah, Georgia. Magnolia blossoms, sweet tea and the hens on the porch clucking their gossip while fanning away a warm and sticky summer breeze. His chest swelled with the memory, then someone picked up. There was a noticeable cough on the other end, followed by a voice saying, "Hello?"

Zach heard the voice, and he unexpectedly became emotional. He hadn't heard her voice for several months during his training, and before that, the eight devastating years he thought her dead. "Mother? It's your boy, Zachary."

There was a squeal of excitement at the other end. Enough for Zach to pull the earpiece back a few inches. "Zachary Ransom!" Abigail exclaimed. "Where have you been? Your aunt and I haven't seen or heard from you in so long since you went away to college."

Of course, that had been the story. College would be next year, but his mother wouldn't know that. Auntie

Emma had known from the beginning and had been the one to support his efforts in Otter One, but she had been sworn to secrecy ever since his mother had been found alive. Zach had made it very clear that when the time came, if ever, he would be the one to fill his mother in on what was really happening in his life. He felt that he had owed her that, but he was sure that it wasn't time yet.

"I'm sorry, Momma," he continued. "School has been a little stressful with study and final exams, and I kind of lost track. Are you well, momma? How is Auntie Emma and all the hens doing?"

"Oh, those ladies are all fine. You know Emma, she's out there on the porch as we speak, holding court like she was Queen Elizabeth, only she doesn't have old George to hold her back on that tongue of hers."

A sudden vision came to Zach of the day last year when his mother was rescued. Her being held up, too weak to walk for any distance on her own. The gauze eye patch wrapped around her unwashed, stringy hair told part of the story—the aftermath of the Japanese Zero crashing into their family's schooner and taking her eye. And for eight years, he hadn't known her pain; he hadn't been aware of her tortured existence. She was now a worn and skeletal shadow of a one-time beauty. He closed his eyes and tried to visualize the scene as it was on that Sunday morning, December 7th.

"And you, momma? How are you?" he softly persisted.

There was a noticeable pause at the other end of the line as his mother turned away to cough again. Zach sensed something off, like she was gathering herself. Finally, she returned. "I'm fine, son. My strength is coming back slowly, but there have been some setbacks."

"Like what, momma?" Zach asked, now more concerned.

"It's really nothing. At least nothing at all for you to be worrying about," Abigail continued. "I've noticed that my vision is just not what it used to be and that things are a little clouded and unfocused, making it harder to read. I think those years in those darkened cells most likely are the cause. Emma is taking me to the eye doctor later in the week, so I think the next time you visit, I will probably be wearing spectacles. So don't be surprised," then she laughed a familiar laugh that reminded Zach of the good times and the overwhelming love his parents had bestowed on him growing up. At fifty-one, she had only been a few years older than her sister Emma, but the ravages of her ordeal had her appearing like she could have been her sister's mother.

"Okay, momma. I'm sure it will be fine," then he heard the clatter of a screen door closing in the distance on the other end and the familiar voice of Aunt Emma speaking to his mother, asking who was on the phone and Abigail responding that it was her only son, Zachary.

"Momma?" he asked in the hope of hearing her voice again.

She came back. "Oh, Zachary, I told you I'm fine. We'll have plenty of time to catch up more later, when you come. Here's your auntie. She's clamoring like she does to speak with you."

"But momma!" he protested.

She heard him and came back on. "It's okay, baby. You know that I love you very much! Here's Emma," then she handed over the phone, and his auntie was on. "Zachary Ransom! Where in God's green earth have you been?"

"Hey, Em. Well, you know I was looking to take some time off."

"Yes-yes…but that was nearly a month ago," then she lowered her voice to a whisper. "What's going on *now?*"

As much as Zach was not willing to divulge to his own mother about his new life, everything in that journey and more, he could entrust to his Auntie Emma. She had been there to pick up the pieces of his shattered life when he thought both parents dead, then also through his growth to manhood. And finally, she was there to see personally what he had become involved in and some of the players, specifically Jack Tanner, Scarpino, and, of course, the lethal Fredrick Simonson, whom both he and she, intimately and regretfully, had become involved with.

"They've pulled me back in, Em. I'm on assignment here in Spain."

"Last time we spoke, you were on your way to the islands to take some time off. This is too soon, isn't it? Are you ready?"

Zach had to think about the last question for a second before responding. "I am, Auntie," he finally said.

A sudden fear for her nephew came over Emma, but she didn't let on. "In Spain?" she said, sounding very much surprised. "My Lord! Now you're officially a world traveler!"

"I guess that's true. It's been exciting to be sure."

"The larger question, Mr Ransom, is are you being careful and staying safe?"

Zach tried to hold back a laugh but couldn't. "Of course, Em," he hated to lie to her, but did anyway. "Just handling paperwork over here. Nothing to be concerned with at all."

There was a short pause from the other end. "Well, you've certainly become a good liar, Zachary. You *do* know that I intend to live vicariously through your soon-to-be many exploits. You would be handicapping my enthusiasm should you hold back the most salacious of details."

There was no fooling Mrs Emma Grandal, Zach reminded himself. "We're on to something, Auntie, but I promise I'll be safe," he replied. At that moment, he was going to say goodbye, thinking he would say more when he had more time. But then it hit him again that there was something else going on. He was going to ask just once, but after a long silence while he thought about it, Emma beat him to it.

"We don't know, Zachary," she said, anticipating the question. "We thought it might have been allergies at first, but then your mother's eyesight started failing at an alarming rate, and it's been causing, we believe, the headaches she's also been experiencing."

"When did this all start happening?" he asked, with his anxiety starting to peak from not being home.

"Everything was fine when she first got here. Abby was settling in, and we were getting along as sisters, filling the gaps in on our years apart, you know…what with her losing Thomas and you, then her isolation. But about three months ago, your mother started noticing little things. She asked me to promise not to say anything to you while you were in college. I couldn't tell her about all of this other stuff you're involved with because you asked me not to."

Zach thanked his auntie and agreed that filling his mother in on the dangers of his new line of work would only worry her unnecessarily. "I will call again in a few days. Hopefully, you will know something by the end of the week," he offered. He thanked Emma again for all that she had done and meant to him, and for taking in his mother.

Emma wished him safe, then added one last thing. "Zachary. You shouldn't wait too long to have that talk with your mom. She's a pretty smart lady."

Although dreading the conversation, Zach agreed with her, said his goodbye and then he gently hung up the phone. For those few minutes, he had lost track of where he was and the job before him. He forced a clearer head and began weighing what was in front of him, which included the pressure of knowing that much of the world would be depending on an agreeable outcome for all who were on the right side of it. It was ever more important that he focus everything on that outcome and not on any troubles, as hard as that would be, back home. This would be his hardest challenge.

Attempting to clear his head, he suddenly realized that he would be an easy target for any assassin who had been near and ready to pull a trigger. Zach refocused as much as his brain would let him and left the booth and moved quickly away from the brightening streetlamps, then, using the shadows, he made his way back to the hotel.

CHAPTER NINE

THE LOVELY MISS DE ANDA

"Hasta que ella te mate."

THE WHOLE DAY had passed quickly with nothing much happening except lost time. Zach had spent much of the day roaming the streets being inconspicuous while practicing his Spanish with shopkeepers and trying not to think of his mother, while realizing that he never did inquire about Jenny Mathews. *Did that mean it was over with Jenny*, he wondered. That whole idea then morphed into the woman at the café—he needed to de-clutter his head again.

He had already been in contact with Miguel, or rather, Miguel had found him just after his call back home, and had given him an update. Now, back in the room, it was already eight o'clock when Zach slid the room key in, turned the latch, and opened the door to peek in. To his relief, Jack Tanner was up, mostly dressed with his pants down around his ankles, and sitting on the edge of his bed. A new field wrap was around his exposed leg.

"How're you feeling?" Zach asked while thinking Jack looked pale and was going to puke at any moment.

Jack stood and balanced himself, then feet already through the leggings and shoes tied, he pulled his pants up and tucked in his shirt. "Don't worry about me, Ransom," he coughed through. "Just tickled the flesh a bit, is all," then buckling his belt, he reached for his sidearm from the nightstand, then turned his dark and baggy eyes back to Zach's. "Learn anything out there in the big bad world?"

"Buenas noches, to you too, Jack," Zach said, laughing, then turned serious. "Turns out our friend Miguel did a little recon of his own. The one we threw into the trunk gave up the new location. A town outside of Constantina. Cazalla de la Sierra."

"Okay, then!" Jack exclaimed, trying to will himself well. "What are we up against?"

"Unknown. We don't have the building yet. He buddied up to a couple of the locals over some Rioja, and—"

"Look at you. You're learning your reds," Jack interrupted.

"And they had mentioned," Zach continued, "some newcomers, who didn't exactly speak the lingo without their home accents, had been lurking around. The locals pointed them in the direction of a couple of possibilities. He thinks these are our guys and spent the rest of the afternoon surveilling three homes just above town, but couldn't mark anyone coming in or out."

"What about the Spaniard?" Jack asked.

"Doing better. Whatever Miguel knows, he knows. That's it," Zach replied. "But he did have a strong suggestion."

"And what's that?"

"Miss De Anda?"

"I see," Jack responded, hesitant. "And?"

"Miguel told me one of the men he spoke to had seen a car driving through town—a man at the wheel and a woman beside him. The driver had stopped briefly to get out and grab a newspaper. The local had said he thought he recognized the woman; he was almost certain she was a flamenco dancer he had once seen performing in Seville."

Jack exploded with a loud scoff. "There are lots of Flamenco dancers *and* singers in Seville."

"This one, the man said, was the most beautiful woman he had ever seen. He knew her as Marcella."

Jack's eyes went blank. "How sure was this local?"

"Pretty sure," Zach replied flatly. "Curves from here to Gibraltar. And the face…"

"Go on. The face?"

"You know. The Helen of Troy thing?"

Tanner let out a heavy sigh and then started taking off his pants.

"What are you doing?" Zach observed with a grin. "You just put those on, and I'm thinking we have to go find her."

"I did, and yes, we do. But where we're going, we need to suit up."

"Suit up?" Zach questioned. "If you recall, we left whatever luggage we had back at the shooting gallery. What I'm wearing is all I have. You too."

"When you dumped me on this bed, did you do what you're trained to do and check out the room? Look in the wardrobe, buddy."

Zach sheepishly looked down and then squinted toward the small closet door to the left. In his anxiousness to get out on the street, he'd missed it.

Walking over, he gave a quick glance at Jack, who was standing and moving over also. When he opened the door, six suits were hanging there, two each of dark blue, gray, and black.

Jack reached in past Zach and grabbed one. "These look more like my size. I'll wear a gray number. So, we don't look like twins, I suggest you go with blue."

"But I like the black," Zach quibbled.

"Where we're going, it's classy, but not formal."

"What's the difference?"

Tanner paused to think about his response. "I guess I really don't know the answer to that. Just what I've been told."

Zach thought back to his aunt Emma and her teachings on what to wear on his first date with Jenny Mathews. "Told by whom? I'm guessing a woman?"

"I suppose we'll just have to research it at a different time," Jack said, indignant. "Just put it on, will you?"

Zach laughed. "Okay, okay. Just wanted to hear it from you, is all."

Forty-five minutes later, a taxi carried them into Triana neighborhood, and let them off in front of El Patio Sevillano, one of the many tablaos that lined the main drag of Calle San Jacinto, their doors glowing with the promise of music and movement. Although, while peering through a water-spotted window, Zach had noticed this particular establishment just seemed to have a tad more going on.

It was bustling with large groups of men and women in their finest, smoking their nicotine sticks, laughing and hustling while waiting for tables inside. Jack handed the driver more than enough pesetas to make the man smile, then he and Zach exited the taxi. As they neared the entrance, Zach could feel the pulse of the event quickening as rhythmic Spanish beats burst, castanets clacked, and a single guitar raged in unison through the open doors, flooding the atmosphere of revelers out to the street.

The place was jumping. Jack led the way past the outsiders and stepped past an ambivalent bouncer and through a wooden-bead curtain. A thick, heavy smoke immediately filled their lungs as they maneuvered through the obstacle course of shoulder-to-shoulder, cigar-wielding, martini-slugging humanity, as well as the tables filled with Saturday night couples. Zach was instantly intrigued, finding himself getting caught up in the excitement.

The newness of the experience that resonated on his partner's face registered on Jack's. "Remember what we're here for," he cautioned.

Zach nodded, and began scanning for anyone who might look like someone who might have seemed like an inconsequential passerby before, but who now appeared dangerous. He reminded himself of the man from the bathroom who turned into an assassin and that he needed to be vigilant. As his eyes scoured all corners of the room, no one stuck out in his memory. Off to the right, a group of American Air Force kids were having a swell time while showing everyone how to be rude in a foreign country. The rest of the house appeared full of locals and those who had an appreciation of the art form. Suddenly, there was a slight separation of onlookers, a parting of the sea of bodies no more than a few feet ahead, and just like that, a thunderbolt hit as he locked in a woman that would forever be etched in his mind.

The dancer spun her traje de flamenco while posing and sensually positioning her movements within the rhythm offered. The skin-tight, jet-black gown with vivid red plumes flowed like crashing waves with every turn. Zach sensed he hadn't taken a breath in seconds, so he inhaled, then took a quick glance around to see if Tanner had been watching him. Turning back, he witnessed the dancer's final crescendo spin, and her arms flinging skyward like rockets that would conclude with exploding firecrackers, and then the music abruptly stopped as if the notes had fallen from space and met the sudden impact of Earth. The room went silent in unison.

Mesmerized by her beauty, Zach watched transfixed as the woman, with her arms still raised, slowly and seductively lowered them while her eyes slowly opened, and she appeared as if searching the room for a lover. She lit the room on fire with her performance, and was very much aware of this. She had penetrated the souls of every man there and elicited equal appreciation and disdain from the women on their arms.

Her performance had brought those fortunate enough to have witnessed it, through her story of dance, to the very end. She then lowered her head, spreading her plumes outward, and curtsied as her smile grew wide, enhancing the eyes that needed no enhancement. The room suddenly exploded with raucous applause. Everyone sitting enthusiastically stood to join those already clapping. Even the women there to appreciate the art and the artist understood the greatness of the performance delivered. But perhaps, they may have been secretly jealous of the adorations their significant others were giving to the one onstage.

The artist placed her hand over her heart, displaying her own appreciation for the love given, and then gave one last spin and gracefully disappeared through the crowd toward the rear.

Jack took one look at Zach's gaze that followed her. He then placed his hand on his underling's shoulder and leaned in. "Yup, my boy. That's her," he said loud enough over the ongoing roar.

A feeble "Holy shit!" was all Zach could muster.

"Yeah. That about sums it up," Jack said in agreement. With another slap on the back, he said, "Let's go."

Jack pointed toward the rear and started politely nudging his way toward a small hallway through the crowd, who were still giving her their ovation. As they reached the opening, a large man with a menacing look got out of his chair and blocked the entrance. Behind him, leaning against the wall, was the guitarist, just lighting up. He was a tall and lean gent whose looks fell somewhere in between Errol Flynn's handsome and Jerry Lewis' goofy. Either way, he could pull the ladies in. Looking up, he noticed the two and immediately came over.

"Why are you here?" he demanded in a not-so-welcoming heavy accent. As he closed the distance, his eyes narrowed. "I know you."

"You do," Jack responded.

"You work with that man. The one people call the Spaniard."

"On occasion, and yes. You're on a roll."

The man took a quick glance back at the stars' door, and then back over Jack's and Zach's shoulders. "The Spaniard, Señor Rodríguez… he is not with you?" he warily asked.

Jack gave a quick glance over to Zach, then back, and sighed. "No," he said reassuringly. "He's been injured."

The guitar player just smirked and said, "Good!" No sooner had the word left his lips, when a velvety smooth voice from behind caught their attention. Everyone turned to the purr.

"Seanito, my darling! Please don't be so protective. Let them through," then with a twirl, Marcella de Anda was again disappearing back into her room. As she did, she tossed her lovely brunette locks back over her shoulder and offered, "You know Mr Tanner is an old friend."

Again, Jack gave a look back to Zach and added a pointed finger at himself as if asking the question of *she remembers me?*

"You obviously made an impression," Zach panned, then pointed Jack to move ahead.

Seconds later, they were offered chairs to sit while the anxious Mr Petitt leaned against the doorjamb. Marcella sat and locked eyes with him through the mirror, then gave him a gentle smile followed by a very slight head tilt as if to say, "It's okay." It was a subtle move that Zach observed and assumed, based on what info Jack had offered earlier, that it was reserved only for a lover. Her guitar player, and apparently much more, returned with a reluctant yet reassuring smile of his own, then retreated and softly closed the door behind him. As if on cue, Marcella stood and turned her back to her guests. "Could you get the clasp, please?"

Zach gave a questioning glance at Jack. "Rock, paper, scissors?" He mumbled under his breath.

Jack quickly obliged with a nod and mouthed, "One, two, three," and they both threw down their offering. Zach won with paper.

Marcella posed with her hands on her hourglass waist. "Whoever won, please hurry. I can't breathe in this thing!" After a second or two, her hands dropped, showing her impatience. "My instincts tell me that the handsome boy won. Is this your first time?"

"No ma'am," Zach said, reminded of Veronica and stepping forward. Then, reaching up, he gently unclasped the hook and hesitated.

"Please continue. I still can't reach."

Zach obliged, pulling the zipper down to the small of her back, exposing her black-laced bra and a small tattoo of a single red rose just below her left shoulder blade. He stepped back.

"Thank you," she said, turning around. Her left hand came up to catch the dress when it slid off her shoulder. "Gentlemen?" she said as more of a declarative statement than a question.

Both men registered the request and turned away. As they did, she let her dress fall to the ground; she unclasped her bra, threw it onto her make-up counter, and grabbed a silk robe off the back of her chair and flung it on.

"Am I to assume, Mr Jack Tanner, that this is not an adoring fan visit?" she said while loosely knotting the tie on her robe.

"We are aware of Ivanski Kalpakoff's reemergence," Jack said bluntly.

"I see," Marcella replied, seeming unsurprised. "And?" she asked while sitting back down and applying cream to remove the rose color makeup from her cheeks. "This has what to do with me?"

"You don't seem surprised."

"I didn't think he was dead like the others. I assumed he would show up somewhere eventually."

"Eventually? Can I assume you were not expecting him here?"

"Here? In Seville?" she said convincingly. "No. Not here."

Still with just an educated guess about the woman in the car, Jack set the bait with a lie. "You've been seen with him, is all, and I want to hear from you what that was all about."

"Someone said that I was seen with Ivan. That is interesting, Mr Tanner. And you heard this from whom?"

That was not a denial, Jack thought. "Reliable eyes," he said.

Marcella swiveled back around to face herself in the mirror, and her loosened breasts noticeably glided with her. "I don't believe you," she said, while taking a hand towel and wiping the cream from her face.

Jack shrugged. "It's all true. What would be the point otherwise?"

"I thought we were friends, Jack?"

"We were slightly more than acquaintances from years ago. As I recall, you were playing the field and I was the referee. You're stalling. What can you tell me?"

"That disappoints me," she said, feigning a pout. "Regardless of your failing miserably with any words to convince. I will play the cards."

"I'll take that," Jack said, finally sitting down and motioning for Zach to do the same. "This is Zachary Ransom. My new partner."

She nodded over to Zachary. "A pleasure for you, I'm sure."

"Your English is near perfect, Miss de Anda," Zach offered. "Very little accent."

"I've had quite a bit of practice, Zachary," she said, surprising them with her informal use of Zach's first name. Then she pivoted to Jack. "What happened to Mr Scarpino? I thought you and he were inseparable."

"Your memory is impressive," he answered, again surprised that she retained information from just one meeting with Johnny. "He took a bullet but is still alive, doing the work back home. His head is going to balloon knowing he left an impression."

"Not sure if it's a gift or a curse that I remember."

Jack knew she was attempting to soften him with small talk and wanted to get her back on track. "Kalpakoff?"

"Yes, of course. Another name I remember."

"C'mon, Marcella. We know it was you in the car with him."

Marcella tossed the hand towel onto the vanity next to her face cream. "So, what if I were? There was certainly no crime committed there. Just two old friends catching up. Like now, with you."

"More," Jack said, waving his fingers.

Marcella tried to appear annoyed, "Ivan contacted me last week through one of his men. He wanted to see me. That's all."

"I bet," Jack scoffed, then pointed his head toward the door. "I don't suppose that sat well with what's-his-name."

Marcella placed a cigarette between her plump lips, flicked a lighter, tossed it on the vanity and took a deep draw. "Sean? No. It did not," she breathed out with the smoke. "He has become used to it, I suppose. I'm sure it hurts, but we have an arrangement that seems to work for both."

"I have no interest in your love life of convenience, Marcella—"

"So, we *are* all on a first-name basis," she interrupted.

"I'm not here about the past, and I'm not here with any government. And I really don't care who's tickling those inner thighs of yours. We just need to locate two Americans and get them safely back home."

Marcella's eyes glared for the briefest of moments, letting Jack know that he hit a nerve. "A Korean couple," she finally said flatly. "And don't act so naïve, Jack. We all work for some government, whether it's clear or not who that government is."

"Yes, to the Koreans. So, you *do* know. What can you tell us?" he pressed, sensing her willingness to divulge. "What are Kalpakoff's plans for them?"

"Jack Tanner, you must know better. I do not ask such questions. I'm, as you know, just a facilitator. I get this person to meet this person. Sides do not matter to me."

Jack attempted but failed to hold back a scoff. "Just the money."

Marcella de Anda hesitated as she calculated her response. "That was very cynical of you, *Jack.*"

"Just an observance, *Marcella,*" Jack equally responded glibly. "So, he told you of the Lees. Go on."

Marcella sighed. "The money is good and certainly helps with my lifestyle. One, as you were clearly aware that had been severely handicapped by the previous war. As far as the Lees… is that their name?"

"It is, and you can quit stalling."

Marcella took another drag of her cigarette. "I was just told by one of my people that there was a Korean couple involved somehow."

"You were seen in Constantina," Jack returned, not wanting to get sucked into a memory lane rabbit hole. "We believe that they are being held captive in a town north of there. One would surmise that you were entertained somewhere near there, and not out in the open. A house or farm, maybe? Just give us that location and we will do the rest."

Marcella spun back to her mirror and crushed her cigarette out. "That is all you need?" she asked, while applying fresh lipstick. "Is your intention to kill Ivan?"

"No intent, but things can get out of hand sometimes, and—"

Zach interrupted. "It's not like he hasn't tried to kill us already—" he paused when Jack put his hand up.

"We just want to get the hostages home. Can you help, or not?"

Marcella's eyes momentarily gazed into the mirror, as if transfixed by a memory, then softly said, "It was very awkward years ago with Javier and Ivan. I liked them both very much and both provided a degree of excitement and enhanced life that intrigued, and, yes, financially benefited me. But it did come at a cost."

"Just a location, Marcella. The history lesson doesn't matter anymore. This is important."

"Doesn't it? I still have feelings, and his life may be taken. I think it matters."

"I can make no promises."

Through the mirror's reflection, Marcella kept her eyes on Jack during a quiet pause. Jack kept steady with his own eyes, then after a few seconds, relinquished what was expected. "Okay. How much?"

"I think ten thousand American should do it," she said, without an inkling of remorse.

"Five thousand, and I'll have it wired in the morning. Address?"

"I do not have an address, but there is a small vineyard in the western hills, about a half of a mile above the town. You need to look for a white villa with a single large olive tree out front."

"There are probably twenty such vineyards on the west side, and they are all white," Jack intervened. "And just about everyone has olive trees."

"Yes. But there is a sign out front by the gravel drive. It reads La Escrabina."

Jack and Zach locked eyes. Both had the same thought that it sounded like one of the homes Miguel described. "What else can you tell us?" Zach asked.

"He *is* allowed to speak," Marcella said, smiling, then let her eyes roam over Zach as if she would have him for lunch.

"I have my moments," Zach followed, uncomfortable with the undressing.

Again, she smiled while giving Zach more than a once over, leaving him feeling naked. "There is a beautiful little courtyard in the rear with a Statue of David fountain," she continued, "…the chair cushions are a colorful tangerine, and the smoked salmon was delicious."

"I'd ask what you had for dessert, but we need more important answers," Jack said impatiently. "Did you see them?"

Marcella lit another cigarette. "No," she curtly said. "But his men kept going down these steps that led under a barn out back. One appeared to have food and a jug of something. If the people you seek are on the premises, that's where you might find them."

Jack stood up. "Before we go, anything else?"

Marcella de Anda took one last drag, pursed her lips and blew the smoke out in a steady stream. "He's definitely planning something big, if that is what you are asking. He said he would be retiring soon. That he'd had enough of hiding and that he would have more than enough money to do so," she paused while glancing at the door where her Sean once stood, then lowered her voice. "And he wanted me to come along."

"Something big, and he wanted you along for the ride. And?"

"Please lower your voice," she quietly pleaded. "I told him that I would think about it."

Jack stepped closer and lowered his voice, but added intent. "I don't give a shit about your live dildo out there, although he's a pretty good guitarist, but you're asking me to believe that you're going to think about it?"

"Well, Jack Tanner. I couldn't very well say no right then and there, could I? What if Ivan felt that I knew too much? Maybe I'm not here today."

Jack didn't need to think long about her answer. He knew that Ivan, like so many other men, was very much fixated on this woman. The thought of killing her would be as remote as setting fire to the Mona Lisa. Especially if he still believed he had a chance to get away and have a life with her. "I don't think so," he said confidently. "The big thing?"

"That's all I know," she started as she took another drag, then crushed the half-smoked cigarette out. "I will tell you that he rarely stays at the same location as his men. But I'm sure you knew that already."

Jack dropped his head. "No. I did not know that. What can you tell us about that?"

Marcella smiled and waited for it. Jack shook his head again. "How much?"

"The same."

"Okay, but only if we get the hostages and Kalpakoff," he said. "If not, I'll expect a refund."

"There are no guarantees in our work, Jack Tanner."

"It's a lot of money, Marcella. I'd hate to put you on my list to visit with bad intentions."

"The town of Cazalla de la Sierra is about twenty-five miles from Constantina. That is where he stays."

"That's not an address, just a large area."

"Twenty-five hundred then. That's all I have for you. Had he been successful in getting me into his bedroom, I would have more."

Jack didn't like the vague answer. "He didn't? Why? Did you become virtuous in the last few years?"

Marcella ignored the question and went back to putting cream on her face, feeling the absence of words would be a win for her. She was right.

Jack felt he was being played, but decided to settle with an "Okay." Knowing that if she came up with the goods, everything would be copasetic. And if not, he would be justified in getting the money back or getting even. Hopefully, Marcella believed he was capable of the even part.

"I shall expect you to keep your word, Jack. I'll check with the bank in the morning for the transfer," she said as she wrote her bank information on a note and handed it over.

Jack motioned Zach up and to the door. "It will be there. But if I find out you sent us on a wild-goose chase, your boy out there will be banging a tambourine in Modelo Prison by nightfall."

Out in the hallway, the smoke thickened as Jack closed the door behind them. Sean Petitt moved quickly up and past them and into the dressing room. But before closing the door again, he managed to throw a furrowed brow and a silent, threatening glare at the two of them.

Jack said, "Let's get out of here," and they made their way through the obstacle course of patrons to the door. Once outside, Zach hailed a cab. A few seconds later, they were climbing into a white Fiat with yellow striping and were being whisked away. Jack glanced over at Zach, who was deep in thought and staring out the window. "What's rattling around in there, buddy?" he asked.

"I still have a lot to learn," Zach replied, almost seeming apologetic for not being up to speed.

"You'll get there. Hell, I'm still learning."

"I just want to catch up quicker, I suppose. You can't be the lead every time."

Jack laughed. "With your debate experience, I'm not worried about you being out there alone. Just keep your head down for now."

Zach nodded back. A few seconds later, he blew out a heavy sigh. "That woman…"

"That woman grew up poor," Jack intervened. "Word has it that she worked the vineyards and sold fruit on the street corners for years while watching aspiring dancers through dirty windows. She self-taught herself the moves of many, then perfected and added her own flair. It took years through poverty while having to battle up through the ranks of some of the greatest Flamenco dancers of Spain, and the world," then Jack let out a sigh as if he truly knew her pain.

"As great as she is, though, there's always been a large chip on those silky and slender shoulders of hers."

"And why is that?" Zach asked.

"I believe it's because she's never been recognized as numero uno. I think that's why she's drifted to the seedier side of the law, not that there hasn't been corruption all over this country, so she's not alone in that regard. Her family are all dead now, the war took care of that. And she hasn't popped out any kids, as far as we know, so money and the thrill of being on the edge is what drives her," Jack turned and peered out his own window. "So, yeah," he said. "She's something, all right. But don't let her fool you, buddy. She's dangerous."

"Dangerous?" Zach followed. "She's scary as hell!"

CHAPTER TEN

SIMILAR PREDICAMENTS

"¿Dónde están nuestros hijos?

THE DECADES-WORN and deteriorated wooden stairs headed treacherously downward in a seemingly endless straight line that darkened with every step. A small flickering candle dripped from its sconce some fifteen feet behind him, and there was another near the bottom of the stairway. The minimal light wasn't much help, as Ivanski Kalpakoff warily extended out his right leg in search of the next support while thinking there should have been one more in the middle.

Unsure of success, he reached for a hoped-for handrail that was nowhere to be found and instead steadied himself with the palm of his hand on the damp earthen wall. Slowing his pace to be sure of better footing, he finally found himself at the first landing and the left turn that would get him closer. As he cautiously made the turn, he was relieved to see another light flickering from below, acting as a beacon while it illuminated the bottom steps.

Dimitri, a behemoth of a man with a bald dome, having heard someone approaching, peeked out from behind the corner, then holstered his pistol while nodding to his boss that everything was fine. Ivanski made the lower hall, filled with racks of wine on both sides, then walked over to a makeshift desk of two round French-oak casks with three, six-inch planks laid across, and Jeoung Lee bent over it with pen in hand. An oil lamp to his near left was barely enough for the squinting man to read what his own hand had written. Jeoung lifted his head up but barely acknowledged his captor before letting his eyes fall back to his work. Nari emerged a second later, readjusting her dress, having apparently just visited the honeypot hidden behind more casks. A bathroom was just one of the many conveniences lacking in their new accommodation.

Ivanski clasped his hands behind his back and moved in behind Jeoung like a professor ready to challenge his student on some physics or mathematical problem.

"Where are we at, Doctor Lee?" he bluntly asked.

Jeoung, who could not help appearing annoyed, grunted, "Not yet."

Kalpakoff sighed, unconvinced. "We need an answer, Doctor. Time is waning."

Jeoung took his glasses off, set them on the papers before him, and rubbed his temples. "It's very cold down here, making it hard to sleep. We need more blankets."

Kalpakoff nodded to Dimitri. "You shall have them."

"And the lighting. It is very difficult to see."

"There is no electricity here. How about another oil lamp, yes?"

Jeoung gave a nod. "That would help."

"See? That wasn't so hard," Kalpakoff grinned, then turned serious. "We need those calculations soon. You have forty-eight hours."

"That's impossible!" Nari blurted from a few feet away. "You are asking too much!"

Ivanski turned and smiled back at her. "Is that so, Mrs Lee?" Then he calmly walked over to her, and just as she was beginning to speak again, he backhanded her across her face, nearly knocking her to the ground. Jeoung leapt up and came to his wife of thirty years just as she began to weep. He placed a consoling arm around her and brought her over to a cot on the other wall and sat her down. He gently caressed the red mark on her cheek that was beginning to swell, then his anger grew, and he turned back to his captor.

"This is not how things are done!" Jeoung fired back. "We are not animals! You must be patient for what you are asking!"

"Patience?" Kalpakoff said with a smirk, then calmly walked over. "Here is my patience," then he reached into his pocket and pulled out three photos and tossed them down at the couple's feet. Jeoung's eyes went wide in unison with a hand-over-mouth gasp from Nari. Two of the photos were of their children, Ji-Hoon and Si-Woo, bound, gagged, and in the trunk of some car. The other showed them among casks of wine—a wine cellar, maybe, they wondered. Their children were enduring a similar fate to theirs, and as parents, it hurt.

"They will be dead at one second past the hour forty-eight," Ivanski claimed. Then, looking deep into Jeoung's eyes, he added, "Your Mrs Lee at two seconds."

Robert Dowling raised his binoculars and searched the upper-floor windows for any movement. The placement of the tracking device that his partner had placed just two days before had initially worked, and they had followed their man to a location on the east end of town that afternoon. But by the time the team was put together, when they hit the brownstone, they were disappointed to find it already deserted. When they followed the tracking device again, it led them to one of their own government-issued Fords, and that really pissed Dowling off even more. He sent several (and as he had previously claimed) *clumsy fucking agents* diving under their collective desks when he threw his stapler.

Fortunately for the department, agent Pimpleton had not been in the room, but rather, and on a hunch, had been at the right place at the right time. Figuring he and his superior had already been made with their government-issued sedan, and much to the chagrin of his wife, he had borrowed her car, the very popular Chevy Bel-Air, to locate the man who had met with Ji-Hoon at the coffee shop just days before.

He had camped out at various times near the two other spots where the mark had been seen for meetings and got lucky. The agent's second stop had reaped the reward sought when; while sitting behind the wheel, he had noticed his mark strolling up to the frequented bench at Burnside Park, in the center of Providence. A few minutes passed when a fellow he had not seen before, wearing a long pea coat and fedora, approached and sat at the opposite end of the bench. No sooner had Jeffrey taken some quick photos than the second man was gone. Half a minute later, his mark had set down his paper and strolled away. He had followed the man to the location that was now being readied for a rescue with twelve agents lying in wait for a signal.

A shade was briefly lifted, and one of the men in the grainy photo that Agent Pimpleton had provided was recognized peering down to the street, then quickly closed the shade again. Special Agent Dowling lowered his binoculars and handed them over to another agent. Then glancing at the photo again and recognizing that it matched the man in the window, he nodded and said, "Okay," then he gave the photo one last verifying glance before stuffing it back into his coat side pocket.

"Tell everyone it's the second floor, west end, corner unit. We go in five," he ordered. He raised his hand with five fingers aloft, and followed with a quick motion to a group of six to circle around to the rear alley. A few minutes later, all hell broke loose with doors banging, windows breaking, a few screams, and several gunshots. The last caused Agent Dowling to grimace while running behind and down an outside stairwell. When he finally reached the bottom and entered the room, there was one bad guy bleeding out on the floor.

"Are we clear?" he questioned the first agent he encountered.

"Yes, sir. We're clear."

He stepped over the soon-to-be-dead dude and went through to the next room. Two other men, one still shouting what Dowling could only assume were expletives in his native tongue, were on their stomachs, bleeding from various points on their bodies while being handcuffed. "Where are they?" he quickly asked the agent kneeling on the back of the one irritated bad guy.

The agent slapped the head of the still-yelling man, thought to be a Russian. "Shut up!" then he head-nodded to a door on the right. "Another flight down."

Agent Dowling, feeling more relieved, went down the last twelve steps and entered a spacious wine cellar. On the left were several single casks with two large, floor-to-ceiling bottle racks yielding approximately four hundred bottles. Up against the right wall, and separated by a high-topped table, were Ji-Hoon and Si-Woo. Both were just getting adjusted to being ungagged and bound, but more importantly, appearing uninjured and healthy. As soon as Ji-Hoon saw Agent Dowling, he cried out. "Our parents?!"

Dowling sighed and shook his head. "Unknown."

This brought immediate despair from the two now-rescued children. "But do you know where they are?" Si-woo cried out.

"All that has been received so far is that they have been moved to the countryside and that they are being held by a well-known arms dealer. His name is Ivanski Kalpakoff. He was taken off our wanted list when he went missing a few years back. Everyone interpreted that as he had stepped on someone's toes and was no longer a viable source."

"What does that even mean? No longer viable?" Ji-Hoon questioned.

"For us, it meant that he was likely dead. We were wrong."

"What do we do now? Just wait?"

"Unfortunately, that is all you can do. Only not back at home," Dowling waved his partner to come over. "This is Agent Pimpleton. He's going to take you somewhere safe. He'll fill you in on the way, but just know that you won't be able to leave the home for a while until things are cleared up. It's just too dangerous. You'll have supplies, so I hope you can cook."

Pimpleton helped Si-Woo to her feet and motioned them both to follow. At the foot of the stairs, Ji-Hoon turned back. "How much trouble are our parents in?" he asked, not really wanting an answer.

"It depends," Dowling replied.

"On what, exactly?"

"On whether or not the boys on the ground get to them in time."

"Who are these people? The ones helping?"

Dowling hesitated over how much he should be willing to say. "This is where it's a little muddy," he admitted, "The United States is not officially on the ground there, but there are others on our behalf that are making headway. We're getting word via a sympathetic and trusted intermediary."

"Who? Can you tell us?"

"I'm sorry, no. Even though we have never met, they keep us informed. We're only aware that to date, they have never been wrong. But when we do hear any word, you will be the first to know. That's all I can say for the moment. You'll just have to trust the process. You have no choice."

The response didn't help ease any worry Ji-Hoon and Si-Woo had about their parents. Si-Woo leaned against her brother's arm for comfort, and Ji-Hoon pulled her in close. "It will be all right," he softly said, trying his best to be convincing. As he helped his sister take the first few steps up, another thought came to him. "What about the other one?" he asked, showing concern. "Do you know what happened to her?"

"What other one?" Dowling asked, perplexed.

"There was another one brought down with us. A young woman, around my age. We tried to communicate through our gags before she was taken away."

Dowling and Pimpleton briefly locked concerning eyes. "We haven't heard anything about another, but if you remember any more details, make sure you tell the agent." Then, he motioned Pimpleton to get moving. "Take them out the back, just in case."

CHAPTER ELEVEN

GET THEM OUT ALIVE

"Eins von zwei ist nicht schlecht."

FIVE IN THE MORNING, the wee hour, and the Adler limo pulled up right on time. It was still dark out, and Zach tried to stifle an oncoming yawn, then cautiously peered both ways before stepping out of the hotel doorway. The street was barren of any headlights or fumes from a parked assassin's car tailpipe, and that's *a good thing*, he thought, amusing himself. *Then again, it would be hard not to be noticed on a narrow, cobbled street, barely wide enough for one car and a fruit cart, to get by at the same time.* Zach scanned his eyes up to a sea of second-floor windows on the opposite side of the street and slowly trailed them from one window to the next, looking for movement or a glint of a scoped rifle's lens. Nothing there. It hadn't taken long in his short time on the mission to understand that his chosen field was dangerous. A few inches here, a few seconds wasted there, and he probably would not be around to ponder what could have been. His short life would already be gone. The caution had never appeared truer—you could never be careful enough. He glanced again up to the windows to see if maybe the sniper had been playing a cat and mouse game and just waiting for him to forget the rule—never-ever be careful enough.

He turned and gestured to Jack Tanner that the coast was clear. Still nursing his wound, Jack gingerly stepped out and, by training, did the same look about, not relying solely on his partner—another rule. Satisfied, he gave a nod, and they both moved quickly to the limo. Zach, acquiescing to Jack's leadership role, went to the front while Jack opened the rear door. The Spaniard was there.

As they fell into the car, both Jack and Zach acknowledged his presence with a nod, then Miguel shoved the stick into first and sped the Adler away. For some reason, Zach had anticipated a few pings off the car's hood from errant shots, but none came. No one had been on the street, in a window or on a rooftop. No one had been watching. The only person seen was a baker, and that too, was through the window of his store while preparing for the day. His look was nothing more than a dream of a passing car. Could *he* even have been an assassin? In this new world he had entered, even old women, dancers and bakers could be killers. You just didn't know until you did.

And that's where Zach realized that the years and experience of having a stable of friends, acquaintances, bartenders, newsboys, bellhops, Matre d's and your average street urchin—that one could find in every village, town or big city, helped in achieving goals and just surviving. He'd seen it with Jack and Javier. He'd seen it with Miss de Anda. And he was now seeing it in him—and he now realized that he was building his own stable. In that mini-second, he felt that he had just achieved a new mental growth spurt. Settled in and more focused than he had ever been, Zach slowed his breath to remind himself that he would now control what was to be absorbed or thrown away, then melted into his seat to just watch and listen. As he did, he was reminded to only speak when there was a purpose. A second later, the drill started.

Jack gave Javier a once-over. "How are you feeling?" he asked the Spaniard.

"Better than expected, and thank you for the inquiry," the ever-optimistic Javier replied, polite as ever. "I can walk without the cane and appear an old man, which is good and bad."

Jack was glad his friend was alive and kicking, but as usual, did not want to let on too much that he had an affection for the man. "I would have thought looking like an old guy with money hanging out his pockets would be the exact look to draw the Mrs Rodríguez number six," Jack said, grinning.

That brought on a half-hearted yet somewhat pained smile from the Spaniard. "Don't worry, my friend. I know you love me. But you may be right. I should have given it more thought."

Jack and Javier gave a longer-than-necessary connected look, then nodded their understanding of the relationship that had endured. Zach sucked it all in while trying to piece together just how friendly these two were, and to what degree they would be willing to use each other. Then, on the other hand, he also had an itch to scratch. He was less connected to the conversation as he was when first climbing in and becoming fully aware of the Sten machine gun on the seat between him and the ever-quiet Miguel. Still, relaxed enough in the moment, he turned to eye Javier and asked, "Is this it?"

Javier pulled open his jacket, exposing not one, but two shoulder-harnessed revolvers. "If we do it right, we will be enough. Our source has assured me that two of the men have taken up residence in town to keep a pulse on anything happening that could affect them. There is a public phone just outside if they were to call ahead," then he nodded toward Miguel. "Our friend here has a man watching for that, just in case."

"That's very comforting," Zach panned.

Javier turned to Jack. "You know…I really like your boy."

Jack returned with a lean-in. "Now *that's* very comforting."

The Spaniard shook off the sarcasm and got back to business. "They typically have breakfast in a café before coming up to the farm and usually arrive around nine."

"And who is this source?" Zach asked.

"So, he's taking the lead now, Tanner?"

"Boy has got to learn, right?"

"I don't want to offend," Zach interrupted. "But I'm not waiting anymore to jump in. I want what everyone wants, but I'm not going to die over a miscalculation that got missed, and I wanted to question, but didn't."

There was no overreaction by Jack or Javier. Even Miguel kept silent, but there seemed to Zach to be an affirming smirk curling from the driver's mouth.

Javier nodded okay. "Very well. One always drinks milk and has eggs over-easy. The other just coffee with a splash of whatever booze he has in his coat. That man never talks."

"Okay. I get it. You trust the source," Zach said, convinced.

Then Javier glanced over and winked at Miguel, who had one eye in the rearview mirror. Miguel took the cue and turned to Zach and grinned. "There will be only two when we arrive," he said in his deep-throated voice. "Small arms."

"He speaks English?!" Zach said, surprised. "And what does *mostly* mean?"

"You never really know for sure in these situations. There could always be more, but do not worry," the Spaniard counseled. "We have grenades, too."

Zach looked over at Jack, who obviously had been listening but was now staring out the window. Jack had to be feeling Zach's eyes, because he turned to him but said nothing. Just an eyebrow squint to say that everything was fine. No words were spoken the rest of the way.

Fifty minutes later, the Adler was slowly rolling through the mountain village of Constantina. It was still dark, but lightening from the sun, which was fifteen minutes away from cresting an easternmost hill. A smattering of shop owners was just beginning their rituals of turning off lights and other preparations for the day's clientele. A young boy, no more than ten or twelve, in an apron and broom, stepped out and began lazily sweeping in front of one panaderia, his eyes barely acknowledging the slow-moving limo. A few less than enthusiastic motions in, he briefly halted and groggily yawned before returning to his chore.

Zach managed a light chuckle as he thought with near certainty that the boy's job had been passed down from generation to generation, like so many other families of the region had for those uninspired to extend their education.

The Adler continued through town, where many of the streets narrowed and stacked row housing with doors opening just feet from the cobbled streets, crowded the road. Every few blocks, a roadway would dead-end into a small and unremarkable triangular park, no larger than the size of two basketball courts side by side, forcing the one driving to circumvent around to find another route. Nearly all would offer sparse trees and shrubs with a small patch of grass for those wanting to picnic, and if one was lucky, a park bench or short stone wall to sit on. *The town was as sleepy as Rumpelstiltskin,* Zach mused.

Another two lefts and a singular right brought them to Calle Pablo Iglesias, where they made a final left turn and gradually headed up the hill and into the countryside. Less than half a mile further, Miguel pulled the car to a lazy stop and peered up the hill while pointing with his crooked index finger that had most likely been broken from some warfare encounter. Javier leaned forward just behind his driver's right shoulder and squinted in the direction where a tall white house stood on what appeared to be a few acres of vineyard. A singular olive tree sat majestically in the middle and out front. He nodded his understanding, then Miguel placed the stick into neutral and pulled the hand brake to full, then, grabbing the Sten, he abruptly jumped out of the vehicle and started jogging down an adjacent road.

"What's happening?" Zach asked, surprised at the sudden abandonment of the vehicle.

"You drive now," Javier said as a command.

"Jump over there, Zach," Jack confirmed.

Never one for a lack of confidence, Zach slid over and then offered a caveat. "I haven't driven in a year, and this isn't a Buick." Then he went to work, taking inventory and studying the center-floor shifter, followed by the dashboard of the foreign setup.

"C'mon, Ransom! It's a stick!" Jack lightheartedly pushed.

Zach shot an irritated glance into the rearview, released the brake, dropped the clutch, slammed the stick into first, then bolted up the hill and jammed the shifter into second.

"Okay, okay, big boy. Not too fast. We want to catch them by surprise," Jack cautioned.

"You can't have it both ways, Tanner," Zach snarked back, but eased off the accelerator all the same. Twenty seconds later, they were in front of a closed wrought iron gate. A wooden sign on the six-foot-high block wall read, LA ESCRABEÑA.

"This must be the place," Jack uttered, playing Captain Obvious. "Pull past and down a little bit further to the right."

Zach obeyed, quickly shifting the car into neutral and killing the engine, yet keeping just enough momentum to roll into a small gravel turnout, stopping against a river-stone wall draped with orange-blossomed bougainvillea. Javier retrieved two hand grenades from the glove compartment, then the three simultaneously emerged from the car, checked their side arms and began looking for anyone who could sound an alarm. It was now just a little after six, and the sun's early rays had already started to brighten the sky.

"We'll go over the wall down there," Jack said in a low voice while pointing to an area ahead on the perimeter wall fifty feet away. "Once we're all inside, we two cripples will enter from the front door."

While moving in earnest, they kept their frames low. Zach followed the two to a section of wall where the road's uphill grade had the wall at only five feet. He raised his eyes just over the river-stone cap and could see that just a few feet away, on the interior, was a tall hedge that would keep them hidden for the time being. He gave a coast-clear nod, then helped both Javier and Jack up and over with a two-handed boost. Javier stifled a painful, low moan when he landed less clean than Jack, and ended up on his backside, barely avoiding a head injury from a large protruding tree root. Zach heard the thud, then followed, leaping as if a mongoose, clearing the wall cleanly with spring-loaded legs, and then landing softly, like a cat, right next to them.

"I'm going," he said, confident that no one would argue, then immediately bolted away.

Javier watched and turned to Jack, who looked amazed. "How does he do that?" he said in a low voice.

Jack shook his head. "Beats me? But when I finally find out, I'll start eating what he's eating."

Both men regrouped and positioned themselves to watch Zach's approach through the hedge. He had begun his circle by running full speed to the large olive tree next to the left walking path, then he waited for any acknowledgement, an alarm, a dog, or just someone shouting at him being there—none came. The grounds surrounding and the home itself were quiet. He turned back to the boys and threw two fingers down, signaling two minutes before their own approach. As discussed, there would be a distraction. Zach made it to the side and had turned the corner, then, with his pistol raised, he slowed his pace to get a peek into several windows along the way, but could not see anyone about. Already, the scene had him thinking of the first attempt at rescuing the Lees. Nobody was home. Ten seconds later, he was at the rear and crouched behind another low stone retaining wall next to a short set of steps that led to the back courtyard. He slowly brought his eyes up and confirmed the observations given by Marcella de Anda. The tangerine cushions and the fountain with David spewing a stream of water from his privates were spot on. She hadn't lied. Zach scanned the courtyard, then the barnlike structure twenty yards further out.

Waiting for the distraction promised, Zach kept still beneath a high open window. Then suddenly, Miguel's head popped out from around one corner some sixty feet away, and near a door at the far side of the rear structure. He raised his arm and waved Zach to come over, then went inside.

"Shit!" Zach mumbled to himself, thinking that Miguel should have waited. Then he heard a loud knock at the front door; the distraction was here. A few seconds passed, then footsteps were heard followed by a female voice. Someone had been home. She said something that sounded like a surprised greeting, then he could just make out that she was asking politely what business they had, followed by the Spaniard kindly asking for the owner. The housekeeper, or whoever she had been, followed quickly with her suspicious reply that they were all out on Holiday and would not be returning until June.

Zach needed to make his move now. He quickly leapt up the steps and crossed the courtyard to a rear French door, reached for the handle, and applied slight pressure. As hoped for, the entrance was conveniently unlocked. Just as he was leaning to slither in, he was startled by the faint pops of gunfire from the barn. It was on. Without hesitation, his instinct had him springing toward the barn door at full throttle. Jack and Javier would be on their own for the time being. Halfway there, the crackling of machine-gun fire was heard in the interior and most certainly would be heard at the front door. *So much for surprises*, Zach thought as he burst through the open door and threw himself down on the floor. The landing was small, only four feet square and a stairway down. With two hands on his weapon and facing forward, he began to slide on his belly down the steps and into the darkness that was only strobe-lit by the gun battle being waged below.

Every step killed his chest, knees and crotch, but he was determined not to be upright when the assailant turned the corner with their machine gun. His body began to swell, as was now expected, when he was under duress, and that was okay by him. Halfway to the bottom landing, Miguel suddenly fell backwards into the stairwell, causing Zach to instinctively fire off two rounds. To his, and more importantly, Miguel's relief, both missed their intended target. The bouncing as he went down the steps altered his aim just enough for his bullets to be errant. If he hadn't finally recognized Miguel, he was certain he would have calibrated enough to have taken him down by the third. Miguel gave a look of "What the fuck?" then turned to take a quick peek around the corner. Zach was standing now and quickly closing the distance down the steps. Once there, he hugged the wall next to Miguel, who was reaching under his coat and pulling out a hand grenade. Without consulting the man next to him, he pulled the pin.

"No!" Zach shouted, then noticed that Miguel was bleeding again. This time from several places. "Are they dead?" he loudly asked, referring to the Lees.

Miguel put on his usual *don't worry* grin, then tossed the grenade. Both leaned into the wall and covered up. The explosion rocked the stairwell, and specifically the wall they were up against, sending pieces of wood and mortar flying around them. With seemingly no fear, Miguel plunged forward into the dust-filled room, and Zach reluctantly followed. Miguel had leapt to the right while laying down a suppression fire, so Zach went left, doing the same. On the opposite side, the machine gun, and whoever had been on the trigger, was silent.

Both Zach and Miguel stopped their fire and lay prostrate on the earthen floor, peering through the sights of their weapons. As the dust cleared enough, to the right, they could see one man down. His head was pinned awkwardly against the wall with his glazed eyes forward. Both his hands still gripped the Russian-made PPSh-41 submachine gun, which rested on his chest. Miguel squinted while aiming his Ruger 9mm, then squeezed off a single round that exploded the man's forehead into the wall. Zach squinted his questioning eyes over at Miguel.

Miguel shrugged. "I thought I saw his chest move."

Zach got up quickly, but noticed Miguel struggling. He reached over and helped him up. "Gracias, *mi amigo*," Miguel offered respectfully, and with the kind of sincerity you would expect from going shoulder to shoulder into battle with another.

The two men surveyed the scene, taking inventory of the aftermath. Suddenly, there was shouting from above, followed almost immediately by gunfire. They both spun quickly around with their weapons raised. Again, like a cougar chasing its prey, Miguel did not hesitate. He lunged toward the stairwell, then surprisingly bounded two steps at a time, up the stairs as if uninjured. Zach's first instinct was to follow, but remembering the mission, he hesitated, then refocused. Only two men were supposed to be there, plus one possible housekeeper who may or may not be working with the group, and who may or may not be good with a weapon.

The boys up top would have to cover it for now. The smoke was beginning to clear, and so he began his search. Where were they? A few moments passed when he heard coughing from behind a few wine casks. He kept his pistol raised in that direction.

"It's okay. You can come out now," he said.

First were their raised hands, followed by their heads, then finally the forms of Jeoung and Nari stood up through the lingering smoke. Zach let out a sigh of relief.

"You're safe now," he said, just as a few more gunshots were heard outside, belying the statement.

"Are you sure?" Jeoung reasonably questioned.

Zach glanced back up the stairs. "Probably," he answered, then commanded, "Follow me."

"Wait!" Jeoung called out. "Who are you? What is your name?"

"Sorry," Zach quickly returned. "No names for now. Let's go," then, turning to leave, he applauded himself inside for being so professional.

Jeoung and Nari warily followed Zach up the stairs until he halted at the doorway and motioned with a palm held up for them to wait. All of the mayhem had apparently stopped—but who won? Zach cautiously went outside and disappeared from view. The couple stayed back and anxiously stood waiting for news of assured safety, then a minute later, they heard the call from Zach that they could come out. The two peeked outside and quickly deduced all that had happened on their behalf. Miguel was kneeling down next to one of their captors, who appeared very dead, and was going through his pockets.

Over by the courtyard and the David fountain, were two men speaking with their rescuer. A woman they had never formally met, but who they presumed to be the one making food for them, lay crumpled in the fountain with her body floating face up and her feet hanging over the stone rim. She was not moving, and there was a pistol on the ground a few feet from her. Oddly funny, David was pissing on her head.

Zach motioned for the Lees to come over. He introduced them to Jack and Javier by saying, "These two men…" then embellished more with them as not belonging to any one particular organization but as concerned citizens. He was quite sure that they didn't buy any of it, but he also figured that, at this point, they probably couldn't have cared less. Being just thankful to be out of their dire predicament and in the hands of whomever was willing to risk their lives to save theirs.

Jeoung was taking inventory of all that was around them. "There was another," he said loud enough to get everyone's attention.

Jack spoke first. "Another?"

"Yes, there was someone. We were all gagged and blindfolded the first night, so we didn't see or speak to him."

"You're sure it was a he, then?"

"Yes. A younger man, to be sure. But he was not with us by morning. When they took our restraints off, he was gone. We assumed they put him in another room."

Jack gave both Zach and Javier a look, suggesting, "Anything?"

"There's no one else in the barn," Zach said.

"And the house is clear," Javier followed.

"Well, whoever it is, we'll have to deal with it later. Can't be chasing ghosts right now," Jack concluded.

Javier quickly agreed, then reminded everyone about the two other bad guys who were in town having their breakfast and would be arriving around nine. He then suggested that it was time to go and ushered everyone toward the car. Jack hesitated. "We can't take everyone in the limo," he said, looking around, then added to Javier, "Where's your man?"

No sooner had the words left his lips, they all turned to face a roar behind them. A newer model, black Mercedes-Benz sedan, peeled around the back of the barn, spewing dirt and gravel in its wake. Miguel was behind the wheel. He stopped alongside them and, badly hurt, struggled out of the car. He had so much blood all over his body, it was hard to tell what was from his injuries or from him rolling around during some hand-to-hand battle with one of the combatants. He stopped to steady himself, then said, "I'm keeping it," then he stumbled around the front of the car using the hood for balance. Just before climbing into the front seat on the other side, he pointed at Zach and said, "You. Time for the hospital."

Zach pointed at himself while turning to the others. "Me?"

Jack helped him out. "You go. We'll get these two to the embassy, then I'll meet you back at the shack."

Zach nodded an "Okay," and got in the Mercedes behind the wheel. Jack walked over and tapped the window. Zach rolled it down. "I'm okay," he said to Jack. "It's an automatic."

"I'm sure you'll do just fine. Just wanted you to know that when he said hospital, he didn't mean hospital."

"Nothing is as it seems, someone told me once," Zach said, then shrugged. "So where am I going?"

Jack nodded over to Miguel, who was motioning to get going. "He'll tell you where to go. Practice the language and make friends."

"And what about Mr Ivanski Kalpakoff? What happens to him?"

"For now? He gets to live another day."

Jeoung interjected from behind. "But what about the papers?"

Jack turned to the professor. "What papers?"

"He has everything."

"What's everything, Mr Lee?" Jack said, starting to feel sick to his stomach.

"They have our children. You must understand," Jeoung pleaded.

Jack gave a quick look back at Javier, then went back to Zach. "Go and handle this, but be ready when you get back. You'll be able to sleep next week. Go!"

"Our children," Jeoung said again.

Jack placed a comforting hand on Jeoung's shoulder. "We received word a couple of hours ago. We have them. They are fine."

CHAPTER TWELVE

RIVERA'S REQUIEM

Pearl Harbor Naval Base Hospital,
April 19, 1942

THE LIGHT had been purposely dimmed to make the room less conspicuous, but the result was discomforting. Octavio Rivera turned away from his microscope, set his glasses aside, and began rubbing his tired eyes. He had been at it for several hours already, and the time spent had followed a grueling ten-hour (but normal for the times) hospital shift checking in on the infirmed and recovering, which, barely four months removed from the Japanese attack on Pearl, had been relentless.

Regardless of his scheduling, he had decided that he would be the one to determine the validity of his theories. No person of perceived higher authority was going to sweep his findings under any bureaucratic rug—and that included his nemesis, Colonel Carl Sherman. The threat given had been delivered by the colonel just nine days before. The words weren't minced and certainly not subtle. He, and on no uncertain terms, was to leave the Ransom file alone or there would be consequences.

Now, with the boy gone and living with his aunt in Georgia, it left him with no additional physical access, and the only ultimate conclusion he was left with was for him to sneak down to the hospital laboratory in the wee hours to continue his own unauthorized investigation. He was very tired, and to say that he was nervous about being discovered, would be an understatement.

The doctor yawned, stretched, then dragged himself over to the door and glanced through the side glass panel down the empty 3 a.m. hallway. Bernie the janitor was the only soul in sight—and he hadn't noticed the doctor slip into the lab. Returning to the sink, he splashed cold water on his face, took a sip, and felt the grogginess lift slightly. Back at his stool, he stared at the largest horn-eyed ghost crab he'd ever seen, drew a deep breath, held it, then exhaled.

The average shell size of this particular decapod ranged from two to three inches, he reminded himself, and this creature was nearly four times that. With body parts already disassembled, the doctor took another one-eyed survey of the crustacean's inner workings, convinced, he pulled away from the eyepiece and began writing preliminary notes. The molting process had occurred months before in what was perceived to be a mature crab, so the muscle had already grown back, which had given the good doctor a great specimen to work with.

His initial writing confirmed two main issues. First, the obvious: that the entire circulatory system was abnormally enlarged along with equivocal bone and musculature structure. Secondly, high levels of radiation poisoning were still evident in the creature's system, yet rather than gradually killing it, as science had taught the world that it would, it had enhanced the creature and, similarly, other crustaceans found at the time—and given what those levels would do to humans, that had been a surprise.

There had to be something inherent to the structure of its metabolic system that either restrained, protected, or enhanced its genetics in some way—but what? And, like the others captured and held in large tanks, there had been offspring. These newbie crabs had remained normal-sized and showed extremely low levels of radiation. He was convinced that the enlarged initial clan had been a one-off occurrence. Other than small amounts of radiation, nothing had passed down from one generation to the next.

The main conundrum was that normal crabs from all varieties were known to be mostly harmless. They never bit and had no exterior teeth to cause any harm, anyway. They had been known to pinch if cornered or would have their territory invaded, but it was still a rarity. And if one *were* to pinch, there would most likely not be enough force behind the compression to pierce human skin. *Did the radiation poisoning create aggression,* the doctor thought on. *Like the madness formed in a rabid animal. And, if so, did it also give the decapod the increased size and strength to enable its pinch to penetrate? And if it were to break skin, how would the radiation be transferred to a new host?* The doctor rubbed his temples as his head was beginning to ache with all the questions cluttering his brain.

He reminded himself that he had not been the only one to document all this, but all involved in the research, him included, were ignored. Their combined reports and most useful observations had been redacted and stuffed away in some vault to be harvested at a later date, or so they were told. Regardless, everyone with access to the information was told no, commanded to basically leave it alone, and that it was being handled by other "higher up" and "more qualified" departments. His brain screamed, *bullshit!*

After his unfortunate collision with the coronel the week before, and the discovery of his own notes being missing from the archival library, he had been scared, wary, and then pissed off! Raised by farming parents, he had toughened up while having to work in the avocado fields outside of his hometown of Morelia in the Mexico state of Michoacán. That, and the childhood fights for respect that were commonplace amongst his peers while establishing the unofficial pecking order for youths in the community, had hardened him to abusive challenges. He had resolved long ago that he wanted to be and live his life as a fair man. And no. He wasn't going to be dismissed or ignored.

Now, he thought back about the young boy whom he had grown fond of over the past four months. *How in God's divine name did this affect young Zachary Ransom?*

CHAPTER THIRTEEN

AN OLD FRIEND JOINS THE PARTY

"¿Cómo me encontraste?"

TOMMY POSTMAN yawned and attempted to reach up with one hand to rub his eyes. The chain around his wrist stopped him short by several inches. "Shit!" he blurted as he winced, then it all came back to him. Franticly squirming, he tried to reach across his body, twisting into it, but the chain on the other wrist prevented that also. The itch was driving him nuts now, so his last alternative was to just lean his head onto his bicep—thankful success. Now the panic set in.

It had been five days since he and his buddies, all just out of basic training, had arrived at Moron Air Base—an unfortunate name to be sure, just thirty-five miles south of Seville. After his best friend Zachary had convinced him over a year ago to stay out of the infantry, he had taken a chance and joined the Air Force. He knew his grades would never be good enough for flying, but it had turned out that he could be a damn fine mechanic, so they had taken him. According to the recruitment officer and the other recruiter working the kiosk, he was goofy enough to contribute in some way. It also didn't hurt when he handed over a nice referral letter that Jack Tanner had penned, with the simple request not to make him look bad.

Tommy and his friends from basic, along with one or two he had met on the transport, had just completed the first shortened week on base. Having finished their initial orientation and gradually getting settled in, they were given an unusual R&R day. The one caveat given was that they were to represent all of the people of the United States and not to act like crude and crass Americans. This was the hoped-for outcome by the brass, but it was acknowledged that it was rarely achieved. The final parting shot by the lieutenant was that whatever happened on their excursion outside of camp, they were to be ready by reveille at zero-four-thirty the next morning—no excuses. At that time, their real tour would begin.

With new experiences on the horizon and opportunities abound, it had been a no-brainer for Tommy and his newfound pals to head into Seville for some good old-fashioned beer chugging and general debauchery befitting nineteen- and twenty-year-olds. Twenty minutes later, and at the researched suggestion by one of his mates, they found themselves at a renowned downtown club. None had ever seen a flamenco dancer before, and the pulse of the place had them throttled up for fun. He remembered that they had gone through several jarrones of Estrella Damm, and that the last dancer of the night had been absolutely stunning. So much so that she had caused all of their mouths to be in various stages of openness, but with little to no sound emanating like before she had taken the stage.

Fifteen minutes following her disappearance back to her dressing room, which had been filled almost entirely with the chatter about her beauty and the explosive performance she had delivered, Tommy had gone to relieve his bladder. Slightly blurred from the drinking and fairly distracted in thought about the woman and what he had just witnessed, he had caromed down the hall, into the restroom and had made it to the one and only urinal. The task completed, and fortunately, there had not been a line, he had come out of the narrow hallway and had been making his way back to the boys when he casually glanced across the throng of patrons and was startled to see what he thought was the back of his best buddy from the States, walking out the door.

At that moment, he couldn't believe that he was halfway around the world and there was Zach! He felt that he had sobered quickly but by the time he had pushed his way through the sea of revelers and made it out to the curb, he had just caught a glimpse of his buddy diving into the front of a limo. He remembered shouting out to him, but it was too late as the limo sped off in a cloud of spewed exhaust. He had been clearly disappointed not to have made contact.

Now he recalled that a few seconds later, another man, a rather large stranger, had walked up and asked for a light for his cigarette, and he remembered frustratingly obliging. It registered as odd at the time that the man spoke with a mottled eastern accent, sounding like every generic communist bloc accent ever heard on television. But he had been more concerned in the moment that he had just missed his best friend. The next words out of the man's mouth after he took a drag and had thanked him had been, "So you know that guy and just missed him, eh?" He remembered nodding, mildly despondent. "Yeah," he had replied. "That's my best buddy in all the world," then he had turned away to try and track the limo as it made a final turn before disappearing around a corner. He remembered being disappointed and then reluctantly pivoting back to reunite with his friends inside. When he made the turn, he was whacked in the head—instant nothingness.

Now here he was. A one-inch knot on his head and already AWOL at his first post. *What the hell happened?* he demanded of his brain to tell him. There was no immediate answer, so he gave a frustrated yank at his leg chains—no luck. He was lying on his back and had his legs spread-eagled. A bowl of something that looked like some sort of porridge sat next to him, but like an intended form of torture, he couldn't reach it. He reasoned that it must have just been delivered while he was regaining consciousness because steam was still rising from whatever was inside.

"You hungry?" came heavily accented words that startled from behind.

"I could eat, if that's what you're asking, asshole," was the captive's quick response. He attempted to crane his neck toward the door to catch a glimpse of the man talking through the peephole but fell just short of the view. Apparently, though, his retort had been enough to stir whoever was on the other side. He could hear the latch being turned, followed by the door creaking open.

A few seconds later, a very large man had his shadow over him.

"You're a big fellow," Tommy said glibly, just seconds before the man harshly slapped him with an oversized paw. "Ouch! Damn! Now, was that necessary?" he painfully mumbled while trying to adjust his jaw without being able to touch it. Then it came to him. "Hey! I remember you! I gave you a light outside that club!"

His jailer leaned down next to him and laid a spoon on his stomach. "What hand eat with?" he asked.

"What?" Tommy answered, then got sarcastic. "Still trying to master the King's English, are we?"

This last comment was followed by another and much harder slap to his temple, causing Tommy to better understand his current situation. He quickly capitulated. "My right, I suppose."

"I free left hand. You try funny business, you get another hand. Understand?"

Tommy nodded, signaling that he understood. The beast—that's the only term he could come up with— did as he said and unlocked one hand, then retreated out of reach.

"You eat, now. I'll be back," then he left and latched the door again. All that was left were the echoes of the behemoth's dwindling plod down whatever dingy hall Tommy envisioned. He let out a heavy sigh, then winced as he patted his swollen cheekbone with his free hand. His stomach growled, followed by survival thoughts that crept in and took over, with the first being to fill his stomach—whatever was to follow, he needed his strength. All that was left after would be to wonder and try to form a plan.

Miguel had directed Zach to drive deep into a barrio section of town, not that far from the safe house he shared with Jack. While navigating and taking in the bleak, sketchy surroundings, Zach thought this area could be the very epicenter of his wounded counterpart's operations. By the looks of the section, he was quite sure that there would be enough scoundrels willing to make a fast buck, dwelling in these dilapidated apartments and row-housing to form a formidable network of necessary information or any other action requiring low ethics or morality to accomplish it.

Another two minutes and a few more turns in, Miguel pointed and grunted, then gave one last direction that led Zach to make a turn down an alley that felt as sinister and dangerous as anything he had felt before.

There were unsavory types at every corner, some carrying weapons and all keeping their eyes on him, his slumped back passenger, and the shiny Mercedes that obviously didn't belong. Miguel opened his half-shut eyes enough, then mumbled for him to stop next to a gate and honk the horn three times.

The forty-five-second wait seemed interminable. Zach had been checking all his mirrors while keeping his weapon on his lap. He was ready to say something to Miguel when, to the right of them, a wrought iron gate, with corrugated sheet metal planks bolted to it, slid open a few feet, and a woman peeked her head out. The gal didn't seem to suspect anything unusual about the Mercedes and the unknown man behind the wheel, and after her cursory study of the visitor, she turned away and appeared to be speaking to someone behind the gate.

A moment later, two men came out, both carrying their own raised weapons and sporting stern faces. Zach was already nervous and on edge about his surroundings and didn't want to be stationary if things suddenly went sideways, so he placed his left hand on the door handle and eased his right forefinger over the trigger. Then one man, the taller of the two, raised his palm to the man in the back seat. Miguel opened his door, and they quickly came over and helped him up, out, and through the gate.

No words were spoken, no instructions were given other than Miguel's last words to him to not leave the car, and to remember that it was his. As serious as Miguel sounded, it still made Zach smile. He felt that he now had a connection with the man and truly wished him a speedy recovery.

Less than thirty minutes later, and still just late morning, he had successfully navigated the maze of city streets and to within a few blocks of the safe house. He found an inconspicuous space just off a side street where an old man was sitting on a wooden stoop a few feet away. He introduced himself to the man and offered him twenty pesetas to make sure the car remained there until a man by the name of Miguel came to pick it up. At that time, he would be given an additional ten pesetas per day.

A wide grin and his hand out to take the money had meant yes. Zach truly believed that the other man's enthusiastic response would mean that he would stay up all night to watch over the vehicle. Satisfied, Zach walked two blocks back to the safe house, where Jack was entertaining Javier. As he walked in, they acknowledged with both of their weapons pointed at his head, then they returned to their momentarily interrupted conversation and half-empty wine bottle. Javier concluded whatever information he was in mid-sentence of, then turned back to Zach.

"Mr Ransom!" Javier called out, sounding truly enthusiastic that he had made it back. "I see you are all in one piece. Please join us. I've brought an amazing grape for you to try."

"It's a tad early for me, Senior Rodríguez." Zach countered politely.

"Sadly, not true. It's always evening somewhere. But I respect your steadfastness. Did you know the French drink wine like milk for breakfast?"

"I did not know that. I guess I'm still learning the ways of the world," Zach replied respectfully.

"More to come, my friend," the Spaniard said with a grin. "How is my Miguel?"

"He is in good hands, I believe. I'm sure the best surgeons pine for working digs in the seedier areas of town."

Javier let out a laugh. "Of course, yes. Appearances as they are. He's been there before, I'm sure you had surmised. But you would be surprised by the service and accommodations offered behind those doors."

"I believe I would be," Zach replied while giving the room a once-over. He quickly locked his rotating eyes on a map on a side table that had been pulled away from the wall for an expanded purpose. He gave Jack a quick glance, then back down at the map, and walked over to get a closer look. The map was topographical, with wide lines for flatter terrain and tighter lines for steeper slopes, along with rivers and small towns he recognized in the Andalusian mountains outside Constantina.

"What are we looking for?" he asked. "I thought we got what we came for with the Lees, but I'm guessing along with whatever the professor gave this Ivanski fellow, we came up short of the optimum objective."

"Yes, and yes," Jack concurred. "The papers were, and still are, our highest priority. According to Jeoung Lee, any fruits derived from his work could tip the Cold War scale to the wrong side."

"So, if the Lees had died…."

"An unfortunate but acceptable trade, had we prevented the papers from getting into the wrong hands," Jack finished the sentence. "That's correct."

Zach was prepared for that answer, and he began to feel more comfortable with the concept. "I'm ready. Let's go. What's the plan?"

"Well, there's more."

Zach watched as Jack gave a quick glance over to the Spaniard. He was sensing something heavier, if that were possible, coming in the next few words. "Okay. Do I need to be sitting?" he said, while already plopping his butt on the end of one bed.

"Do you remember Marcella mentioning that Kalpakoff never stayed with his boys?"

"I do. So, you're looking for something around Cazalla de la Sierra because you think he's there."

Jack's face turned serious. "You also remember the Lees talking about someone else who had been an apparent hostage also?"

Zach looked confused and worried. "Yes. An unknown," was his measured reply. "And our understanding was that person had apparently been moved."

Tanner pulled a folded flyer from his shirt pocket and handed it to Zach. "Maybe not so unknown. We believe that person to be Tommy Postman."

"What?!" Zach exclaimed while unfolding the flyer. On the page was an Air Force ID photo of a pal, Thomas Postman. The words in both English and Spanish only described him as missing and that he was last seen around eleven p.m., at a nightclub downtown: the El Patio Sevillano.

"Tommy was there!" Zach exclaimed.

Jack continued, "I've already made a call over to the base commander's office. The word is, he's been missing for a couple of days. He and some other newbies just got stationed there at Moron and were out busting loose, and as it happens, they were at the same joint we were at. Some witnesses say he came running out like he was looking for someone, then was attacked by a couple of guys and thrown into the back of a car. A black Fiat sedan."

Zach couldn't believe what he was hearing. It was surreal, a dream where you just knew it couldn't possibly be true. "And you two believe that he's there? There with Ivanski Kalpakoff?" he asked.

Jack shrugged, then gave a look to Javier. "Best guestimate?"

"It, as you Americans say, connects all the dots." Javier agreed. "Your friend came running out for someone. Someone he knew, or why else? We now have to assume that you and Jack had been followed. Whomever it was didn't have a plan in place, but was left with an opportunity that was too hard to pass up."

"All of these players are looking for leverage, an ace in the hole," Jack added.

"Insurance, per se," Javier concurred.

"So," Zach said, while gauging both of them for a solid agreement. "You think that by holding on to Posty that Kalpakoff will have a chip to use, if needed."

"That's the gist," Jack confirmed, then added, "Or he's dead."

Zach shook his head as if to say he didn't believe the last words and Jack knew immediately that he had gone too far. "Sorry, Zach. Yeah. Of course, he's alive, probably," he offered apologetically.

"He has to be considered an asset, right?" Zach said, while trying to build confidence in his own head. "So, what do we do?"

"Well, my friend here and I agree that we need our own bargaining chip."

"And who would that be?" Zach asked. Before one of them could respond, the answer came like a lightning bolt. "No! How are you going to get her to do it?"

The Spaniard furrowed his brows. "When it comes to national and possible world implications, serious men must make serious sacrifices."

Zach thought he knew what the words meant, but had to ask anyway. "And what does that mean?"

"It means…" the Spaniard started. "…that she will be given no choice."

CHAPTER FOURTEEN

—✵—

CAUGHT BY SURPRISE

"Come one, come all."

NEARING EXHAUSTION after three electric performances and the clock ticking just a few minutes past eleven, Marcella de Anda needed a drink and a bath—and in exactly that order.

Tonight, she had not been required to sing and mockingly thanked God for the reprieve as her vocal chords had strained the past few performances. Her dance choices had always been rigorous. Performing for her adoring fans was exhilarating, yes, but the effort to reach her very best always came at a cost. This was what her audience paid their hard-earned money for. Achieving the level of perfection that brought fame required years of preparation and relentless practice—just as it does in any profession. Again, the preparation would also meld into her personal life. Preparing, as she had before every opportunity of work or indulgence, and sometimes both, she had created a routine that was both comfortable and, most importantly, satisfying. In truth, as she acknowledged, it was essential for the balance of her own well-being, and tonight would be no different.

The water had been drawn hot but would cool enough to be tepid while she undressed, slipped into her robe, and went through the process of applying cold cream to her face for the removal of unneeded makeup. Some would remain, of course. Eyeliner and lipstick were essentials, but her undeniable and natural beauty would trump any other enhancements. The door to her bath was, as required, left just slightly ajar when she bathed. This was primarily to let the steam out, but also to facilitate her little game she liked to play with her lover on the nights it would be needed. The plan had been that tonight would be one of those.

The room was seductively darkened with only three flickering candles to illuminate, heightening the ambiance for whatever would come later. It had been nearly two weeks since she last released the tension that came with the dance, and although initially tired from her night's work, she felt enough energy and desire remaining to fulfill at least one immediate gratification.

Already downed was the first glass of her favorite white cava, and with the second one poured, she set the glass on a side table next to a chaise lounge adjacent to the footed tub. Dropping her robe on the floor, she stepped over and eased her curvaceous body down into the perfectly warm water with her favorite sudsy lavender soap, then let out a tension-releasing sigh. Her knees and breasts rose like islands, and the plentiful bubbles formed like a sea of air balloons around them. She let out a thought, *if there was a heaven, this would need to be a part of it.* As she melted into her environment, and as she often would, Marcella allowed her mind to drift over her life and career. More often than not, she would lament that her biggest disappointment had been that, as great and adored as her fans made her feel, she had always felt second best to the incomparable Carmen Amaya, who by all accounts was the greatest of them all. Carmen had been the one to represent the art of Flamenco to the world, and somehow this had bothered Marcella tremendously. *Why hadn't it been her?*

Taking another gulp of wine, she brushed the recurring mind-fuck away like an annoying gnat, then began reminding herself that the last forty-eight hours had been more stressful than anticipated. With all that had been going on, how she would ever manage to compartmentalize enough to put together any performance, boggled even her mind. Ever since she had essentially traded wealth for the life of a past lover and a man who had contributed greatly to her status and financial stability, she had been feeling guilty about her failure of allegiance to Ivan. But then, on the opposite side, she had an incredible fondness for another who had nearly been as prolific a lover and ally—Javier Rodríguez. *And,* she admitted with a grin, *Javy was more fun and not nearly as serious. Besides,* she continued to justify, *wouldn't Mr Kalpakoff dispose of her if his life and security depended upon it?* Then, wouldn't *Javy* also? *Fuck!*

Marcella let out a deeper, even more lung-clearing sigh, reached over to her glass and took a larger gulp, nearly draining it while letting the nectar drip down her throat like honey. A light fog started to wash over her as the alcohol was beginning to reach its intended mark. Then, and always a pragmatist, she began systematically shaking off the thoughts of things that could not be changed, only endured, and began the soothing process of which the term "bathing" ultimately suggested: to cleanse oneself. *Maybe,* she thought, *I could somehow cleanse myself of these terrible thoughts.*

Fifteen luxurious minutes had passed, and the water was just beginning to chill, when something suddenly came over her. She had been so comfortable and on the fringe of sodden euphoria that she had almost forgotten. First, the slight sound of a hinge barely moving as if nudged by a tiny field mouse, then a shadowed movement followed… a presence; one that was like a spirit taking inventory of its next possession. She was now the prey. The vulnerable bunny caught in the open that might freeze the moment before an attack, but this bunny would not.

A chill came over her as she feigned ignorance, then she allowed her eyes to trail upward to the drawer that held a small twenty-two, garter pistol, then continuing, they rolled up to her makeup mirror that had been placed purposely for such a moment. The door, barely two inches ajar, was filled with a dark shadow. She was being watched by a well-known voyeur, and this excited her as much as the watcher. She continued the charade, slowly and seductively touching and rubbing all of her sensual places to pique the shadow. Her perfectly shaped nipples hardened in expectation, while not a sound was made from the door.

Finally, she lazily raised both arms and stretched, arching back just enough against the porcelain tub's backrest. Her breasts rose in unison through the remnant suds. Then, as if performing another dance, she let her arms fall back behind her slender neck and let out a pleasing sigh while holding still for a moment to listen. She could now make out the heavy breathing of the watcher. It was enough, and satisfaction was soon to follow—but not too soon. She allowed one hand to slowly slide back down into the water and to her inner thigh. Then she closed her eyes and moaned.

"Don't move," the tenor voice at the door instructed.

This heightened Marcella's lust as she wanted to be instructed; so she obeyed and held still. The door slowly opened, then was closed, followed by the figure sliding into the room and behind her. She kept her eyes closed as two hands gently landed on her shoulders and began kneading them, then moved caressingly up to her neck, working both sides with two fingers on either side. She half opened one eye to peek in the mirror. His bathrobe parted enough for her to notice he was halfway there, and this excited her more. She allowed her head to fall to one side in a growing ecstasy, then let her own hands fall over his and pulled them down to her buoyant breasts, and he willingly cupped them. She moaned throatily and wanting, then her eyes half opened, and she smiled up at the man who could always be counted on to fill her needs without condition. His own bathrobe loosened, exposing his now full and throbbing manhood.

"Sean, my love," she purred as she reached up to take it in hand to gently squeeze its power.

"Yes, my dearest," he responded through a reciprocal moan.

"Please hand me my robe. You have much work to do before breakfast."

"I do?" he retorted, continuing with the role that had been played numerous times before. "What could I possibly do more than play second-fiddle to your brilliance?"

Marcella thought for only a moment about whether, or not, that last comment translated to jealousy and their placement as partners.

"You'll see," she softly said. "I'm quite sure that you are up to the task of handling all my little chores."

CHAPTER FIFTEEN

THE CALL

IT WAS still very early in the morning, and the sun was just rising enough to lighten the small-town square. The call had been prearranged, but the conversation had not taken place. Too many moving parts, too many unexpected events in between had changed the narrative. Ivanski Kalpakoff held the phone close for several seconds, waiting for the voice on the other side to capture the essence of their conversation and to respond. Not a man to wait, he felt it was taking too long.

"What did they say?" he asked impatiently.

The man on the other end of the conversation was Sergio Barberia. He was a product of the northern Basque hills above San Sebastian and known in his peripheral world as "The Barbarian." But in the rarified inner circles of the criminal underworld, he was just referred to as "The Barber." A moniker not given for cutting hair, but throats. The Barber had no fondness for

Russians but respected the business of making money from whomever provided the opportunity. "Twenty-four hours," he finally responded.

"Twenty-four hours!" Ivanski bellowed, then fell quiet while looking around to see if there were those close enough to the public booth to listen. "We did as asked!" he said in a lower voice. "In twenty-four hours, I plan on being on a boat heading to a beach somewhere in the Mediterranean!"

There was a heavy, if not exasperated, sigh from the other end. "This cannot be helped. You must be patient," Sergio replied. "There are many movable parts to this, and the ones that pay are the ones moving them."

"I don't care about the others. They are your problem," Ivanski said in a calmer voice. "My arrangement was with you," he then partially lied, knowing there may indeed be others, but they had not surfaced yet. "If you cannot perform, then there are those who are more than eager to get their hands on the product."

There was hesitation from the other side as Sergio carefully chose his words. In an ominous voice, he said, "That would be a mistake, with consequences."

Kalpakoff knew what those last words meant. He had used them himself many times, and the outcome was never pretty. "It needs to be handled over the next eight hours," he said. "There are many getting close; I've already lost five men. This needs to be resolved as quickly as possible," after his own pause for whatever persuasive effect it might have, while also allowing for a calculation on just how far he could go, he added, "The Koreans have the money and have made it clear that they will pay."

What he did *not* add and probably did not need to, but knew to be fact, was that those same Koreans would be just as happy to kill for the formula and keep their money. Not that other representatives from other countries wouldn't do the same, but the Asians tended to be less reluctant to kill. Ivanski Kalpakoff knew that any transfer would need to be orchestrated for safety and a clean escape, then, and only then, would he be free to just evaporate like a fart in the wind.

The breathing on the other end and the tension it brought was palpable. Then the long silence ended, and the Barber sternly said, "It would be in your best interest to not let anyone else interfere. We will contact you. Twenty-four hours," then the line went dead.

Kalpakoff continued listening in semi-disbelief, hoping the voice of the Barber would return, and that the negotiation would continue. It did not. The Russian uttered an expletive then suddenly exploded in rage and began to pound the receiver in the mounted phone booth until it splintered into unusable pieces. He yelled a few more expletives and then turned to exit the booth. An elderly woman with a sunken face resulting from a mouthful of bad gums, looking to use the phone, had managed to get within a few feet without being noticed. She stood wide-eyed and frozen—her toothless mouth agape at the destruction. Then, realizing the phone would no longer be of service for the foreseeable future, the woman shook her head in disgust and walked away mumbling, *cabeza de mierda.* And those words Kalpakoff understood.

He stepped out from the booth and closed the bi-fold glass door behind him, and watched the woman waddle away. She looked familiar. Could she be one who worked for others? A few seconds later the old woman ducked into a small carniceria and disappeared. Kalpakoff felt he was becoming paranoid. He raised his hand as it trembled, a reaction not of becoming frightened of Sergio Barberia, aka "The Barber", but from the anger that was now raging in him. He knew he was so close, and whenever close to executing any deal or transfer, he became the same nervous scum until it was completed, and he was a country away.

Most times, it would simply take some bar or tavern to pop into, then a stiff drink to return to control, bringing him back to the best opportunity for him to be sharp. He's had this pressure before, he reminded himself, but with no available drink to be had, the next mechanism was to let out a loud and bristly scoff, then walk away and think of all the ways to best the Barber.

In between deep sleep and consciousness, his dream took him back in a feathered sequence of him to that December day back in 1941, lying bruised and exhausted on that Oahu beach. His eyes closed, and then they began to flutter, and he grimaced as his subconscious reminded him of the two piercing jabs on his calf. He reacted by reaching one hand down to rub the scars that remained. Not as sensitive as they had been the first year, but they still tingled when touched. Zach grumbled, then, still in wake-up mode, he kicked off the comforter that weighed annoyingly heavy over his toes.

He had always slept well, mostly on his right side, but would maneuver over the course of seven hours to his back, then left side. It was on his back with toes upright that his discomfort would come. Something about the light pressure on the tips bothered him, and he wondered why he hadn't kicked off the bedding before and freed his toes from the beginning; he thought he was smarter than that. He rolled his legs over to a sitting position and rubbed his face. More alert and still in touch with how the dream had ended, he again reached down, and this time as his fingers caressed over the raised ridge of the upper mark. He gave a deeper thought as to the why and how that one moment in his life had come to be.

Months earlier, he had already made up his mind. Regardless of others and their endless explanations, the escaped radiation from the site had first hit the local wildlife and then, somehow, transferred to him. He trusted that friendly Doctor Octavio Rivera—the only one seriously concerned and offering solid, if early, information—had been right. Rivera had noticed the changes while doing his own unauthorized research. But then he vanished, only to turn up dead under unexplained circumstances—another mystery waiting to be solved.

Zach was certain now that whatever sequence of events collided on that beach, a tad over eight years before, had somehow transformed him molecularly over the following five years, then suddenly it all stopped. He was nearly seventeen when it did. He had remembered wondering why, but had continued to brace himself for the onslaught of painful events to return. They never did, or at the very least, not the painful part. The swelling of his muscles still would overwhelm when induced by stress or anger, but not the pain. And the longer that time would pass, the more he felt relieved that that part of his life was mercifully over.

Zach breathed deeply, then oddly flexed his left bicep and pressed his right hand against the granite-like muscle. He *was* stronger by all accounts than the average. *I'm not invincible, though,* he cautioned himself for the thousandth time. Quick thinking and reaction combined with muscle might help to avert danger or overwhelm an attacker, but those attributes could never stop a bullet or a knife's pointed edge. He needed to always be sharp and aware. He needed to duck. Zach yawned back to the current reality, then began going over what had transpired the night before.

Everything was in place and ready to move on, but the decision to move quickly had been abruptly halted by Jack Tanner. As frustrated as Zach had not been to immediately go to the rescue of his friend, the news of the Lees' children being found and recovered safely, along with the Lees themselves, coupled with his lack of sleep in the previous forty-eight hours, had made a solid rest the pragmatic move in order to be fresh and alert. *It made sense*, he had thought. Not long after that, his exhaustion had taken over, and he slept, and he was grateful for that. His eyes now fully opened; he stared at the ceiling above. A few seconds later, there was a gentle knock at the door, followed by Tanner poking his head in.

"Good! You're awake!" Jack said enthusiastically. He stepped in and handed Zach a steaming cup of the local java. "If this doesn't get you going, nothing will. Strongest coffee bean to date."

Zach blew a stream of breath over the cup, then took a sip, making sure not to sear the roof of his mouth. "Thanks," he said. Picking some loose grounds from his lip and flicking them away, he began firing off all the questions circling in his awakening brain. "What's the latest, how's it going down, and when?"

Jack looked at his watch. "Soon. You'd better get dressed," he said.

Zach blew again across the rim of his cup, and after taking another less cautious sip, he set the cup down and started dressing. No sooner had he had his pants up, socks on, and the first shoe laced, that Javier Rodríguez came to the open door, still supported by a cane.

"They're here," he said, then looking over at Zach. "You look rested, young Ransom."

"I am, thank you."

"Good! We will need those brains and muscles shortly, but we need to move now," then Javier hobbled over to a nearby wooden chair, grabbed the shirt draped over it, and sighed as he tossed it over to Zach. "Slightly wrinkled. We will have it pressed later."

Ten minutes later, the three of them were at the curb waiting. The weather had turned to an overcast gray, unusual for the time of year, and the cool mist had the men turning their collars up. They carried on in a more intimate and familiar conversation like men waiting for a bus in their hometowns, then the familiar red Adler appeared around the near corner and pulled to a stop just out front with the seemingly indestructible Miguel at the wheel. A new passenger sat quietly in the back with her face pressed against the window and looking away on the opposite side. It was Marcella de Anda.

Zach mumbled to Jack, "He's healed?" then followed with, "What is she doing here?"

"There has been a change in our plans, apparently," Jack said, sighing. "Well, not really a change, just an implementation of what we spoke of last night."

"Our plans?"

"When in Rome…" Jack followed. He opened his door and eye-rolled over to the Spaniard, who was getting in on the other side and motioning Marcella to move to the middle. "No. His. You sit up front," he said over his shoulder.

Zach climbed into the front seat and gave a nod to Miguel, who actually offered a partial smile back. "¡Buenos días, mi amigo! ¿Cómo está usted?" Zach asked, while noticing Miguel's shirt was puffed up in several places where wound gauze was used.

"Bien," Miguel said with a shrug. "Morphine." Then he slid the stick into the first position and bolted the Adler forward, quickly shifting up to speed down the avenue. A few turns more and he was heading out of Seville toward Constantina and beyond.

Zach threw his elbow over the seat and craned his neck around. Marcella, in a long dress, only exposing her ankles and wearing a coat, was definitely not happy with her current predicament and was giving a look of being severely inconvenienced. She shot an annoyed look Zachary's way. "What?" she said.

"Oh, nothing, Miss de Anda," Zach replied, surprised she actually felt compelled to initiate words with him. "I'm just happy to see you again."

"Why?" was her quick response. "Do you want to fuck me?"

It was an obvious ploy to show she was not happy with her situation, but Zach was still appropriately taken aback by the crass return from a woman who had exuded grace. He was quiet for only a few seconds while he thought of a response, which under normal circumstances (and with none of the current gentlemen around) would most likely have included a "Yes." Instead, he decided to just smile and turn back around.

That left Marcella to turn away with her own grin at her perceived power over the men that infected her life. "I guess I win," she said just loud enough to be heard. "You will never be at the level necessary for such an accomplishment."

Zach winced inside at the insult but then gave himself credit for not laying out a hurtful comeback. He was raised to be humble but was very much aware that he had veered from being just that. He knew he was smart and good-looking enough, and over the past months, he had used those traits to his advantage. Strengths and weaknesses are what you make of them; his auntie had taught. He had wanted to give this Marcella de Anda a 'what-for' but held steady while conjuring a fond thought back of his chemistry teacher, Veronica, and the red dress she wore the night she seduced him. *Now that was a night to remember*, he thought.

Losing his virginity to someone as beautiful and alluring as her had definitely given his confidence a boost. He remembered the moment clearly—and he knew it hadn't been out of sympathy. Veronica had wanted him. The thought amused him, a private little triumph he had no intention of sharing. The laughter escaped him before he could stop it, drawing curious looks from both Jack and Marcella. *Apparently, he had managed to reach that level after all, bitch! That was one hell of a prom night!*

CHAPTER SIXTEEN

THAT RASCAL TOMMY

"오직 탈출만이 유일한 길이다"

EVERYTHING WAS dark, and the shroud covering his head itched terribly. Being alive, though, was a huge plus and mostly helped in providing the calming effect he needed for his current predicament. Now, and with his hands tied and unavailable, Tommy Postman rotated his head back and forth to try and bring relief to the annoyance.

Lying fetal and bound was not comfortable in the back of a truck bouncing around on a rain-rutted road. It was also very cold. The seemingly relentless rain pelting the canvas top, combined with the rear canvas covering that was left partially open, didn't help. With the winds whipping around, it had felt like a meat locker. He shivered violently, then tried to bring his knees further up to his chest to create more of a barrier to the wind. It had been the third time he'd been moved over the past two days, but this time involved a degree of travel. When he and Zach had found time to catch up, Zach would always share his newfound knowledge. One thing he had said was that during his training, he was taught that when captured, you had to force yourself to remember every detail. All sights and sounds, words, steps and train whistles—everything. Right now, he was in that moment, and God knows he was trying to focus, but with the environment creating enough distraction, it had been difficult, but he was managing. He had never really counted on having to call on this training, but here he was in this most unenviable position, being forced to implement it.

He guessed he'd been in the truck for about an hour. No one had spoken since the man who'd given the order to move out. Apart from the jolt of the road, the creak of the springs, and the scrape of wooden crates shifting around him, everything was silent. Before, there had always been several men on the watch, and they had always talked and laughed among themselves when the boss was not around. Now, there had only been the driver.

Maybe thirty minutes in, he had calculated, the truck had driven past a farm, or some herder in the road, for he'd heard sheep *baa*-ing. At an average of forty miles per hour, he had figured they had traveled around twenty miles outside of town and were somewhere rural.

Tommy took a deep gulp of air to try and pull more oxygen through the burlap shroud, then his stomach growled, reminding him of just how hungry he was. *When did he eat last?* Then he figured that it had been a good twenty-four hours, and just having his brain tell him that made the hunger worse. Just then, his attention was drawn back again to his current situation as he could hear the truck's engine throttling down, followed by the grinding of brakes that led his mechanic's mind to believe that they were nearing replacement.

I hope they can stop this apple cart from going over a hill, he thought. A moment later, the truck came to a complete stop, and he heard the low mumble of the driver speaking to someone on the outside. Now, two men. There was some sort of grunted acknowledgement that resulted in the truck moving forward, followed soon after by a sudden hard left turn that rolled him over and into a crate of onions and other produce that he had been smelling since he was dumped into the bed of the truck.

No more than a minute had passed when the truck rolled to a stop again. Tommy listened intently to try and pick up any clues. He quickly registered the flowing sound of what he surmised as a large nearby stream. The rushing water came from the right side, conjuring up a picture of a wooden forest with perhaps a cabin. *Not another cabin*, he thought to himself, reminded of what he had endured with Zachary a year ago. Then, a few seconds later, the driver was out, not closing the door behind him. What did that mean? Maybe they weren't staying long? A few seconds later, the bolt latch on the tailgate squeaked its rusty slide-through, and it dropped with a clank as the heavy chains anchored on both sides came to full extension. Two meaty paws grabbed hold of his ankles and forcefully pulled him out. He crashed hard on the muddy ground; only the burlap protected his face from being covered with the muck.

"Where are we?!" he yelled out, though muted through the shroud.

The paws again clenched him by the back collar and dragged him through the mud a few more feet, forcing the wet ground uncomfortably into his pants. Heavy rain began to fall as he tried to get his feet under him, but the momentum brought to bear was too quick and forceful. Just when he managed to get one foot braced under, he was abruptly let go. Unable to bring his bound hands forward, he face-planted into the muck again.

Tommy attempted to purge the mud that had been forced into his mouth from the fall. "Come on!" he finally bellowed. "Was that necessary?!" he said, shaking the collected mud from his head.

"On knees!" the driver commanded in broken English.

"What?!" Tommy replied frantically, although he understood.

The driver grabbed Tommy's collar again and lifted, almost choking him. "On knees!" he said with more emphasis than before.

Something was different from the previous days, and Tommy Postman was beginning to sense his imminent demise. He immediately began pleading. "I don't know what this is about!" he shouted. "Whatever it is you think you have in me, you're wrong! I don't know anything! You have the wrong person, I swear!"

There was a long silence, only the pelting rain. For Tommy, the nightmare was everything he had gleaned from the more disturbing books and movies he had seen or read. He heard the slop and suction of another person sloshing through the mud as he approached from behind. Had another car been waiting, and was this man number three? Or did the second man just walk up?

Still more silence, the newcomer mumbled a few words to the driver. They sounded different from before, deeper. And still, these were words and language he could not understand. Suddenly, he heard the click of what could only be the cocking of a pistol that was being prepared to fire, and his whole body shuddered. This sound was as familiar as his mother's peach pie and something he was most certain of. The hair on his neck immediately sprang up to attention like tiny needles. He cried from within, this was it.

Then the newcomer finally spoke. "Jack Tanner, Javier Rodríguez and Zachary Ransom. You know these men?"

Tommy didn't understand, yet he did. The why, how, and what of the ask, had taken him by surprise. But two of the names he did know. "Why?" he managed, while setting the motion of the other slapping the back of his head.

"Okay, okay!" Tommy relinquished. "Take it easy!"

"So, you know these men?" the voice said sternly and with purpose. "Answer!"

Tommy gave in, hoping it would allow him to see his parents or anyone else again. "Yes," he answered in a trembling voice. "I don't know any Javier but the other two, yes, I know these men, but…" was all he could get out. The merciless shroud of darkness came quickly.

CHAPTER SEVENTEEN

AND IT BEGINS

June 25, 1950

THE NEWS came fast and furious in every outlet imaginable. Barely a tick after five a.m., and the local newsboys were already shouting in their native tongues and from their respective corners. *"KOREA AT WAR!"* Children as young as eight years old flailed their limbs and the pulp they held high above their adolescent frames in the daily competition of procuring coins.

Restless the entire night and unable to get any quality sleep, Zach had been lying on his back staring up at the ceiling with his thoughts for nearly an hour. He remembered thinking it a record of some sort to be awake before the indomitable Jack Tanner, but had given his partner a pass for being a little injured and stupendously drunk from the night before. When the news finally broke from the street below, he had gone to the window to check out the commotion. At every corner, the newsboys and their high-pitched preteen voices selling their wares, were yelping like puppy, cocker spaniels. His understanding of Spanish was initially put to the test, but once the basic idea had hit, he had rushed past a half-asleep Jack Tanner—who grumbled a "What's going on?"—out into the short hallway and down the back stairs to the street to grab a copy of the print. As he had stood there at the curb reading the first paragraph, his first thought had been that he couldn't believe what was happening.

North Korea had crossed the 38th parallel into South Korea. *For God's sake!* he wondered. *Didn't the world learn anything from the last war?*

Zach rolled and tucked the paper under his arm and made it back upstairs in minutes. When he entered, Jack was back to his symphony of mouth breathing. Rather than waking him, he filled a pot and poured grounds into the basket, then set it on the room's hot plate. While the coffee heated and began to percolate, he sat down by the window to read while the strains of Jack's snoring gave a mild distraction from a few feet away.

The first article read about President Truman and America's quick response through the United Nations, in which the United States was the primary military force and that Truman's intention would be to petition

Congress, a formality, to join the war in support of the free democracy of South Korea. In addition, one reporter had already heard from an unnamed source that General Douglas MacArthur would be placed in charge of all three branches of the military. It would be just five days later that all of this would come to fruition: there would be a rapid mobilization of US troops, and they would land at the Korean port city of Inchon.

Zach felt Jack's presence over his shoulder and responded without looking up. "It's happened. Just as you said."

"My pupils haven't yet reached full clarity, "Jack managed through a drawn-out yawn. "But yeah, I can see that. Sooner than expected by a few months."

"You knew this was going to happen? How?" Zach questioned.

"I've been tied into, you know…socializing and mingling for nearly two decades longer than you, Zach. I know people, is all."

Zach stood to relieve his bladder. "And those people know people and on and on. I get it," he said, while moving to the toilet.

Jack stood there in his tidy-whites and poured himself a cup of the just-brewed coffee while listening to the solid stream coming from the open-doored bathroom. He took a cautious sip, then sat down on the edge of his bed and blank-stared at a cheap, cheesy, watercolor painting on the wall ahead, depicting some generic street scene. His mind was coming back into focus, recalling the conversation with the Spaniard that had taken them to half-past two in the morning. Zach, having succumbed to full at first, then intermittent sleep before midnight, had not been able to keep up, but the talk had continued. Somehow, Jack had sobered up enough or the news had been sobering enough, to pay attention.

Jack had been stewing over Marcella's abduction two days earlier, eager to get the full story. But when he pressed for details, Javier refused to share, believing it was safer that way—if anyone got captured, they couldn't reveal where Marcella de Anda was being held. That logic didn't matter much to Jack. What bothered him was that the plan hadn't been discussed with the Otter One team—especially with him—and he would've preferred some say in it. He'd only mentioned to Javier, during an earlier conversation, that it might be smart to have their own bargaining chip. Still, furious as he was, he thought better of confronting the Spaniard about it.

The one caveat that Javier Rodríguez gave, and only because it amused him, was that when the crew Miguel put together to grab Marcella snuck into her apartment, apparently her guitarist and man-toy, Sean, was there also and had put up a decent struggle. But having been naked and frantic to dismount his in-the-throes-of-passion position, Sean was not able to fight off the two masked intruders. At gunpoint, he was allowed to get his trousers on and his oversized Johnson tucked in, then was bound, gagged, and taken hostage as well. But once outside of town, he was unceremoniously dumped on the roadside, next to a field full of grazing cattle. He was not happy and managed a middle-finger salute as the kidnappers drove away.

The other conversation was about when they, meaning Miguel with Miss de Anda in tow, had picked him, Zach, and Javier up the other day; that they had only made one stop before realizing their plan had to be postponed. The initial plan, though everyone knew it was a long shot, had been to use Kalpakoff as leverage—trading him for Marcella, or for whatever papers he possessed. The problem was the presumed barrels of money that other suitors would likely offer the Russian—a serious threat to any negotiation. The real question: what mattered most to him?

The stop just outside Constantina had been to connect with one of Miguel's trusted informants. A simple cobbler by trade, the man had appeared humble, quiet, and didn't have the appearance of one who would be aware of anything other than his work and feeding his family; all this made him perfect for the job that helped supplement his and his family's existence. Appearances aside, it was soon learned that he was more talkative around town than his appearance had led Miguel to believe, and with his buddy's input, he had been obviously well informed of most of the comings and goings of the town and surrounding areas. Once the requested information had been retrieved, he had the unique ability of becoming the quiet cobbler once more and a real asset.

Unfortunately, the news had been troublesome. The man, who had gone by the name of Gallito, because he also raised chickens and his friends taught him to cluck and be cocky when he spoke, reported that Ivanski Kalpakoff had stealthily moved on from his hideaway and that no one knew where to. This had returned to Gallito, along with some paper money handed over, and a snarled grunt from Miguel, who had felt that he had overpaid. At that point, there had been a short discussion with the outcome, concurred by all, that the only course was to go back and rethink.

Back to last night, at around 12:30, there had been a knock at the door followed by a blank addressed envelope being slid under. Both men, Jack and Javier, and again with pistols drawn and Zach still in and out of his dream state, had held still for seconds before Jack had reached for the note. It had been a coded telegram message from Johnny Scarpino that required deciphering. A few minutes later and the task had been accomplished; the message that followed was read by Jack.

The basic translation had been that the hidden figures financing Otter One were very concerned and were now offering a sizable donation of their own pooled resources to the cause of retrieving the formulas in question. Added to the offer was the "get out of jail" card of a clean getaway for Ivanski Kalpakoff. Although neither man was happy about Kalpakoff going scot-free, at least now they had *three* things of value to throw into the pot that might sway the Russian.

The singular and most pressing problem, at that point, had been a number of questions: Where was Kalpakoff? When, or if, he was located, how long would it take to reach him? And then finally, would they be killed trying to get him the offer and, for all of this, would it ultimately be too late? Tommy Postman was never mentioned, and Zach regretted not showing more concern for his friend.

That was yesterday, and now is now, Zach reminded himself before interrupting Jack's train of thought. "I see the wheels spinning. Did you and the Spaniard come up with something?"

Jack rubbed his temples. "I have a headache," he said. He rolled his eyes up to Zach and attempted a painful laugh. "More than you know, mi amigo. Have a seat."

Zach did as he was told and pulled up the window chair. Ten minutes later, he was up to speed on all that had transpired while he was out. "Jeez!" He exclaimed. "I only slept for a little less than four hours! What now?"

"Before I answer that," Jack started. "I know you have other concerns, so let me get this out of the way…" This brought on a cringe of "What now?" from Zach. "…going in there had been a package. A package that didn't leave with the group."

"A package being, what? Are we talking Tommy?" Zach asked, putting it together.

Jack confirmed with a reluctant nod, but before he continued, he was interrupted by a loud honk from down on the street. Jack went to the window and peered down at a waving Miguel, then he checked his watch. "A few minutes early."

"Early for what?" Zach asked, desperately wanting to get back to the conversation.

"Finish getting dressed. You and Miguel are going to get a head start. Miguel and his network have been going at it since last night. He's got guys all over those mountains. Hopefully, by the time you get out there, someone will have seen something."

While Jack was explaining, Zach had dressed himself in the anticipation of having to move quickly. He finished lacing up his last shoe and then waved down to Miguel that he was on his way. Rushing past Jack toward the door, Jack grabbed his arm. "Forgetting something?" he asked. He eye-pointed over to the nightstand where Zach's shoulder harness and weapon were still out.

"Oh...," Zach said, "...can't forget that," then he quickly pulled off his coat, neatly slipped on the harness, then pulled the coat back on. "Anything else?" he asked with a barely perceptible grin.

"Yeah. Two things," Jack offered. "You need to focus on the main priority."

"And?" Zach said impatiently.

Jack grinned back at his partner. "Try not to get killed."

CHAPTER EIGHTEEN

A HUMAN SHELL GAME

"Wo oh wo, kann er sein?"

THE BARBER swiped the eight-inch blade a few more times across the sharpening stone, then slid it back into its worn leather sheath on his lower calf-strap. Then, reaching down, he picked up a Mauser Luger that he had confiscated from a German SS officer six years before. The man, whose only offense in that moment, other than the obvious, had been that during his interrogation, he had offended him with a disparaging slur about anyone of Spanish descent while the Barber had been in one of his surlier moods. The interrogated did not survive.

Sergio Barberia's current mood had not reached that point yet, but he was certain and actually was anticipating that it could get there. Shaking the though, he rose and walked across the room to a large, windowed door that led to an expansive second-floor veranda where clay-potted bougainvillea sparsely flowed up, over, and through a short wrought-iron railing. Outside was a trio of men drinking coffee and laden with shouldered bolt-action destroyer carbines. As he emerged, they quieted and then respectfully, and warily, parted to various corners of the deck to continue their low-key conversations while keeping an eye out for a nodded command from their boss.

Sergio grunted at the men as they appeared nervous around him. *Why should they be nervous*? he thought to himself. *I've never even hinted at hurting them or anyone in their families. Did I not buy Fernanan's papi a truck for his melons? And the old man loved that truck!* The thought annoyed him that it should even have come to mind. He knew his men loved him, or so he had made himself to believe.

He turned back to them and attempted a comforting smile, but unwittingly it came across sadistically evil to the men, and they retreated further while forcing awkward smiles. Sergio sighed. *I was never liked in school either,* he thought. Standing by the rail, he stared out at the arid expanse of shallow rolling hills and then took in a deep and cleansing breath. As he circled in a 180-degree turn, he rested his eyes over the large reservoir and across to the Melonares Dam, a half mile away and at the southwestern end. The dam was only fifteen kilometers, as the crow flies, from the small town of Cazalla De La Sierra and their previous hideout, but he had been well satisfied with the layout and the seclusion of their selected new location.

The main paved road that brought them here ran across the eighth-mile span of concrete over the reservoir, and if one should cross-over and continue into the barren and high-desert horizon another one hundred yards past the second turn on the near side of the dam, they would come across the wide boulder-obscured gravel road that led to the Hacienda that he and his men now occupied.

The elderly husband who had retired several years before and longed for the peaceful seclusion of his farm would no longer greet the rare visitor with his broad smile and alert eyes. He was now lying face down with his throat cut under a boarded floor in the one outbuilding that held farming tools and a single milking goat behind the modest, Spanish adobe home. His terrified wife survived the horrific, wee-morning mayhem, and was in the kitchen after being ordered to cook up some food with whatever meager supplies she had in storage. Still trembling from the night's event, she could barely move in the wake of her personnel carnage. But the men were hungry from their middle-of-the-night move and takeover of the small farm, and no choice had been given.

Sergio turned to nearing movement from behind. The more courageous of his men, the one he had admittedly feared would move on him at some point, Rene Guerra, came out onto the verandah and approached him.

"She is still cooking. I left Sandoval with her," he reported. "What would you have us do?"

Sergio thought for a moment as he took cautious inventory of the young man's posture. From the look in his underling's eyes, he concluded that this one was not afraid. He turned away, giving the man his moment—as if daring him to take a knife to his throat. Seconds passed, and again nothing happened. *He is not ready yet*, he grinned while thinking to himself. Then he glanced at his watch and turned back to face Guerra.

"They will be coming, but not for a few hours yet," he said, hoping it would be enough.

"The others…they are tired."

"Let them eat, then they can rest," Sergio thoughtfully said. "They must be ready and alert when the time comes."

"Señor. And when that time comes, what is it that we should be ready and alert for?"

A slight grin formed over the Butcher's face. "What you have been trained for," he said.

The soldier, Rene Guerra but called "Mule" by the others, gave a look of uncertainty. "We've been trained for much, Señor. The men would prefer you to be more specific?"

Sergio turned away, but his soldier caught a side glimpse of what he perceived as a satanic grin. Then his boss abruptly stopped at the door and turned back, then said, "Death, of course."

It had still been dark out when they started off, but now at sunrise, the truck ahead, carrying a small two-man fishing boat that hung out past the open tailgate, was moving at an ill-advised pace for a rutted gravel road. Miguel had somehow managed them, and Zach knew enough not to ask where it had come from, a Peugeot D3 van. A heavy terrain vehicle it was not and with every rut and pothole that the van hit continued to prove that it was absolutely not designed for anything other than a paved road. And this was all the more apparent by Zach's jaw rattling and ass hurting from the lack of a proper suspension.

From the beginning, the man they had been following, the one behind the wheel, had been driving a reasonable fifteen miles an hour over the harsh terrain while keeping an eye out for crossing sheep and goats. Then just in the last few minutes he had taken off, as if wanting to get his part of the escapade over as quickly as possible. He had been veering back and forth at a nerve-racking thirty miles an hour, making the two of them wonder aloud whether or not it was even advisable to keep up. The recklessness had been so evident that on several sharp turns it appeared that the truck's tires had come off the ground, causing both Miguel and Zach to wonder if there was a calamity just seconds away. Then, in just as unpredictable a move as the kind the driver had been making thus far, he suddenly stopped. The spewing of gravel, dirt, and truck brake lights surprised Miguel into a jolting stop of his own.

"Well, that was uncomfortable," Zach panned while quickly scanning about for anyone or anything. "Is your man sure?"

Miguel did not respond. Instead, he just gave a look back to Zach that read as "Are you really still questioning me?" then he jumped out and jogged like someone that was fully recovered, which Zach was assured of that his friend was not. A few seconds later, Miguel was up to the truck where the driver was already out and untying the three-quarter manila rope that had kept the boat from flying out of the back. Assuming this was going to be their jumping-off spot, Zach exited the jeep while squinting ahead. The morning light was now cresting over the hills in the distance, making it easier to see that the conversation between the truck driver and Miguel was brief and that Miguel was now helping pull the boat off the truck's bed. It landed with a thud, followed by his partner handing the other man some undisclosed amount of paper money, followed by the driver jogging back to his truck and churning his tires away.

The Viar River was the main tributary that came down to fill the large Melonares reservoir. It had been dark on the hour and a half drive that only covered twenty miles from their starting point of Cazalla De La Sierra, but it had been important not to approach via the main road for fear of lookouts. So, the suggested route was to follow a series of small dirt roads—paths, really—that intertwined in a random serpentine pattern yet followed the river south toward the dam. Only the ranchers and small homestead farmers used the roads—and typically on horseback. Zach figured that the not-so-straight line had added another four or five miles to the drive.

Up ahead, Miguel was animated, waving Zach up. He quickly obliged and was up and surveying the boat and reservoir shoreline in seconds. "How far?" he asked.

Miguel grunted, "One, maybe two miles."

Zach gave the boat a once over. "Doesn't look very seaworthy."

"No ocean here."

"I don't see a motor," Zach followed.

"You are, as they say, very quick. I'll row," Miguel continued glibly.

Zach really liked his partner's ability to access his wry humor, but not too many people would dare to question his own masculinity, and he was having none of it.

"I get your humor, *Kee-mo-sabi*," he said, but also with enough respect for the man that had proven himself several times over. "But I'll do the heavy lifting on this one. Besides, you're still recovering. Grab the front."

Miguel didn't respond other than to do as suggested, and this had Zach secretly thinking that he had earned some form of mutual respect from the man. The two muscled the boat to a clear launch point just forty feet ahead, then Zach jumped in and quickly moved to the bench seat and oars. Miguel gave a final push out then followed him over and in. Zach began cranking the oars front to back in a steady rhythm, and they were on their way. The straightest line would have made them obvious intruders, and thus targets, so Zach made sure to hug the coastline. Miguel sat in the rear and faced forward, looking over Zach's broad shoulders. After a minute or two, he reached under the bench seat and pulled out a pair of binoculars from a satchel he had tossed in before pushing off, and he began scanning the left shoreline ahead.

"How many do we expect?" Zach asked between rows.

"Four," his counterpart answered. "Could be more."

"Wonderful," Zach replied, then added, "I'd feel better with the odds if we had some larger weapons."

Miguel turned back and reached down to a clump of worn fish net and threw it back, exposing a single carbine equipped with a sniper's scope.

"That'll work," Zach said with a grin. "You've thought of everything."

Miguel gave a grunt like "Thank you," under his breath, while his eyes never left the shoreline ahead.

Zach kept up an impressive pace that created a steady wake behind them for another ten minutes, while Miguel maintained a concentrated awareness forward. Finally, he lowered the binoculars and pointed ahead. "We stop here."

That sounded right to Zach, so he immediately reversed one oar and pointed the boat's nose toward the shore. A minute later, they had the boat up on a shallow mud bar, securely hidden behind some reeds and were stealthily moving toward a small homestead just a few hundred yards ahead. The sun was just up as they neared the Hacienda's outer grounds, and without the darkness, their optimum cover was now gone. Miguel noticed a shadow at the second-floor corner of the building they were moving on and he signaled a closed fist up, to stop. They both quickly knelt behind a large yucca bush facing the rear west side of the main structure and watched for more conclusive movement above. They could see the south end of the front second-story railing and the two men who occupied the post. Zach motioned to Miguel to stay low and to move further toward the rear of the property. No sooner had the two agreed when Zach held Miguel back and motioned with his eyes to the north side of the structure and the large cloud of dust approaching.

The men watched as the two lookouts reacted simultaneously then quickly disappeared out of view. The moment could not have been better, so they moved, crossing several hundred feet in a dead sprint to the rear of an auxiliary shed. Miguel leaned the scoped rifle against the wooden structure and pulled out his firearm with a silencer already attached. Zach nodded his understanding that the rifle wouldn't be very good this close in and pulled his own weapon and spun on his own silencer. Just as he was turning away, Miguel grabbed his arm.

"Who is this *Kee-mo-sabi*?" he asked, looking confused.

"The Lone Ranger?" Zach said in a low voice and wondering if it was worth the effort. "You know. It's a show on American TV. That's what his trusted friend, Tonto, called him."

Miguel just shrugged that he didn't get it. "Never watched TV," then he turned away. Zach shook his head, wondering where that had come from, then he went to the opposite corner and slowly peeked around. The vehicle that had created the commotion and diversion had stopped, and all four doors of the sedan were open. Behind each door was a man with his weapon drawn. *Was this to be an attack, or was there a deal taking place?* Zack thought. Then he quickly cruised through the other possible scenarios. *And if a deal was in the making, and if it should go sideways, then maybe there will be fewer men to contend with? That would be a good thing*, he thought. Then the second and less appealing thought came that all eight men could join up and turn against them. "Let's take option number one," he mumbled to himself.

Up ahead, a new motion began with one weapon being lowered and the man holding it standing to expose himself. Zach recognized the man from a photo Jack had showed him several days back. It was Ivanski Kalpakoff. The Russian took several confident steps forward and would most likely be dead if that had been the intention of whomever was at the other end. Any more action from these armed men would now require Zach to expose himself also to see what was happening. So, without looking back, he threw four fingers up to let Miguel know the new number of men. Then turning to confirm and suggest Miguel approach from the other side, he froze. Miguel was there on his knees with one unexpected goon, seemingly very military with a serious face and holding a gun to his partner's head.

His thoughts racing, Zach put together that apparently the plan had been for the man to maneuver himself into some sort of advantageous position. He could have come from the home or been dropped off by the men in the vehicle a few hundred yards back. Regardless of which side he was teamed with, in the process of circling or approaching the man, he had discovered Miguel and was most likely wondering the same thing. *Who were these guys?*

The newcomer was all business and motioned Zach to lower his weapon; he slowly obliged, while looking for any distraction. Just then, as if on cue, a fly buzzed the man's ear, and he instinctively moved to flick it away. That was all Zach needed. Before dropping his weapon completely, he raised it and fired one shot, the explosion sending the man's head and stunned eyes violently backward. The man, though, did manage to squeeze the trigger before blackness. The round luckily just missed the ducking Miguel's head, while piercing the side of the shed, exiting through the thatched roof, and most likely burrowing into the arid dirt-and-sand terrain a quarter mile away. But more alarmingly, the round had done its job of alerting everyone on the other side of the home that something was amiss. All hell broke loose.

A frenetic barrage of gunfire commenced as Miguel was back up on his feet and brushing his head for a graze that wasn't there. Then just as quickly he moved, circling with his back against the shed, to the opposite side. He took one quick peek and was gone. Zach did the same from his position. As he sprinted the fifty feet of open ground to the rear of the main house, he could see Miguel crossing on the other side just ahead then kneeling at the corner. A second later, he was doing the same and trying to guess what had happened out front in the last twenty seconds. The battle was still on, but the initial barrage of rounds had slackened to intermittent single shots. Men were obviously moving for sight-line positions and cover. Zach quickly scanned the Kalpakoff carrying vehicle. Two men lay prone and unmoving, appearing to be casualties. One man on the rear right side behind an open door-panel, looked like he had taken a hit but was still in the battle and searching for targets. Kalpakoff was not visible. Another round was fired from a carbine rifle that hit the door panel just below the shattered window and the ducking combatant's head. Then, just as suddenly, orders in Spanish were shouted and all firing stopped.

Zach took a chance and peeked around the corner in the hope of getting a clearer picture of what was happening. Below the balcony overhang he could see in the shadow Ivanski Kalpakoff kneeling with his nine-millimeter weapon pointed upward and swaying back and forth. Next to him, but a few feet further out and in the now full morning sunlight, was a crumpled mass of what Zach recognized as one of the lookouts from the balcony. Fallen from above, he had been one of the initial casualties from the mayhem. Above Kalpakoff, but further to the left, was a man that he had not yet encountered who was kneeling behind what appeared to be another fallen comrade and pointing his weapon downward. Zach could not tell if the prone man was dead or just severely wounded. At any rate, the count of men down was four, possibly five, with the one he took out moments before. That would leave a more manageable three to four combatants left. Just then, he witnessed Miguel's head popping out like a gopher watching for a predator, around the opposite corner and just long enough to see Kalpakoff, the carnage, then a nod over to him—and then he disappeared again. Zach had become in sync with his partner and assumed that he was repositioning for an advantage or looking for another entrance. A few seconds went by, then finally someone yelled out orders. It was Kalpakoff.

Zach could just make out a few of the words, which were clearly Russian. But putting two and two together when the shooting suddenly stopped, it had clearly been an order to cease fire. Then following in broken Spanish, Ivanski called out to the man remaining above him. "Are you still there, Sergio? Or are you dead?"

The man above inappropriately laughed at the question. "I am not dead, but you soon will be for starting this chaos. Russian scum can never be trusted!"

Ivanski responded quickly. "It was not us, you Spanish pig! You laid the trap and now two of my men are dead!" Then he quickly glanced over to the two men down, searching for movement. "Or at the very least, wounded enough to be out of this debacle."

There was a long silence as both men calculated then registered what was going on. Sergio was the first to speak. "What can you see down there?"

"Only my man," Ivanski responded. "And you?"

Sergio stared down at the lifeless body of Rene Guerra. His eyes locked with the open but dead eyes of his man, then he raised the fallen man's head a few inches then let it fall back down, confirming there was nothing left. "My man here will survive his minor wound and can still hold his gun, but nothing else from here," Sergio yelled his lie. "But I have others about and more on the way."

Ivanski knew enough not to believe the Barber, so he opted to play his own tricky move to try and ascertain how many men Sergio really had left. "Send one of your men back through the house to check that we are alone!" he yelled up to the balcony.

There was another silent pause as Sergio calculated his own chess move. "Do you still have the papers, or are you waiting for your other men to sneak up?"

"Do you have what was promised?" Ivanski asked in a voice designed to deescalate the tension.

Sergio was quick to respond. "As promised. Yes, it is here."

Ivanski squinted out at his remaining man who now held a rifle and was aiming up at the balcony. He nodded to him, then taking a deep breath followed by a surge of courage, he stepped out from under the balcony, fully exposing himself. Sergio still had some protection, being now prone behind the fallen with his back deep on the balcony and against the wall. But he was definitely not happy about the rifle training on the angle necessary to take him out should he rise.

"Tell your man to lower the rifle and allow me to go inside. We will meet there!" then he yelled down to no one. "Rene! Jesus! Lower your weapons and do not shoot! Check the rear for anyone else!"

Ivanski followed with his own command to his man, then added for him to retrieve the papers from the trunk but to stay back until asked. The man lowered his weapon, then with eyes closely watching for any attempt to double-cross the ongoing negotiations, he stayed as low as possible and made his way to the rear trunk and popped the lid. Reaching in, he retrieved a leather-bound briefcase and set it on the ground then began alertly watching everything around him. In the meantime, Sergio reacted to the moment and quickly crawled back through the windowed door and inside. Up on his feet now, he swayed his nine-millimeter back and forth through the large room. Finding no combatants, he cautiously made his way down the stairs. Once he reached the halfway point where his legs were exposed, he leaned over to survey the room. Off in the corner and standing behind a large high-backed chair was Ivanski. He had one hand around the neck of the old woman while the other held a gun to her head.

"Take it slow, Sergio," he said with caution.

This brought another abbreviated guffaw from Sergio. "First names. I guess we have reached that point, Ivan," he continued. "The woman has no value to me. Shoot her now, and let's get this thing over with. Remember, there still may be other forces we are dealing with, and where there may be some, soon there could be more."

Ivanski knew that Sergio was right. If anything more were to happen, it would be soon, and nothing could be done about it. He let the old woman go, and she immediately shuffled quickly, whimpering into the kitchen and out the back door. As she tearfully emerged, she was met by Miguel who quickly pressed his palm over her mouth while putting a finger to his lips for her silence. The woman managed a terrified nod, then still overwrought with emotion, she continued as fast as she could out toward the shed. Obviously looking for refuge when she opened the shed door, she found her husband of forty-plus years and let out a bloodcurdling scream that had Miguel spinning his weapon toward the shed.

Inside, both men in the standoff were also alerted by the scream but managed to keep their eyes on the other.

"Ah yes," Sergio said with a sigh. "Don't mind the woman. She has just found something that was not good for her to see."

"And what might that be?"

"Her husband, of course. It had been necessary," he said matter-of-factly, "Please put your weapon on the chair."

Ivanski slowly reached around over the arm rest while his eyes were cautioning the other to do the same.

"Tactical intentions aside, I'm trusting that you are the last man standing?"

Sergio feigned putting his gun down while stepping down the rest of the way. The motion had the desired effect, and Ivanski released his weapon onto the seat. No sooner had he done this than Sergio leapt out and pointed his weapon at the Russian.

"You lying piece of shit!" Ivanski yelled out while crouching.

Sergio stood steady, and although still holding his weapon, he lowered it enough to help calm the nerves from the other side of the room. Something he has done many times in the past right before shooting another dead.

"Don't worry," Sergio offered. Despite what you have heard about me, I have no intention of causing a reason that would sever ties with those that could make me rich," then he pistol-pointed over to a small breakfast table with an opened briefcase sitting on top. "It's all there. And while your gun remains on the chair, you may go and verify if you like."

"So, I am to trust the Barber not to kill me?"

"What would possibly stop me from killing you now? That chair? I think not, my friend. Go. Have a look."

Of course, this had all made sense to Ivanski Kalpakoff. If Sergio had wanted him dead, he would be. Unless, as reported by others, the Barber was playing one of his sadistic games: maybe a fun little tease to allow him to get halfway across the room before he pulled the trigger, then watch as the others' dying eyes questioned "Why?" The old parable of the turtle and the scorpion raced through his head. It no longer mattered, he concluded, and slowly made his way over to the bag while resisting a wary look back at the man who could kill him. Once there, he quickly peeked inside, then followed with his hand to fan one of the bundled papers.

"So, tell me," Ivanski queried the Russian. "How much will you be getting?"

Sergio sighed. "How interesting that you should ask," he said while calculating the consequences of telling his counterpart. "Why not?" he reasoned out loud, thinking he had truly nothing to lose with the answer. "The negotiated amount is twice what you have there."

Ivanski let out a laugh that reflected that either he didn't believe it, or that he felt stupid for not asking for more. "Twice," he muttered. "I suppose that I left quite a bit on the table."

"Don't get greedy now," Sergio replied with his own grin. "What's there is more than enough for that nice life somewhere in the Mediterranean you have longed for. Take it and be happy."

Ivanski steadied himself then moved to the door and waved to his man to come forward.

"Tell him to bring his weapon but to put it behind him in his belt."

Ivanski was surprised that Sergio would allow that to happen. *What was going on? What was he missing?* He really couldn't see a play to be had so he did as instructed. A minute later, Ivanski's man was at the door, where he stopped to cautiously look inside. His boss was back, standing at the table with his ill-gotten gains, and there was Sergio at the base of the stairs pointing his weapon at his head.

"Set the briefcase down and slide it over," Sergio commanded.

The man gave a quick glance over to Ivanski, who gave a nod back, confirming it was what needed to happen. Then the man knelt down and gave a muscled push of the leather briefcase and slid it across the

Spanish-paved floor to Sergio's feet. Keeping an eye and gun on the man, Sergio knelt and opened the case. Then opening a single journal with Professor Lee's inscribed name on the cover, he flipped through the first few pages of notes and calculations. It was all in Korean. "What is this? I can't read this. How do I know it is what is looked for?"

"You don't," Ivanski responded with confidence. "But as I had, you will have to trust."

"Trust is not something that comes easily in these situations," Sergio said, appearing slightly more agitated than just seconds before.

"Regardless, it is exactly what you paid for and is exactly what the others will be paying *you* for. And whoever those people, or country could be, they will be the ones to figure it out. And they will pay."

Sergio gave no more thought to it. "You are right," he said. "If all goes well, the next time we meet we shall have a drink and laugh."

Ivanski couldn't even manage a smile. From where he stood, he still felt at substantial risk of not getting away from there. "What now, then?" he nervously asked.

"Are the keys in your car?"

Ivanski glanced over to his man, who nodded an affirmative.

"Good," Sergio said. "Now, you will take your money and your weapon over on the chair. There is a truck behind the rear shed. It has enough gas to get you where you need to go, and the keys are on the counter next to the kitchen sink. You and your man will leave out the back door and battle what may be there, if anything, and hopefully have a safe and pleasant journey to whatever that destination of your choice will be. I will take my chances out the front. Do we understand each other?"

"Do I have a choice in this?"

"No. You do not."

Ivanski nodded back. "Then, I do," he said.

"Good," Sergio returned. "Then you should go now and not waste any more time."

Ivanski and his man gave a quick 'what now' look then Ivanski grabbed the briefcase, ran for his weapon, then he and his man disappeared into the kitchen. Sergio picked up the briefcase and strode to the front door and waited. A few seconds passed before he heard what was anticipated but dreaded: the muted popping sound of one weapon followed nearly simultaneously with several louder, non-silencer rounds being fired. Another gun battle was being waged behind the home. *Were there men waiting to cut me down also?* he thought.

No time was to be wasted if he was to have any chance at all, so he burst through the door and outside into a sprint toward the Russian's car. He was halfway there when suddenly he heard a loud command from behind. "I would stop right there, if I were you!"

His escape temporarily halted, Sergio Barberia stopped in his tracks. His face felt flush with the failed conclusion of his plan. As he stared ahead, another approaching vehicle was kicking up a cloud of dirt and gravel as it neared. *So close but yet so far from a life of freedom,* he thought. The voice from behind came from a man neither Spanish nor Russian and had come from the upstairs balcony. Whomever was there had obviously scaled up somehow and had his weapon pointed at him. If it was a rifle then he would probably die. If only a pistol, at sixty, or so, feet, he had a chance of a miss. The other car was closing, and with every foot closer, his chance of survival was dwindling. He dropped the briefcase. "Okay," he offered, insincerely. Then, like a springing mongoose, he dove to the left and attempted to roll.

In his very short time with Otter One, Zach had bought into what he had been taught; and that being to not trust anyone. He had been ready with two quick bursts from his weapon with the conclusion of both hitting their mark with pinpoint accuracy. One in the upper chest, the second in the lower abdomen. Sergio Barberia cried out in anguish but still attempted to raise his weapon. He managed an aimless shot into the sky, just before being forever silenced with a final round through his left temple.

Zach went over the railing and dangled six feet from the bottom railing post, then he dropped to the ground just as the trailing sedan was pulling up, but stopping well short of the carnage. Jack Tanner, who was behind the wheel, was the first to exit, weapon drawn. The Spaniard, still recovering, followed slower.

"Are you all right, Zach?!" Jack called out.

Zach waved them up. "We're okay!" he yelled back, but spinning with his weapon ready to make sure no one else was lurking.

Jack and the gimpy Javier, ran up. Jack knelt down and flipped over the lifeless man, then leaned back in surprise. "Holy shit! Do you know who this is, Zach?"

"No clue. The guy who tried to shoot me?"

"This is, or was, the infamous Sergio Barberia."

"The Barber," Javier mumbled just before spitting on the dead man.

"Who's the Barber?" Zach asked.

"Kalpakoff's equivalent, only a Spaniard," Jack answered first.

"A one-time competitor," Javier followed. "But not anymore," then he gave a concerned look around. "Where is Miguel?"

The question hit Zach like a thunderbolt. *Where was he?* He thought. *Miguel, the man with a thousand lives, would have shown himself by now.* "Shit!" Zach exclaimed and then took off in a sprint to the back of the home. When he reached the rear corner, he stopped and prepared to catch fire. Slowly, he peered around and just in time to see the truck with Ivanski in it, churning up a cloud of dirt as they sped away. Then he gave a quick scan and found what he was searching for. In the center of the dirt and brush landscape, between house and shed, lay two men—and one was his friend. He quickly ran out while searching for anything moving that may take a potshot at him. It was all silent when he reached Miguel. The other man was face up, glassy-eyed, and quite dead.

Miguel was face down as Zach knelt and pulled him over just as Jack and Javier were hobbling their way up.

"Is he dead?!" Javier asked gravely.

"He's breathing," Zach said as he watched Miguel's chest heave. Then suddenly his friend's eyes fluttered open, and he tried to speak. Zach leaned over close. "Take it easy, Pal."

Miguel reached up with his hand behind Zach's neck to try and pull him even closer.

"What is it, Miguel?" Zach asked while leaning in closer to hear.

Miguel struggled through a series of heavy coughs and then managed to blurt out, "It was Ivanski."

"Okay, my friend. Take it easy, now," Zach comforted as he reached out to hold the dying man's shaking hand.

Miguel squeezed tighter and tried to pull Zach in again. As he did, he managed one last attempt to speak. "*Kee-mo-sabi….*" he said in a weakened breath. No sooner had he managed the words that would be his last, his eyes rolled one last time and his chest ceased to move. "He's gone," he said as he laid Miguel's head down then stood up.

Javier collapsed next to his most trusted ally and placed a caring palm on Miguel's chest. "There were none better, my dearest friend."

Jack turned away from the scene, having been there himself on two occasions. The last time with the Simonson affair, he almost lost Johnny Scarpino. He remembered how it had affected him. Losing a partner like that always carried a burden of sorrow never to be lost. He turned to Zach, "What did he say?"

"It was Ivanski."

"If it was and any exchange happened, he took the money and left the bigger prize," he said while holding up the case. Then kneeling, he opened it just to verify the contents.

"What about Tommy? I didn't see any indication that someone, other than the old woman, had been held here. Do you think…?"

Head down and focused, Jack was already deep into what he felt carried the most weight at the moment, but he still managed an unconvincing "He'll show up somewhere, or…." he didn't need to complete the sentence. Then, taking the journal out, he began flipping through the pages. As he went along with everything written in Korean, his pace quickened into a near frenzy.

Abruptly, the pages had become blank until just as suddenly, he came to a section where the pages had been torn out.

"What's the matter?" Zach asked.

"He's got them!"

"Who's he and what does he have?"

"All of this is in Korean. Professor Lee told Johnny back home that he had also translated everything into English."

"And now Kalpakoff has it," Javier chimed in and was already thinking about what comes next. "If we don't find him quickly, he'll make his own deal with whomever."

"The fucker got the money and the goods to get more," Jack added. "That's going to make it pretty hard to negotiate, and that's if we're able to catch up to him."

Zach was still processing the loss of Miguel but managed to bring himself back to the immediate. "How long do you think we have?"

Javier locked eyes with Jack. "Yesterday."

CHAPTER NINTEEN

THE ROCK CREPT FROM UNDER

"Und du dachtest, ich wäre weg."

The Western Caribbean Sea

SHIP'S STEWARD, August Eriksson, lowered his binoculars and headed down from the second-tier railing just below the bridge. Youthfully bounding several steps at a time over the two open flights of stairs to the boat deck, he paused to take another look to confirm the land mass that had finally appeared at the far end of the horizon. It had been forty days since the Swedish cargo ship the Veendijk, had embarked from Casablanca, Morocco, heading for Panama City. And now, having finally reached the western edge of the Caribbean, he was fairly certain that the seldom-seen passenger would want to know.

The steward had come from a German mother and Swedish father. When he was young, and at the behest of his father, his family had migrated from Germany back to Sweden in the mid-1930s. Both mother and father had witnessed the rise of Adolf Hitler, and although mother was thoroughly committed to the Fatherland and the leader who would eventually become a maniacal dictator, at the time, family had won out. As the years passed and Hitler had manifested into what he was to become, many of her political allegiances changed but not to her country. Once settled back in father's home port of Stockholm, both parents, following a wise stance of neutrality for profit in the country of his father's origin, had managed to maintain an arm's length through the big war. His father had procured a job as a radio operator for the Johnson Line company and over the following years had served on a series of cargo ships, while mother had taken up in a local bakery shop. Over the next decade or so, the family prospered. But it had always been apparent that mother had never quite reconciled that her homeland had lost, thinking they would return one day to help the rebuild. Unfortunately, it was not to be, as tuberculosis eventually claimed her life at the young age of forty-two, leaving father to fend for himself and his son. Before she had passed, though,

Gerda (Muller) Eriksson had made it her mission that her son would fluently speak the language of her forefathers.

Somehow, August had reasoned, speaking two languages had been a boon in his profession and additionally had made it almost obligatory in taking the money and helping the stranger with the German name. And in doing so, the caveat of making him feel he had given back to the country his mother had loved. The steward allowed an almost whimsical and easy smile to come over him as he thought of his mother and that somehow, she was aware and approved of his efforts.

New to his apprentice chores, the steward warily ignored them to be able to apprise the stranger that his journey would soon be over. He continued toward the foredeck while thinking that the city of Colon would be at the beginning of the canal and thus an easy off-ramp for the stranger to start his new life. But in their previous and brief conversations, mostly allowed by the stranger because of the loneliness that came about from the long voyage, Panama City on the Pacific side would be the man's disembarkation at the end of the fifty-mile canal. The stranger had been very adamant about and had paid a hefty sum in advance to secure the final destination and the once-a-day food, water, and occasional bottle of wine or bourbon that would sustain him on the journey. From there, nothing was gleaned about where the stranger would eventually end up. The German Swede had assumed that a man requiring that amount of anonymity would certainly find the least conspicuous destinations in Central or South America—but he had never asked that question. His own knowledge of Argentina being a preferred destination for those of Germanic heritage that wanted to avoid prosecution, notwithstanding. And other than the occasional dusk to midnight excursion up to the open deck for fresh air, the passenger with the obvious limp rarely ventured from the forward hold.

Hustling to not be noticed, Steward Eriksson ducked inside, clambered down another two flights of stairs and down a long hall of crew cabins and through another man portal, and then down another single flight and finally emerging into the main frontal hold. Nowhere were there any indications of a living soul among the large wooden crates and large baled, cloth containers that were stacked floor to ceiling. The steward went further toward the front then hung a sharp left past the last sixteen-foot-high stack of crates carrying Moroccan coffee, then stopped. The overwhelming aroma of coffee beans was intoxicating, but at the same time quite wonderful, he thought. Then, anxiously looking around for any indication of life, he said quietly in German, "We're nearly there."

There was a short pause then a subdued response back in the same language. "How long, my friend?"

August had never really developed any lasting friendships while growing up, and it pleased him to hear the word *friend*, regardless of whether it truly kept any heartfelt sincerity.

"Another four hours to reach the entrance," he replied dutifully. "Then after registering the paperwork, it will take another ten hours to get through the canal."

The stranger let out a sigh. "Very well, then. It's been a very long journey under these conditions."

"You still may disembark here, if you could be persuaded to do so," the steward added.

"Tempting as it would be, my destiny lies elsewhere, my friend," the stranger replied.

"Yes. I understand," August said respectfully. Then he nervously glanced behind him to see if anyone was following. "I do need to get back. May I get you anything right now?"

The stranger stepped out from behind a stack of wooden crates. Tall and striking, late forties no doubt, but appearing tired from the journey. A month-old beard, ginger with a hint of gray formed scraggly around what had been a chiseled face at the beginning of the voyage. His eyes appeared narrow and focused as if fully ready for whatever came next. He held a cane for balance, and in the other hand was a large burlap sack.

"You are very kind," he said, "You have shown to be a loyal and caring tribute to the Fatherland."

The sentiment gave the steward a warm feeling. "Thank you, sir," he said sincerely, offering a partial bow.

The stranger smiled then extended the bag. "Would you be so kind as to have these cleaned and pressed for me?"

The steward took the bag. "Certainly, sir."

The stranger registered another warm smile. "You have done your job as contracted but also exceeded my own expectations. Inside the bag, you will find something extra in the hope that you will hold our little secret till the end of time."

Ship Steward August Eriksson smiled back, then stood erect while letting his chest puff out in prideful acknowledgment. "I will, sir," then, turning away, he stopped and pivoted back. A look of duty and responsibility to the one before brought a frown to his face. "My apologies, sir. I did mention our little agreement only to my father back in Stockholm. He is infirmed with cancer at the moment and I'm afraid has not been given much more time."

The passenger let out a noticeable sigh, then nodded while taking a moment to digest. "I see," he replied, trying unsuccessfully to show the degree of disappointment he felt. "And at still quite a young age. Very tragic and I am sorry for your troubling news."

"Thank you, sir," the steward said, feeling relieved for doing so. "So, you see, your secret will be kept."

"Yes. I am quite sure that in the end, it will. And besides, he is your father."

"And who could be trusted more than one's own father?" the steward said proudly.

The stranger smiled back at the young man. "Indeed. Who else?"

The conversation had turned, causing the young steward to feel emboldened. "Sir?" he started. "Under the circumstances, might I ask your name now?"

The stranger fell silent for a few seconds as if weighing consequences. "You are a very brave young man," he finally admitted. "I should hate for anything of serious consequence to happen to you from this knowledge."

"But sir, what could ever come of this knowledge now? You have been so kind to me, that I would truly take any risk that would come my way."

"I suppose you would," the stranger replied, then reluctantly, "My name is Fredrick Simonson, and you should be the only one to know that name."

"Fredrick Simonson," the steward repeated. "I will honor you by never speaking of it again. But thank you, sir."

Simonson watched as the young steward turned to head back up. "Oh," Simonson suddenly called out to him. "Before disembarkation and when you return with my clothing…"

"Yessir?"

"Would you be so kind as to bring me a simple carving knife?" He held out his two palms separated by an estimated eight inches. "About yay long?"

"Absolutely, sir!" the crewman responded. "May I ask what for?"

"You may, kind sir. But I'm almost embarrassed to say."

"Well. I wouldn't want you to feel pressed to be in a position of being uncomfortable, sir," the steward replied.

Simonson set his cane aside against the crates then limped forward and placed both hands on the steward's shoulders. Then giving a warm look of assurance into the steward's eyes, he smiled as if he had been the young man's father. The move was designed to reassure yet also to create curiosity in the seaman's mind about what could have been had he been willing to take a chance. Homosexuality was viewed as a crime in his home country up until 1944, and certainly on the high seas, even with it being a known issue among a small percentage of merchant seamen. August Eriksson had been a late bloomer and not yet willing to experiment on the off chance of being ostracized by his peers. He politely drew back.

"My dear August..." the stranger softly offered.

"I...I...I'm not quite sure..." the steward stuttered. "You know my name?"

"Of course. Those that I feel important to me; I make a point of knowing."

"I'm not sure, sir."

"I see," said Simonson. "It can take time for one to succumb to his true self. To be free of those chains will be quite something for you to look forward to."

The steward stepped back with what could only be described as his own, and unnecessary, feelings of shame. "I'm sorry," was his needless apology.

"No, my dearest August, it is I who should apologize. I'm afraid that I have put you into a position of questioning a moment you were obviously not ready for," then Simonson smiled a reassuring smile once more. "You are still very young and have a lifetime to blossom."

"Yessir," August replied, still nervous about the conversation and its openness. Then turning away, over his shoulder, he asked, "Anything more, sir?"

"Just the knife, I would remind," the stranger said loud enough for the quickly retreating seaman. "Just the knife."

CHAPTER TWENT

—ⅿ—

A LITTLE LUCK NEVER HURT

TIED TO a wooden chair, his face swollen and bloody from the last thirty minutes of a beating, the captive dropped his head and spit out the blood that filled his mouth. Trying to steal a few breaths and hoping for a reprieve that he knew would never come, he grunted, "Nyet."

Showing no mercy, the Spaniard again pressed the end of his wooden cane deep into the man's wound, prompting another series of gritted teeth screams that made both Jack and Zachary wince.

"Tell us!" Javier yelled while twisting harder. The man bellowed one last primordial scream then began to sob uncontrollably. "I'll talk! I'll talk!" he yelled in Russian. Zach was the only one to understand. "He wants to talk," he told the others.

It had taken less than an hour of mild—at least by Cold War standards—torture to push the man to the brink. When by the car, wounded, and out of the action, he probably had wished he hadn't cried out so loud, bringing attention to himself back at the Hacienda. Zach, Javier, and Jack had just loaded their friend Miguel into the Adler, not wanting to leave him behind, when Zach had heard the painful cry for help. One of Ivanski's men had survived the firefight. He had taken one in the shoulder, and as he lay on the ground trying to get back into the fight, his exposed leg took another, and he was done.

"Ask him what the plan was if things went to shit," Jack directed his eyes at Zach.

"That's a little more than I can put together, Jack. Only two months in on the language, remember?"

"Give it a try. We're hanging on nothing here," Jack encouraged.

Zach pinched his lips then squinted his eyes to look as evil as he could, then reached over and placed the man's right nipple between his forefinger and thumb and started to pinch. "You better speak some fucking English right now, asshole!"

His blood-soaked clothes meant he was in deep shit and needed a doctor, and now he was getting titty twisted. The man had put up a good fight, but now his face was turning beet red in unison with the deep pain he was now feeling. He held for a few seconds, then blurted out, "Okay-okay, I speak English! Please, please! No more!"

Zach turned back to Jack and Javier and gave them both a satisfied raised eyebrow. "That wasn't so hard, was it? Have at it, boys."

Jack jumped in. "All right, dipshit! Where were you all supposed to meet after the deal went down?"

"No meet," the man said through a bloodied mouth. "The boss, he leave us our pay at church."

"What church?" Jack demanded.

"In Seville. The priest there was to give money."

"Why would a priest get involved?" Zach questioned.

"The answer would be that he had no choice, am I right?" Javier intervened.

The man nodded back. "We were made aware that any failure to complete task that there would be specific consequence."

"Your English is getting better," Zach said, noticing a more complete use of the King's English.

"Two years at Boston College. My parents, both Russian immigrants, didn't have a pot to piss in, so I was recruited fairly easily. The money has been good."

"I bet it is," Jack jumped in, "I feel a deal coming."

"Freedom and I give you the church. There's very little time."

"How about we get you to a doctor and you don't die?" Javier interjected.

"Freedom is all I have. Jail will mean death. They will find a way."

"Two years in isolation at a location of our choosing. Arizona or Utah and you are in constant communication. You go missing and we hunt you down, and I don't mean the US of A feds. I mean us. The guys with no rules and dealing with scum like you with extreme prejudice."

Zach knew this was really a giveaway and with no real authority to do or to commit to anything being offered. Otter-One wasn't even a known reality with the Pentagon or American government, although those that funded the support team and agents did have indirect ties to those same entities. The reality was that people knew but didn't, or at least not officially. Basically, this guy was fucked either way.

"The church!" Javier demanded while pointing to Zach to reach for his nipple again.

"Iglesia de Santa Ana!" The goon managed, then pleaded. "Please, a doctor!"

Jack and Zach both pivoted and bolted for the door. Jack turned back to Javier. "If you have anybody you can call in Seville, you had better do it. Kalpakoff has almost an hour on us. I'll call once we get there and once we know if he has gotten there ahead of us."

"Remember…" Javier said. "He probably stayed off the main roads. That will certainly have slowed him down. You may still catch him."

"And if we do?" Zach asked.

"Once you get control of the papers, then it's up to you," the Spaniard replied. Then his voice took on a more serious tone. "The man has many friends, and he cannot be trusted to not have a plan using those friends. My belief is that if you have an opportunity, you should eliminate someone who would have no qualms about doing the same to you."

"And what will you be doing?" Jack asked.

"I will not be far behind," Javier answered. "I need to make one call to those who need to know what is happening, then also to pick up something we will most likely need."

"And what about him?" Zach asked, not confident about what the Russian stool's fate would end up being.

Javier waved the two to get moving. "Don't worry. I will take care of him."

"You promised!" the Russian blurted. "We make deal!"

Jack nodded then followed Zach out the door. As they jumped into the van a single gunshot rang out from behind. The two exchanged glances, then they sped off with Jack behind the wheel.

Zach wanted to ask about the Russian they left behind but didn't. This was the business he was in; he counseled himself. To be effective and give yourself the optimum chance of success, at times, would require certain choices. He was certain that he could live with those choices.

"So, who does Javier need to call?" Zach asked Jack. "And what is it that he thinks we need?"

Jack made a sharp left turn then pressed down on the gas. "I'm wondering about the call myself," he said, sounding intrigued. "But the item to be picked up would be Marcella De Anda."

Padre Diego Martinez turned back to the sparse congregation, those few elderly women still holding the faith for their family members that were not as willing to make the early Mass. As he stood there surveying the mostly empty pews, the church door suddenly opened, and, facing east, the morning sun briefly burst in like a bolt of lightning, nearly blinding the priest. Several of the flock craned their necks around to see who had shown up late to their ritual but quickly turned back around. When the door slowly creaked its way shut and the shadows returned, in the back was a man that the padre had recognized but had also dreaded a return from. The man nodded then disappeared behind the right narthex column, bringing a sweeping chill over the padre while he pondered how his God would allow a henchman of Satan to enter His house of worship. He took in several shallow breaths to steady his nerves and then said in a lower-than-normal but still controlled voice, "The Gospel of the Lord."

The smattering of women responded. "Praise to you, Lord Jesus Christ," then the Padre kissed his Bible and bid the remaining faithful a good morning. He moved to the front and, as he stood at the door and warmly shook hands with each congregation member, he felt the presence of the man in the shadows waiting in the side vestibule. Then, when the eldest finally made her way out, just as he had done a hundred times before, he helped the Señora Perez down the steep steps. Releasing her off one final time, she thanked him and shuffled away. Giving a final wave, he then quickly made his way back up, then closing the door behind him, the Padre began searching the shadows for the man he feared. Although the latecomer was nowhere in sight, the sense of him being there, like some apparition sent chills up his back and caused the hairs on his neck to spike. Stealing himself then mumbling an inner prayer of deliverance, he made his way back to his office. The man was there.

With his back to the doorway, Ivanski Kalpakoff stood next to the lone sash window staring out across the narrow brick cobblestone street to the modest, tree-lined park between an apartment building and a small carniceria mercado. In his right hand was a leather satchel while his left arm dangled at his side with a blood-soaked towel tied just above the elbow.

Preferring to stay in the doorway, Diego did not move. "Señor. Are you hurt badly?" the Padre asked.

Ivanski turned around. His worn and tired face showed something different, but he shook his head no. "Where is it?"

"It is there," Diego replied, pointing to a kneeling bench in front of a small praying altar.

Ivanski caught himself in mid-swoon then leaned against the wall for balance. "Please get it now."

Diego nodded then moved quickly to the bench seat and lifted it, exposing stacks upon stacks of cash. "What would you like me to do with it?"

"Put half of it in this bag," Ivanski said, pulling the bag off his shoulder. "The rest is yours."

"But what about the others?"

"They will no longer be needing it."

Diego thought he understood but still could not bring himself to fully grasp what was happening. "This is too much. What shall I do with it?"

Ivanski had to laugh even though it hurt to do so. "Whatever, I suppose, is in your heart, Father. Do you not feed the poor when given the opportunity?"

"Señor," the Padre followed, "In this town. On these humble streets we are all poor. Only the Lord's word and our goodwill in His name will make us rich."

"Well now...." Ivanski began before coughing to help clear his throat. "Now you have the paper riches to aid in your goodwill. I trust your silence will follow this gift?"

Diego sighed before acknowledging with a nod, followed by Ivanski tossing the satchel over and the padre hurriedly filling it.

"Where will you go?" Diego asked, not thinking if his answer would put him in danger.

Ivanski slowly stepped over to the Padre, who was still kneeling by the bench. He leaned over the man's shoulder to make sure that the satchel had been filled as asked. Then reaching around to his back, he retrieved his revolver causing Diego to let out an audible gasp.

"No, Señor!" he pleaded, with palms raised and fully stretched out.

Kalpakoff stood back erect, then his eyes turned quizzical. "I'm not going to kill you, Padre," he said while seeming surprised that the Padre had gone there. "Right now, you and maybe your God, are the only friends I have," then taking the bag being handed to him, he felt the weight. "I noticed a door to the rear avenue," he continued, while muscling the bags' shoulder strap over his head and keeping his weapon-hand free. "How do I get there?"

Diego pointed to the left. "All the way down past the organ. There are stairs leading down on the right. They will take you to a door that leads out to the street," then the Padre remembered the vow he had given and summoned up a courage that had always been there. "Señor. Please offer your confession before you go."

Ironically, Ivanski Kalpakoff had been raised Catholic but had long since been removed from it. The unexpected offer actually had him giving brief and considered thought to the request. Then he sighed before answering, "No."

The Padre continued while feeling more confident in his commission to do so. "Are you certain? Life is an unknown and short for some. Please, Señor, think about it. For your soul, please."

A few more quiet and thoughtful seconds passed and the padre, sensing the confusion and turmoil in the man before him, relinquished saying, "Then I shall pray for you."

Taken slightly aback, Ivanski wanted to say thank you, but the words never formed. So instead he offered back a last and silent confirming nod then turned away and began the short journey that would be slower and more painful with his injuries. Down the hall he hobbled, past the organ, down the short flight of stairs, and out into the sunshine. He slightly stumbled when the weight on his leg nearly weakened and gave way, forcing a brief need to lean against a nearby statue of Saint Luke. He wondered about the blood loss but calculated that it had been comparatively minor to other wounds he had sustained over the years and that he had more than enough strength to continue.

Glancing both ways and not finding anyone to bring alarm, he tucked his weapon back into his belt and began making his way down the several short, narrow pathways leading to the Canal de Alfonso, where a motorboat would be waiting.

CHAPTER TWENTY-ONE

FINALLY, THE LIGHT

Miraflores Locks, Panama City, Panama
"Una cucaracha es difícil de matar."

THE HUMIDITY drenched his clothes, and the salty air fell heavy on his lungs, but he was invigorated, nonetheless. Fredrick Simonson had stealthily made his way up the several flights of stairs and was now waiting patiently for the scorching sun and all its Ecuadorian heat, to slip down beyond the Pacific horizon before quietly slithering off his floating home of the past three months. Many things had changed during that time, and unequivocally, he rationalized, his appearance had been one of those things that did.

The deep hold, the forward belly of the freighter, and all the heat and humidity it held had helped in a guestimate-loss, he had figured, of at least fifteen pounds more or less. He had made that calculation earlier, and in preparation for his debarkation, he had pinched his waist handles and squinted into a small, handheld mirror provided by his steward friend for shaving. His new figure was gaunt, and his once short, wavy, ginger hair, although it had grown longish from the journey, had thinned and showed enough gray now to add a dimension to what he had always considered a formidable profile. He thought to himself that he would assuredly be nimbler with the weight loss, and with the newly chiseled face, he was still a devilish specimen. This tickled him into a single chuckle. *Ladies beware*, he silently mused.

With the sun dipping and dusk settling in, he quickly scouted in both directions and noticing the side deck clear of personnel, he pulled down the hat borrowed from Steward August Eriksson's lifeless body and then stepped out from the portal and made his way stealthily toward the gangplank that swayed ever-so-gently at a steep thirty degrees downward. Following a few unbalanced steps on the planking, the moored freighter rocked suddenly from a passing tug's wake, and he had to quickly reach for the guide rope along the plank to steady himself. A few cautious seconds and his footing back beneath him, he adjusted his shouldered duffle for balance then using his cane with one hand, he maintained constant contact with the roped handrail with the other. Finally reaching the stationary pier, he again righted the duffle and the meager belongings within, then began surveying his surroundings. It had been a long and uneventful journey, and he was glad to be on landfall, but now the second leg needed his full attention. He scanned again for contact of any sort because none had been given, only that he would be watched for, then back up to the freighter and its tiered decks. With a large contingent of personnel already on dry land and enjoying their initial leave time, there remained only a skeleton crew behind. He had not been noticed, and for that he was grateful.

He had studied the Panamanian government and was already quite understanding of that Panama City was a dive at best. The government, or lack thereof, consisted of a string of presidents more prone to hiding and hoarding money for themselves, rather than applying it to the infrastructure the citizens so desperately needed. The current and recently elected, authoritarian leader, Alcibiades Arosemena had shown promise but ultimately had been no different. Fear had ruled the day for decades, but his ways of handling unrest would appear in more covert ways. Silence the subversives and all would be well: that had been the order of the day, and that was something he could lean into. Through research on the country and its government, he had determined it to be a perfect fit as a landing destination. He could hide in the shadows or move through the upper circles while looking as corrupt as the rest of them. How long he stayed was yet to be determined.

Still not sure in the direction to go, the stowaway gave another glance in both directions, when suddenly there was a child's voice from behind.

A young boy, no more than eight or nine years old, shouted "Señor!" enthusiastically while trotting up. Dirty and appearing malnourished, the waif had sprung from hidden shadows and was now grabbing the stranger's arm and tugging. Then again, "Señor! *Por favor*, this way!"

"Yes. Of course," Simonson said, obliging the boy. "And in which direction shall we proceed?"

The boy gave a quizzical look. "*Por favor!* This way!" he repeated, while now pulling with both hands.

"I see," said Simonson as he moved with the boy, realizing the words repeated were probably all that the child had been taught for the little escapade. "I will follow you," he replied, while motioning with a nod and a pointed cane for the boy to continue. Then with a cherubic grin, the boy tugged harder, and they were off. Down the boardwalk they went, past another moored and much smaller freighter in from Libya, and the occasional merchant closing down their rolling stands for the evening. Finally, the boy stopped in front of one alley and pointed. "There!" he instructed.

"Down this way, then?" the stranger said, baulking while wishing he had spent more time learning Spanish instead of French.

The boy nodded and again pointed down the alley. Simonson again obliged by stepping up and peeking down the narrow and very foreboding space. No more than fifteen feet across, the alley was lined with overflowing trash cans forming an obstacle course of debris to navigate and hiding places for the sinister types that would need them. Dusk had turned the corner to early evening darkness by now, and the alley that traveled between two three-story apartments was almost completely dark with the exception of two lit, oil lamps from second-floor sills at the very end, which, at best, brought only the most basic dim illumination.

Simonson didn't feel anything other than that treachery was afoot, should he go down that alley. He hesitated for a moment longer then let out a reluctant breath. "So I am to go down there?" he asked again of the boy.

The waif seemed to understand and shook his head in affirmation. Simonson managed a strained smile down at the waif and then took the sailor's cap off his head and placed it on the boy's. That brought another grin from the child. Then turning back to the alley he squinted down to the end while reaching into his pocket for some miscellaneous coins from three different countries. He was certain that the boy had already been paid in some form, probably in bread and cheese, but he had neither. Giving one last gaze down at the child, he placed the coin into the outstretched palm of the boy, who then smiled up like he had just won everything in the world and then scampered off.

The stowaway with a Germanic accent, glanced away from the alley's shadows just long enough to watch the boy disappear down the boardwalk. Somehow, it had made him feel good to bring a misguided balance to whatever evil he had most recently inflicted. The steward, August Eriksson, had been an unfortunate casualty: but such were his ways when appropriate. *But to a child*, he thought quietly, *he could be good when the opportunity arose.*

Simonson peered down the alley again then let out a steadying sigh while reminding himself that it had been a long journey and his time away from the action had been difficult. But he was here now. No missteps would be allowed going forward—he had to be mindful of everything. Two-thirds of the way through his planned trek was no time to fall victim to a young grifter and whomever the scoundrel he had taken orders from who may now be lying-in-waiting for his next victim. Simonson reached behind to his waistband and retrieved the yay-long butcher's blade that still had a tinge of August's blood caked on the handle.

"Very well, then," he said, steeling himself. "Let us see what we shall see," then with forced confidence he strode down the alley and into the darkness. As he neared the opposite end of the alleyway, he could see that it tied into another walkway running left and right that led to several back-alley doors of the wretched apartments that lined the waterfront barrio. At any time, one such door could open, and an attempt could be made to remove his head from his shoulders. He squeezed the grip of the knife to remind him it was there. When he reached the end, he again questioned the foolishness of going further. As he stood there contemplating the direction, he sensed movement followed by a dark figure suddenly appearing like an apparition, becoming visible near the middle and down the left wing of the alley. The figure seemed quite large from a distance, and in his estimation equated to near giant status were the figure beside him. *A freak, to be sure, like something from a traveling carnival*, he thought. Nevertheless, he feared an unwanted confrontation and began searching for the next option. He gripped the knife tighter, then glanced down and into the shadows on the right side. That corridor was even darker with absolutely no illumination, possibly a dead-end. Not one to panic, he turned back to the enormous figure only to find the nearly seven-footer had stopped in his tracks about forty feet away. This was not for him, he surmised, now realizing the boy had been a ruse in the trap before him. He abruptly turned to retreat when he was startled by another figure standing just five feet away. He quickly brandished the blade in full view of his possible assailant and swiped it left and right, causing the other to widen his own stance in possible defense but also throwing a cautionary open palm toward him.

"Simonson?" the man asked with a heavy accent.

"I am," he responded somewhat relieved.

"Do you have the money?" the man continued.

Simonson slowly lowered the knife while quickly glancing behind to check on the giant. He hadn't moved closer. "I do," he replied. "Do you have the weapon?"

The other nodded and Simonson relaxed his stance while the man reached into a burlap sack, producing a Mauser P.08 Luger—known as the "Black Widow"—and handed it over. Simonson checked the Luger's mechanism then stuck it into his belt. If the man before him had been in a different frame of mind, he could have used the weapon on him, but thankfully, he had come as advertised. *Miscreants come in all shapes, sizes, and warped temperament,* he had cautioned himself. *You never knew who could turn in a moment of greed.* For now, he needed to trust just enough. He then reached into his pocket and handed over several large-denomination paper pesos.

"You will find that to be the amount as agreed upon," he said, then pointed toward the entrance of the alleyway. "Please. Lead on."

The man stuffed the bills in his pocket while studying the man before him. "You wish a hotel in the Casco Antiguo district?" he asked, knowing that it had been requested.

Simonson nodded.

"You carry much money, Señor?"

"Enough," Simonson said cautiously.

"Very dangerous, Señor," the man said with a grin that heightened the stranger's alertness even more than it already was. "La Concordia, Señor. The very best for you."

"Well done," Simonson said and then glanced back at the giant. "And him?"

The guide laughed out loud. "Him? He doesn't leave the shadows. He is a very large cockroach, that one. Light scares him terribly."

"Hard to believe," Simonson panned.

"Don't worry, Señor," the contact said, "he will make sure no one follows."

"Of course," Simonson acquiesced with a half-hearted grin, "since you are being so accommodating…"

"Before you assume, Mr Simonson," the guide interrupted, "You have paid me well, but one who pays like this most assuredly has more. I could just as easily afford myself to what is left on your person."

"My apologies, and I stand corrected," Simonson replied while instinctively placing a hand near the grip of the Luger and preparing himself for anything. "It has been a difficult journey and I long for a hot bath, a worthy meal and some, let us say…female companionship. Is this something you could provide? For a reasonable fee, of course."

The man eyed the freak behind Simonson, then waved him off. "This way," he said, followed by a giggle reminiscent of a teen flipping through the pages of his first porno mag. "You will be well taken care of," he offered, "I know just the one for you. She's clean."

Fredrick Simonson guffawed, then pointed his guide forward. "Being taken care of, well…that's all I've ever wanted."

CHAPTER TWENTY-TWO

WHO ELSE?

"La linea de la muerte es larga."

IT WASN'T a surprise for Johnny Scarpino to see the obvious company vehicle parked there. Nor for the two people sitting in the front seat attentively staring at the building across the street. He had a well-placed mid-level man in the FBI for the past two years who had been keeping him apprised of most things at the agency, at least the ones that weren't classified so secret that it might get him irreversibly compromised. So he was already aware of Special Agent Dowling and that he and his underling, Jeffrey Pimpleton, would be keeping tabs on the Lees. These two had been taking turns with another pair for the past week in watching the home for any comings and goings; but would be the most likely agents on the stakeout—and they were.

Johnny glanced at his wristwatch, it was 6:45 and right on time for his, unbeknownst to the Lees, planned seven o'clock appointment with the family. The question would be if his plan, and the character enlisted, would perform as instructed and get the result intended. People on the fringe were occasionally dependable, at best, and were a dime a dozen and more than willing to make a buck. The lesson learned a few years back was never pay up front.

Charlie, or "Charlie Beefeater" as he had been nicknamed for his favorite gin, had been used before and had earned the right to be at the top of the list of useful persons. The problem had always been finding him and what condition he would be in when found. Charlie liked to party and would frequently be found either in the gutter or passed out on one of his many stool friends' couches. Surprisingly, though, once found Charlie had a unique ability to sober up quickly. A real plus.

Johnny Scarpino felt anxious, though, a rarity for him, of the still-possible prospect of failure on behalf of his chosen drunk. The negative thought had him inexplicably checking his watch again, followed by him shaking his head as if to chastise himself for doing so. *A few minutes to go. There was still time*, he reminded himself.

He regrouped to clear his head of the current task until needed, allowing one eye to stay trained on a singular hedge across the street while his thoughts morphed into how his whole chosen field had worked. Specifically, Otter One and how the powers behind the scenes had been super stealthy on the creation and deployment of resources for the projects committed to. He was also fairly certain that the FBI were also aware of them, *some* group, or at the very least, someone who had been heavily invested in the Lees and the secrets that the house supposedly held. And it was important to remember the fact that that person or group was on the good old US of A's side, or that was what was assumed, according to his inside man. Still, you never knew who would be willing to turn for a donation of life-altering money, and that would include his boy floating around the halls of Langley. But to everyone concerned, all the recon and watchful eyes had made sense regardless of whose head those eyes were imbedded in. Protect the good old U.S. of A. was all that had mattered.

Johnny stopped himself from checking his watch again. Then, sensing a presence across the way, he looked up and caught a glimpse of movement at the eastside walkway of the home. Right on time, a man wearing a dark shirt and a black beanie stood then stepped out from behind the large corner hedge and looked like he was up to no good. Charlie had been on time and was earning his twenty-spot. Better yet, and as hoped for, both heads in the FBI's vehicle also zeroed in on his man. Apparently, the coffee had done its job and kept them awake. Charlie did as he was told and made himself conspicuous for long enough then took off running down the street like he had already completed something nefarious. Again, as hoped for, Special Agent Dowling and his partner fired up the engine of the company car and took off after him.

The window now open, Johnny Scarpino stepped out from behind one of a line of mature magnolia trees and crossed the street. Striding with purpose, he made his way up the steps of the brownstone just as the FBI boys' vehicle had reached the end of the street and was turning onto Olive. By the time they cleared and paralleled the vehicle with the road, Charlie should have already climbed into a waiting parked van and disappeared from view. It would take approximately ten minutes, he had calculated, of constant searching by Dowling and Pimpleton before they returned or gave up on the night. He and the boys would deal with them returning should it occur before they were finished, but the hope was that they may just go home. For now, he needed to be sharp because the whole attempt would be improvised and fluid once he knocked on the door—he did. A few anxious seconds passed before he could hear steps approaching and the latch being turned. The door slowly opened and an Asian man, late twenties and surprisingly not Jeoung Lee or his son, in a suit, tie, and looking very much part of some serious organization, was standing there with a broader than necessary smile on his face.

"May I help you?" the man politely asked. Again, surprisingly, with an American accent that suggested he was schooled in the States. Johnny quickly surmised that he was probably Ivy League and, most assuredly, recruited by his home country. Johnny gave a quick study of the man's face, bone structure and eyes. *Yeah, he's probably Korean,* Johnny figured.

And while he was giving the man before him the final quick overview he was also peeking over the man's shoulder for others. "I have an appointment with the Lees," he replied with his own nonchalant smile. "Are they home?" Then, eyeing the family sitting in the formal living room by the fire, he pointed over. "Oh, there they are! May I come in?" and not waiting for an answer, he brushed past the man.

Both Jeoung and Nari Lee were sitting on the sofa with daughter Si-Woo on Jeoung's left. Ji-Hoon sat in a high-backed chair across. The man at the door was not alone, though. Another more menacing looking man stood behind Ji-Hoon with one arm hanging down behind his back like it was attached to something lethal. Johnny stopped short of the room.

"I am so embarrassed," he apologized, "I think I got my days mixed up. It *was* Saturday, right?"

"Jeoung and Nari looked at each other momentarily, then Jeoung bought in on the charade. "I'm afraid it is our mistake, Mr.—"

"Johnson," Johnny was quick to provide.

"Right. Mr Johnson," he said, "I need to apologise. These are my sister's boys from California, and they have given us a surprise visit. We were just catching up, and I forgot to call you to reschedule. I hope you can understand."

Johnny Scarpino nodded his understanding. "Sure, no problem, Mr Lee. The Kirby Company appreciates that you have given us an opportunity to show you just how great our vacuum machines are." Then, with a quick scan to assess the overall situation, Johnny felt it would be better for everyone to retreat. "How about I get back in touch with you tomorrow and we'll set up another time. Would that be okay?"

"Certainly," Jeoung said, while unable to stem a slight tone of uneasiness.

Johnny turned for the door and stuck out his hand to the one blocking his way. "Enjoy your time with your aunt and uncle," he offered.

The man shook Johnny's hand while stepping aside. "We're sorry that we inadvertently messed up your appointment," he said convincingly. "But we are only here for one day, and it has been some time since our last visit. We really wanted to see our cousins."

"No worries," Johnny said, smiling. "I'll come back at a later time," then as he reached the door, he caught the figure of a third man in a reflection on a glass-covered art piece depicting an Asian rock garden with an ornamental wooden shrine in the background. The figure in the glass was on the right side of the doorway, just peeking out from an adjacent dining room. Now there were at least three of them.

An obvious professional and clearly suspicious, the man at the door couldn't let it go and fired one last salvo. "But you didn't bring this fantastic machine with you?"

Johnny let out an awkward laugh. "Yeah, those damn things are heavy!" he replied. "American built like no other. Besides, the Lees already took a test drive the other day," then he whispered to the man, "It's kind of a done deal."

"I see," said the man as he followed Scarpino to the porch. "Well, good luck tomorrow," he offered, then closed the door behind him.

Not looking back, Johnny gave an over-the-shoulder riposte, "The machine sells itself, my friend," then he stepped off the landing of the home and quickly down the steps, all the time thinking that the man at the door wasn't buying any of it. Across the street the FBI boys had returned and were parked, their eyes locking in on him. He feigned not to see them and moved briskly down the sidewalk. Once past the next two homes and out of view from any of the Lees' front windows where he was sure that eyes were still on him, he sprinted across the street and stealthily made his way back up to Dowling's car. Never out of sight, both Dowling and partner Jeffrey Pimpleton quickly emerged with hands inside their coats and coming toward him. Johnny stopped in his tracks and threw up his hands.

"Easy boys," he said. "I believe we're on the same team."

"Don't think so," Dowling followed, while sizing Scarpino up. "Who are you, and what is going on with you and the Lees?"

"All good questions. Skepticism is good in our line of work," Johnny glibly replied.

"And what line of work are we in, again?" Dowling asked.

"Okay. I get it. First off, you are not getting my name. It's bad enough that you now have a face to go with a voice. Suffice to say that I am thinking America protection and support."

"Or we can just take you in and get your name then?" Agent Pimpleton chimed in. "I'm sure you're carrying some form of identification?"

"I am not, but that would be another way to go," Johnny panned. "I would be remiss, though, if I didn't divulge the main and more pressing issue."

"Which is?" Dowling said impatiently.

"The main thing you need to be aware of is that the Lees and their children are being held hostage by a Korean unit inside."

"What?!" Pimpleton interjected. "We've been keeping tabs here for a couple of hours!"

"Regardless, now is not the time to get into your skill set on surveilling. You will need to trust me in this. They're inside and most likely trying to get their hands on what everyone else is trying to get their hands on."

"Including you?" Dowling asked.

"Not me. Well, technically yes. If there's something to be found or had, my people only want to ensure it stays in American hands. We just need to take care of business right here and now. Are you in?"

"It would greatly help if you told me who you work for."

"Not going to happen, Agent Dowling."

Agent Dowling scoffed. "So, you're asking us to trust you?"

"I am."

"And how is it you know my name?"

"That, and your partner, Pimple…something?"

Dowling gave it a thought then glanced over at Pimpleton, then back at the home. "You can't tell me who you work for?"

Johnny's eyes followed the agents. "We don't have much time. I think they're on to me."

"Okay," Dowling agreed. "How many are there?"

"Three for sure. All of them are wearing suits like they're going to a funeral."

"Weapons?"

"Oh, I am quite sure of that. Unseen, but there."

Dowling sighed. "Do you have a plan?"

"It's forming," Scarpino said, not believing it, then added, "If I only had a vacuum."

The car screeched to a stop just in front of the Iglesia de Santa Ana, scattering a flock of pigeons, and getting the attention of pedestrians and early morning park goers. Zach and Jack burst out and bound up the stairs with guns drawn. Once inside, they were met by Father Diego, who was moving between pews, straightening hymnals and sweeping. When he saw the men and their weapons, with no persuasion necessary, he emphatically pointed to the rear of the church and blurted out, "As of five minutes ago, I know nothing," then he hurried away to seek whatever shelter he thought might be necessary for his safety.

"You go!" Jack told Zach. "He has to be heading for the water! I'll get the car!"

Zach bolted toward the rear while Jack did the same toward the front. Zach made it down to the rear in no time, then leaping the six steps and landing on the five-by-five tiled entrance, he busted out onto what amounted to a pedestrian walkway. From his pre-study of the city map on the way, he knew that the Canal de Alfonso was only one street away, and he headed for it. Breaking through to the one-car-width avenue that ran along the canal, he began searching both ways. Suddenly, his ears perked up as he heard a motor growl just ahead, coming from the inside of a small boathouse on the other side of the road. He bolted for it. As he was turning the corner of the boathouse he heard the same motor whine in a higher pitch, and then there it was, a small skiff steering away and heading out into the canal at full speed. Ivanski Kalpakoff was at the tiller looking back at him. The chase was on.

Zach pulled his weapon and thought about taking a shot right then, but there had been too many innocents on the other side of the canal that were in danger of taking a stray bullet, and there wasn't another boat in the slip to commandeer. His fear that Kalpakoff would escape was peaking when, from the roadway, he heard Jack yell his name. Zach raced around the boathouse and saw Jack waving him over to the car. He rushed over and ducked in while pointing ahead. "He's in that boat!"

Jack stepped on the clutch while throwing the shifter into first and squealed the car away. The road was narrow, and although their car was much faster than the small outboard they were chasing, they were losing ground for fear they might hit unsuspecting pedestrians. Finally, they reached a man bridge no more than eight feet wide and designed for foot and cycle traffic.

"Stop!" Zach yelled.

Jack slammed on the brakes, almost sending his own head into the steering wheel. Zach jumped out and ran for the center of the bridge. He could see the launch with Kalpakoff aboard was nearing, so he climbed over the stone railing and positioned himself to jump. Kalpakoff saw him at the same time and immediately drew his weapon and pointed. It didn't take Zach any time to realize his attempt would be a mistake, so he quickly leapt back over just as two shots rang out, both rounds taking chunks of stone and mortar out of the century-old arched bridge. Kalpakoff motored under, and when he came out a couple of seconds later, his weapon was pointed up and ready to pick off anyone who exposed themselves. Zach let out a frustrated yell, then hunched over and keeping low, he ran back to the car where Jack had positioned himself over the hood and had just squeezed off several futile shots of his own at Kalpakoff, hoping to get lucky.

"Now, I could have used a rifle!" Jack yelled, getting back in the car.

"Go! We're going to lose him!" Zach commanded as he climbed in.

Jack sped forward again while keeping one eye on the path ahead and the boat in the canal. Several walkers leapt out of the way with their faces looking like frightened gargoyles. Just then, Kalpakoff took a hard right and disappeared into a small tributary canal. Jack pressed hard on the brakes again. "Can you see him?!"

Zach sighed. "Shit! No," then looking over at Jack, he said, "Does anybody know where that canal leads to?"

"We're in Spain, Ransom. Whoever would know is not in this car or close by," then he jolted the car forward again. Staring intensely between the one they were chasing and the road ahead, Jack could see that the next vehicle cross-over was another quarter mile away. By the time they passed the crossing, then traveled back the same distance to the canal, it appeared the chase was over. Frustrated at being so close but ultimately losing Kalpakoff, they rolled down several adjoining side streets that ran perpendicular to the canal but parallel to the one in question. And at several points, they got out of the car to walk the maze of alleyways that mapped the surrounding area. It was akin to being lost in Venice without the romance.

Finally, they gave up hope, and Jack pulled over to a bank of phone booths. Zach anxiously watched as his partner left the car and went over to place the call he was hoping to not have to make. A minute later, Jack was hanging his head and the phone at the same time. The news had been bad. His second call was to be the Spaniard. Zach continued to watch through the glass while feeling like it would be the first time he had failed at just about anything, and he didn't like it. Just then he caught Jack suddenly getting animated inside the booth, flailing his arms around like some trapped chimpanzee. Then he hung up the phone and hurriedly retreated back to the car with a wide grin on his face.

"Okay. Why the happy?" Zach had to ask.

"First off, the boys back home weren't too happy that we may have missed our chance to stop World War III. But the good news…?"

Zach hated being slow rolled. "What, already?!"

"Our friend the Spaniard has him."

"He has him? What does that mean?"

"Well, not *has* him, but knows where he's going."

Zach leaned back and briefly closed his eyes. "Seems ambiguous, if you ask me. We've missed this guy more than once."

"Where's your trust, Mr Ransom? We haven't missed a location; we just haven't caught the man. Third time's a charm, remember?"

Zach felt like he was still learning but at the same time wishing the knowledge and insight would come faster. He was certain that he could handle it. But then, he reasoned that it was going to take time to build his own network of colleagues, acquaintances, and to reach a seasoned resume to help him in his work. Out of nowhere he let out a laugh that provoked a glaring look from Jack. "What?"

"I'll tell you later," Zach said, while continuing the thought that brought it on. He was only going to be twenty-one, what…next week? He had plenty of time to catch up, didn't he? But then again, waiting was not his strong suit.

Jack gave a second glance over and held it a little longer. It seemed to him that his protégé was in one of those moments of deep thought.

"What's going on in that head of yours, amigo?"

"Nothing that a little more action won't cure," Zach replied.

Jack didn't really want to understand, or agree with the request for more action, but he understood the adrenaline rush that their work could create. "Is that right? You're looking for a little more danger, now, is it?" he said, as he pushed the stick into gear and took off. "I'm not sure that's a good thing."

"Yeah, that's right. Only all of that danger has been, up to this point, has been dictated by others. And up to this point, I've been reactionary. Not anymore. It's time to take it to the bad guys."

Jack gave a loud "Uh-huh," then reminded his partner, "Just remember that not all actions are good, especially when one has their partner following that action. Someone, or more specifically, me, could die."

Zachary stayed silent while staring out the window for a few seconds. "Maybe," he mumbled just loud enough to set his partner's mind wondering.

CHAPTER TWENTY-THREE

—‹‹‹›››—

NOT EVERYONE LIVES

Providence, Rhode Island

AGENT DOWLING placed one more phone call and within twenty minutes, six company vehicles had arrived and disgorged fourteen agents with shotguns and small-arms firepower. They were then tactically dispersed all around the entrance and exit points surrounding the Lee home and adjacent streets and alley tributaries. From Johnny Scarpino's vantage point, the quick mobilization had been impressive.

His guy inside had always referred to the younger bureau boys as testosterone-laden grenades waiting to be launched. And with all newbies mostly restricted to mundane paperwork and data fill while they sat behind their pine desks, he had firmly believed that the bureau managers had set the kids up with the fuse to be lit with any possible call to action. This had happened less than thirty minutes before, and the pent-up levels that had already been at near breaking point welcomed the reprieve with youthful and explosive confidence. And, as a bonus, they may just be able to use their guns. In their collective eyes, nobody would be able to escape. The only question that had Scarpino worried would be whether or not the whole hastily planned endeavor would end clean or in a bloodbath.

Johnny Scarpino was digesting all of this and hoping that Agent Dowling had a handle on it. He was at the rear of one car, mid-street, and out of sight of the Lees' home, his two-way radio on the back seat with the door open for him to hear the chatter of men getting to or reaching their positions. Agent Pimpleton was with him and reaching into the trunk to pull out his wife's vacuum cleaner. "It's not a Kirby," he said.

"It'll have to do until I get inside," Johnny replied.

"Try not to, you know…break it, or anything."

Johnny wanted to laugh but his nerves wouldn't allow air to fully fill his lungs, so he forced an awkward smile. "I'll do my best," he said. "But should it go sideways, and we lose it in there, I'm sure your Fed coffers will cover for a new one. And if they don't, I will."

"But what if you're dead?" Pimpleton said, in an attempt at humor.

Johnny didn't answer, opting for just a shake of his head. Then taking the vacuum from Pimpleton, he walked down the sidewalk then veered up the walkway to the Lees' front door. To both his left and right were men at each corner behind shrubs and at the ready. Johnny took a deep breath then leaning to his left to glance in the formal sitting room while reaching to knock, he noticed the room was empty. He quickly pulled his hand back and motioned to the lying-in-wait men to hold back. He peeked around the corner again, but this time curled his eyes around enough to make sure that no one was lurking. Again nothing. He set the vacuum down and slowly checked the doorknob—it was unlocked.

Johnny motioned to the others that he was going in and to follow. The door swung freely but surprisingly quietly as he and the others stepped inside with their weapons at the ready. One of the agents motioned that he was taking upstairs, and for the other agent to head for the kitchen, and for Johnny to move down the hallway toward the rear. Johnny cautiously made his way as instructed. As he crept forward, at the opposite end of the hallway by a service porch at the rear of the home, Johnny noticed another agent entering through a window. They both gave a quick nod of acknowledgment, then Johnny thought to himself that if they should fall into battle at close quarters, the odds were in their favor. Now halfway down the hall he came across what appeared to be a closet door. Johnny opened it, allowing a burst of light to fill what essentially turned out to be a stairway leading down to a small, dark basement. Immediately, a flash and three shots rang out. Two of which missed their intended mark, while the third clipped the door frame and caromed into Johnny's hip, sending him to the ground in a crumpled heap.

"They're here!" he yelled while grimacing in pain and thinking *not again!*

The agent from the window rushed to his side and pulled him away from the opening and leaned him against the wall. He quickly checked Johnny's wound. "Looks like a graze."

"Well, it feels like more!" Johnny winced back while pressing against the wound. "Not that much blood, so it didn't hit anything important. You better engage before they come back up."

The agent had already turned then saw that the other two agents had joined the party at the other end of the hall. He pointed to the door that led to the basement and the agents approached. A moment later the first agent curled his weapon around the corner and fired two quick rounds downward. No return volley came. The agents then silently entered the stairwell in hi-low defense and again receiving no in-coming, they slowly made their way down the twelve steps. Just as they reached the last two steps, the agent out front noticed the soles of four sets of bound legs. Fearing the worst, he leapt down into the open and swung his weapon into the space. All of the possible combatants were gone, and the Lees appeared bound and alive. Along the south upper, street level wall, an old cast, coal-hatch, just large enough for an average sized man to squeeze through, was propped open. There was a stack of wooden crates just below, suggesting the method of the men's escape.

He quickly went to the window while the other agents were already with the hostages and freeing them from their binds. Several shots were heard just outside and he instinctively ducked. Then, just as abruptly, there was silence. By the time the agents made it back up to the street, there were two of the men in handcuffs and one in a pool of blood in the street. Johnny Scarpino was being attended to inside as they waited for an ambulance and was in good spirits when the Lees made their way up the basement stairs and past him.

"Hey, Professor Lee!" he called out. "Did they get anything we should know about?"

"Nothing to get. I burned everything I had two days ago," he replied then pointed to his head. "Aside from what's floating around in Europe, everything is up here."

Johnny nodded his approval. "I guess then, we need to hope for success there."

Jeoung had devised his own plan while feigning work when in the custody of Kalpakoff. Knowing things were at risk, he had disposed of his calculation prior to the trip, then written in Korean and then transcribed into English, the formulas had been adjusted to be just off enough so that anyone not a mathematician of some higher degree would be oblivious to the accuracy. "Yes," Jeoung replied proudly, "Or the world as we know it will be in deep shit."

Johnny smiled with the now known knowledge that everything was safe, then his face turned into a concerned frown. His friends were putting their lives in danger where now they needn't be, and this was dangerous, and he knew they would not be where he could reach them to warn. Deep shit, was an understatement and the world may not now be in it… but his friends were.

CHAPTER TWENTY-FOUR

THE CHASE

"Todo el infierno se desata!"

THE TAXI DRIVER powered down the last bite of his Tortilla Española, then glanced at his watch. It was almost time, and he needed to hurry. Forcing a last swallow, almost choking in the process, he waved a goodbye to his friend who ran the small neighborhood tapas restaurant and hustled to his cab. Stepping on the accelerator, he swerved away from the curb, then one right and two left turns later he was at the pre-arranged alley that ran through to the canal.

Thanking *Jesus Cristo* that it had taken even less time than he had planned for, he gave a look skyward followed by a sign of the cross over his chest and a quick kiss to his hand. Then pulling forward a car length past the entrance of the alleyway, he whipped his head around and as previously instructed, backed into the alley so the front of the car faced outward. Checking the time again he let out a sigh of relief. The man had told him: a minute late and the deal was off, and his family would be in serious jeopardy. He had three minutes left.

Summoning up a youthful inner joy, he began to whistle a boyhood tune that his *abuelita* would sing to him. "Un Elefante se Balanceaba," for whatever reason, had always brought joy and a reason to smile. Then, leaving the keys in the ignition, he got out and started to walk toward the connecting road. After a few strides, he could sense a huge weight being lifted from his shoulders, and it propelled him into doing something that he hadn't since he was just a young boy begging for food along Calle Sierpes Street. He started to skip. He would have been a sight for anyone watching. Then the further from the car he strode, the more he thought about the envelope forthcoming and how the unexpected riches inside would give his wife that indoor washing machine she had always coveted, and he would get a new taxi with automatic windows and air-conditioning. He was definitely soon to be blessed.

He turned the corner and was a few steps south when a man whistled over to get his attention. The man, unknown to him as the whole mysterious escapade had been from the beginning, waved then dropped an envelope on a nearby doorstep and walked briskly away. *He was paid also*, the taxi driver thought. He quickly went to the stoop and picked up the envelope and anxiously opened it. Fanning the paper money out, his grin widened into a gleeful surprise as the amount counted appeared to be almost double what was agreed upon! He gave way to an uncontrollable yelp, then spun around to see if anyone had heard him. *Did I count correctly?* he wondered. He started to count the bills again, then stopped as an eerie silence came over the neighborhood. No terns flapping wings or huddling for breadcrumbs thrown by old men. No happy chatter from the street children. He turned to check his surroundings again to make sure that no one was closing in on him. Then, off in the near distance, he recognized the sound of an outboard motor winding down. *It's time to leave*, he told himself, and now before the miracle turned into just another dream to be washed away by the waking. Or worse, a bullet to the head. The driver jammed the envelope inside his worn tweed coat and began jogging to get away as far and as fast as his tired legs could carry him. His hope for a new life renewed, while also relieved that the hope for never having to meet the man responsible for his good fortune still intact. One could never know, he reminded himself—he may want the money back!

Zach flipped over the street map, then back again. Slamming his finger into the print, he called out. "We're here!"

"I don't care about the *here*. How much further?!" Jack fired back.

"Just up ahead behind that green truck. You're going to take a right, then two streets further, another right."

Jack did his own quick calculation. "We shouldn't be too far behind. Another ten minutes, fifteen tops."

"That's pretty thin," Zach followed. "How long does it take to board and take off?"

"Shit! You're right! Better speed up!"

"This airport doesn't even appear on the map as an airport. Just a plane icon in the corner legend with a number," Zach said, frustrated. "It took forever to locate it on the map, but there it is. Surprisingly called Seville Airport. Ridiculous."

"Settle down," Jack chided. "Occasionally, you need just a little bit of luck. We just need to get there before he gets in the air."

"Now you're calm. How far out was Javier?"

Jack nervously glanced at his watch but then wondered why. "Unknown," he said. "There's apparently no one to call. It's a private airport."

"Then I suppose it's all up to us."

"I suppose it is," Jack said as he dropped the shifter down into second through the turn, then pressed hard on the gas going through and then into third coming out of it. The engine wailed and he yelled over it. "Let's try not to die!"

With his window open, Zach held tight onto the upper frame of the door as the force of the turn had him leaning. "That would be my fondest wish!" he shouted back.

His throat dry as the Sahara, Ivanski Kalpakoff wished he had brought a jug of water. He jumped from the boat with the briefcase full of the paper that would make him rich. Then, not bothering to tie it off, he pushed the skiff adrift and then ran up the steps to the alley. His eyes reached the plateau, and he saw the taxi at the far end—as instructed. He let out a brief sigh of relief, then bolted for the car, then, throwing the briefcase on the front seat, he slid in behind the wheel. His whole world, his existence, and life going forward hinged on his escape and disappearance from the life with the contents of that case. He was ready, but ten minutes away from the beginning of that life.

He slammed the shifter into third, but as with the men chasing him, with all the slowdowns, turns, and pedestrians, he could never get into fourth and full speed. Finally, a long stretch ahead got him going. He was still a few minutes away, but he could just see the top of the airport's traffic-control tower. He wondered just how far behind the men wanting to stop him were. And, more importantly, was the Spaniard and his lethal friend with them or nearby? He thought about that for a second. Maybe the Spaniard's man didn't survive the firefight at all. In the frenzy of the moment, he assured himself that they had both taken hits. Maybe he had gotten lucky. Still, his primary hope was that they thought he was still in the boat and heading for open waters. Could they have guessed his destination? He needed some luck.

Another quick right and there suddenly appeared the rarely used secondary gate, the one typically just for mechanics, of the private airport just up ahead. He powered through the unmanned gate's entrance and across the small parking area restricted and exclusively used for airport personnel and pilots of non-commercial aircraft. Then he cranked a hard left around a small, wheeled baggage cart and made a beeline for the furthest hangar where the twin-prop Cessna AT-17 Bobcat sat ready. Purchased with illicit money, it was a five-seater training plane from the last war. But as fate would have it, there was only one passenger today. His training and ten hours of actual flying time over the last year would finally pay off. He was ready.

Just as he was screeching to a halt at the hangar's wide-open doors, he checked his rearview mirror and could just make out what appeared to be a red limo bursting through the same entrance he'd come through and slamming on its brakes. *Only someone chasing him would have made such a demonstrative entrance*, he thought. They were on him and most assuredly had help in doing so. Again, whatever forces were in on what was happening, the Spaniard was definitely involved. And the driver would most likely be in a frantic search, wondering which way to go. He had time. He rushed to exit the taxi and grab the briefcase, then before disappearing into the hangar, he gave a last glance back. They had seen him.

Kalpakoff sprinted for the plane and the short rolling stairs that would get him on the wing and inside. He tossed the briefcase up onto the wing, then, stepping on the first step, he heard a voice from behind.

"That will be far enough, Ivan!"

Kalpakoff froze as he could feel the hair on his neck spiking. He knew the accent and the man behind it. It had been a very long time, but the Spaniard had finally found him. He turned to confront his counterpart while gripping his Luger and forcing a grin that vanished when he saw what he was up against. Javier Rodríguez was not alone. Standing next to him, and with his own weapon pointed at her head, was Marcella De Anda.

"Marcella?!" he cried out.

"I'm sorry, Ivan," she said as sincerely as she could. Then, noticing his bloodied shirt, she cried out, "You're hurt!"

"I'm fine," he said, meaning to calm her. "But I can see that you are now in danger."

"Yes," Javier said, confident he had the upper hand. "So choose your next movement wisely."

"You would never harm that which you desired as much as I, Javier," Ivanski declared. "Let her go! This is between us!"

The Spaniard let out a laugh. "You have seen too many movies, my friend. Does anyone ever let them go?" Then he became more serious. "You are most likely correct in your assumption, Ivan. But would you wager on it?"

"Most likely?" Ivanski questioned.

"Well, there are always limits to everything when pushed," Javier replied while noticeably pressing the barrel more firmly against Marcella's skull. "Would you not agree?"

"So. It is the woman or the money? Is that the game?" Ivanski asked rhetorically.

Javier frowned, then cocked his head to one side to fully focus on his counterpart. "Not necessarily," he said. "I always intended to win the money. Marcella just became, let's phrase it as… a convenient insurance."

Ivanski scoffed. "Insurance? I value her more than that!"

"A-ha!" Javier laughed. "Then maybe I was correct! Your love for her appears to have been your downfall!"

Ivanski thought for a second that the Spaniard was probably right. Marcella had been his love, or at the very least the prize he had most longed for. *God, she was something. But there is no time for that no*w, he thought in a forced head-bend. He had to calculate all current possibilities in the reversal of this untimely turn of events. He had a response, though, but before he could give it there was the roar and screech of the chasing vehicle just out of view of the hangar opening. Focused, nobody turned to see. They already knew the scenario and the players, including Javier. For Ivanski, he was decidedly at a disadvantage.

Still holding a firm grip on Marcella, Javier kept his eyes trained on Ivanski. "I can see the wheels are turning in that head of yours, Ivan, but it will be of no use. The men outside, as you are aware, are with me. You are outmanned."

"So you say," Ivanski countered, while in full understanding that his options were limited.

"There is still another scene in the play before us," Javier stated confidently. "But you must first drop your weapon."

Ivanski allowed his weapon hand to slowly roll around his hip for a better position but kept his arm down to appear less threatening. "Or I can just start the final battle in the hope that my lead finds you before yours finds me," he said defiantly. "Marcella would just have to take her chances at being collateral damage."

"Now that doesn't sound like you, Ivan. Remember, as I recall, she chose you the last time."

Marcella squirmed. "That's not true!" she cried. "End this madness! I have feelings for you both!" Then she feigned escape, forcing Javier to tighten his grip.

A moment later the heads of Jack Tanner and Zach were taking turns having quick peeks around the corner. Then Jack bellowed, "What are we looking at, Javier?"

"All is well and in control, Mr Tanner," he answered. "You and young Ransom can enter."

Jack with Zach close behind, warily entered the hanger with weapons up. Then seeing that both men were engaged in a weaponized stand-off, they spread wider, Jack going left and Zach right. Both had their firearms trained on Kalpakoff.

"As you can see, Ivan, your run is over. Now, please drop your weapon. I won't be asking again!" Javier demanded.

"And if I don't yield?"

"Well, you will die and I, well…I will get the spoils."

"What does that mean, Javier?" Jack interjected.

"I misspoke, my friend. We will get what is sought and returned to safety. Is that better?"

"Better," Jack said, but the words still made him wonder why he had given it a thought at all.

A few seconds passed before Kalpakoff realized his attempt to escape had failed. He sighed in capitulation then slowly lowered his body and let the Luger drop to the hangar floor.

"I do not see your man, Javier," Ivanski said, "Is he infirmed or dead."

"Dead," Javier said while motioning for Zach to go and retrieve the Luger. "A shame, really. You, of all people would have appreciated him, and this would have been a moment that he would have enjoyed."

Zach did as he was told, then once in hand he glanced over at Jack who motioned for him to also go and get the briefcase. He quickly did. Two long strides put him at the stairs, then up and onto the wing where he knelt next to the briefcase. He pressed the latches and opened it where he found the missing pages sitting atop of what he quickly calculated as a mixture of several hundred thousand American dollars, English pounds, and Spanish pesos. Three separate passports were under the fold-down divider: all displaying photos of Ivanski Kalpakoff but with different aliases.

"It's all here," he acknowledged, then, closing and re-securing both latches, he climbed back down with the case.

"Thank God!" Jack exclaimed, sounding relieved. Then he and Javier moved in on Kalpakoff. "So what's the plan, Javier?"

The Spaniard sighed. "That part is in flux, Mr Tanner."

Ivanski's rigid posture was now relaxed. He had given up on any idea of a getaway to any beach-front destination but still carried with him the idea of love, or at the very least his admiration of his Marcella. "Please, you can release her now, Javier," he said. Then he stared over and affectionately into her eyes. "I am sorry, my love. I was hoping that a life existed for us somewhere. I was wrong."

Javier released his grip on Marcella, and she immediately walked up to Ivan and let her eyes match his emotion. Then reaching up, she caressed his face then kissed him on the mouth. "This is goodbye, I'm afraid, Ivan," she said convincingly. "Our time was special and if given different circumstances, maybe a life was there to be had."

Ivan smiled as he gazed into her eyes. "I do love you, my darling," he said in a softened voice. "I'm sorry as well."

"As I am also, Ivan," Javier said while gently pulling Marcella away. "You were formidable," then Javier calmly placed his weapon against the Russian's head and pulled the trigger. Blood splattered the dress of a stunned Marcella, and she stepped back visibly shaken and gasping, trying to hold it together. She wanted to scream out "Why?!" but the audacity and brutality of the moment had her trembling uncontrollably, and she couldn't form the words.

Jack Tanner could. "What the hell!" he yelled, while reaching again for his weapon, but it was too late with the unexpected turn of events. "We were hoping to keep him alive. Killing was supposed to be a last resort!"

Javier had quickly raised his weapon out and straight while stepping close enough to both Jack and Zach but not so close that the more agile men would overtake him. "Easy, gentlemen. I know this is sudden and not what one would expect from a friend," Javier admitted.

"Not even close!" Jack blurted. "What's going on here, Javier?!"

"Do you not remember what I said yesterday?" the Spaniard questioned them both.

Zach thought for a second as a quizzical look came over Jack. Then he remembered. "You said that when you had the opportunity you should always eliminate those that would have no qualms of doing the same to you."

"Well done, Mr Ransom. Your memory serves you well."

"And whoop-di-fucking-do, Javier!" Jack said sarcastically. We've known each other for nearly fifteen years. Christ! I was at two of your weddings!"

Javier smiled. "And that is why I do not plan on killing either of you, my friend."

"Well, that's a relief. I mean, what are friends for?" Zach said glibly.

"But I also can't have you moving too quickly to prevent my exit and ultimate happiness," Javier said before commanding them both to drop their weapons. When they did, he pointed his weapon at Jack's leg and fired again. Jack yelled, "Dammit, Javier!" then grabbed his leg in anguish as he crumpled to the floor.

"I do apologize for that," Javier said, seeming genuinely concerned. "That wasn't as easy as it looks. It does appear, though, that I missed the bone."

"But you fucking shot me!" Jack yelled back through gritted teeth.

"I did," Javier responded, "The main point, though, would be that in doing so you will realize that you will survive this ordeal."

Zach slowly raised both his palms in submission while looking for any counter that would get him out of the situation alive. He definitely did not want his leg shot, or worse, and Jack would certainly not be any help in preventing that. Debating seemed the best approach.

"I'm hoping we have become friends enough over this short week, Javier," he offered in a friendly tone, then added, "Because, in general, you must know that I've grown to like you."

That made Javier laugh out loud. "Clever try, young man," he said with a hint of a grin forming. "I have grown fond of you also, Mr Ransom. I have no ill will toward you, and certainly no plan to kill you," then he motioned for Marcella toward the plane, and she went immediately like someone who knew the plan. Reaching the opposite side, she went behind the wheel stanchion and into a crate positioned there and retrieved several lengths of cord. No words were spoken as she returned and began tying Zach's hands behind his back.

"No, my dear. In front," Javier instructed. "He would not be able to sit."

Jack Tanner winced up at Javier then gave a death stare at Marcella. "You're fucking kidding me?!" he said grimacing. "All along?"

Javier shrugged. "Well, not from the very beginning."

"When then?"

"Does it really matter, my friend? There is a lot of money at stake. Plenty to make everyone happy, even you and Mr Ransom here, if you were to be tempted. I could use a few good men that could be counted on."

"And?" Zach added, while flexing his wrist and forearm muscles outward in the hopes it would eventually create more space on his binds.

"And, whatever you may think of me…" Javier continued. "I'm not a greedy man."

Now both Zachary and Jack laughed. Even a slight grin formed over the usually stoic Marcella.

"Could have fooled us," Jack managed, still gripping his leg.

"I guess that I just knew what the answer would be, should I have suggested," Javier replied. "Was I wrong?"

Zach gazed down at his friend lying on the ground in pain, and Jack gave him just the slightest semblance of a wink. "No. You were definitely right about that bastard over there," Zach said convincingly. "But me? I'm still young, impetuous and wanting to cash in."

"Why, Zachary Ransom. What does this mean to me?" Javier followed, surprised.

"What it means is that he doesn't have any qualms about taking the money and disappearing," Jack answered for Zach. "You're a rat-fuck, kid! What would your dad say?!"

"I guess it doesn't matter anymore, does it?" Zach replied. "He ain't here now, is he?"

"Well, I guess I always knew you to have a tinge of evil in you, kid. I just didn't realize how much of an effect losing your dad had on you," Jack said, playing along. "I had thought you to be better than this, though."

"The truth is, Jack, I tried to be," Zach continued the charade. "I guess I'd rather be rich than dead."

The exchange left Javier just confused enough that he leaned toward not believing either one but allowing for an open mind. "Well," he started, "…we shall see, won't we? The next chapter begins now," then he gave a look over to Marcella, who was already motioning with her head that it was time to go. "Shall we, my dear Marcella?" he asked.

Marcella turned and grabbed the briefcase and headed up the stairs, onto the wing, and into the open hatch. Once she had disappeared inside, Javier waved his weapon at Zach to follow. "It's time. You're next, so let's go."

Zach moved to the steps, then gave a last glance back at Jack Tanner. "Sorry, Jack. I just don't see getting rich doing what we do," he said.

"Go to hell!" Jack grunted back, "You were already rich!"

"True," Javier interjected. "But not like this. Goodbye, my friend."

Zach had heard the last words as he made his way up the steps and onto the wing. He gave one last look back down at his partner, then he ducked into the plane where Marcella was waiting with her own gun in hand but keeping her distance. She pointed to him to sit in a forward seat, and he did so. As he kept his eyes roving for something, anything, he felt her presence behind him, then more chords being lowered over his head and shoulders. By the time Javier had made it aboard and the hatch closed, Marcella had further bound him to his seat.

Javier glanced at Marcella then came up to him and checked the bindings.

"It's not my first time," she said, smiling, then kissed him as she had done to Kalpakoff.

Zach watched while thinking that Javier's reaction had seemed off, somewhere between enjoyment and wariness. It hadn't felt like her with Kalpakoff and he sensed that there was no love there: just convenience and wanting to end up on the winning side.

"So who is flying this contraption?" he asked.

Javier sighed at the question and didn't answer. Instead, he moved toward the cockpit, strapped himself in, and cranked the props. Then after checking his instrument panel, he craned his head around. "Better buckle-up, my dear," he said to Marcella. Then he rolled the plane out of the hanger and began his taxi. A few hundred yards later, Javier had the plane in position at the head of the runway and was now on the radio requesting takeoff.

During those sixty seconds, Zach had been scanning the interior of the small space, but there hadn't been much to see. "Would it be appropriate to ask where we are heading?" he asked loudly toward the open cockpit. No response came, only silence.

Another thirty seconds went by before there was a crackle from the radio speaker followed by a garbled "clear for takeoff," from the tower. Javier dialed up the power and the twin propellers ramped up, then the plane began building lift-speed down the runway. A few more anxious seconds passed then Javier pulled back on the tiller and the plane angled up and took flight.

Once in the air the plane veered westerly, putting the sun behind them. Zach had a great memory and a clear understanding of the world map, specifically Spain and Portugal which he had studied on his flight coming over. They were definitely heading in a westerly direction and most likely toward the coast of Portugal, possibly the port of Lisbon where a seaworthy transport had probably been arranged. He quickly calculated that as long as the plan was not to toss him out of the plane over some mountain, he had about an hour to figure out his next move.

As his brain rattled around through the different scenarios, he heard Javier call out to Marcella who was still sitting in the seat behind and across from him.

"Marcella, won't you join me up front?" Javier politely asked while dispensing his jovial spin of what? Me worry?"

Marcella called back loudly over the drone of the propeller engines. "I'm coming but with all of the excitement, I've developed a thirst, my dear. Would you like to share in a little celebration drink with me?"

The weight lifted and the plan coming to full fruition, Javier was feeling sublime. And a real warmth was beginning to flood his senses. "Sounds wonderful," he said.

The plan had really come together, and with only a few minor hindrances, it had worked. He had regretted shooting his friend and wondered if Jack Tanner would hold it against him should they ever meet again. A ludicrous thought, he heckled himself. Then he gave a quick, over-shoulder look back to verify all was still good in the cabin, then returned forward to the clear blue sky ahead of him. He took a deep breath while thinking, *only just a few more steps to the finish line*. A smile creased his cheeks, and he daydreamed of piña coladas with little umbrellas draped on their rims. He doubted the ingredients were onboard, but a gin and tonic or any other concoction worthy of the moment would work just as well.

A few minutes later, Marcella joined Javier in the cockpit. She handed him a whisky tumbler, then gave him a peck on the cheek before scrunching down next to him in the co-pilot's seat with her own drink. They smiled warmly at each other then brought their glasses together in a celebratory *clink*. "To our new adventure," Marcella offered, "the Caymans should be wonderful this time of year."

"So you finally decided?" Javier smiled near euphorically. "I thought for sure it would have been Jamaica."

"Too much violence for my taste," she said, smiling back, her pouty lips inviting seduction. Then, further reveling in the moment, she threw her hair back and let out a gleeful, schoolgirl laugh. The move would send Javier into a perpetual state of happiness. She gave him a wink while raising her glass. "To us," she toasted, and both downed their drinks.

"How about another?" Javier asked, still unable to control just how happy he had become.

"Really?" Marcella questioned. "You'll still be able to land the plane, right?"

"My love. It would take a lot more of these to affect the skill necessary to land."

That was enough for Marcella, and she shrugged an 'okay' back at him, then proceeded to mix two more tumblers while checking one more time on their bound hostage.

Zach managed a snarky, "Having fun up there?"

Marcella did not respond but rather returned to the front looking as serious as ever. When she finally sat back down, she and Javier nursed their drinks this time while for the next hour they joked and spoke of future plans for the next twenty years. Neither wanted children this late in the game, but a villa with a live-in cook and housekeeper, overlooking a secluded beach, was easily agreed upon. When the conversation drifted into a mildly inebriated and comfortable silence, both were left with their happy faces and a big, blue, cloudless sky in front of them. Occasionally, Marcella would crane her neck to give a glance back at a still-restrained Zach.

For his time, Zach had kept his eyes forward and steady for that glance. And in between, he had been alternately flexing and relaxing his muscles in an attempt to loosen his binds without being noticed. At one point, he even leaned forward and with both hands he reached under the seat in an attempt to find any sharp edge on the frame, but there was nothing. Now, with time running out, from the cockpit he heard Javier trying to communicate with an airport tower. They were preparing to land, but he registered something off in the cockpit. Javier had coughed lightly at first then seemed to get it under control before wiping sweat from his forehead. Then, just as suddenly, he began violently coughing again, followed by Marcella asking him if he was okay. His response was that he was not feeling well. It meant something. Something that could give him an advantage once on the ground. More than likely, Zach projected, they would land and taxi to the most private of areas. That could mean fewer people to deal with, which could give him an opportunity over one that was not in perfect shape. He was beginning to form a Plan B for when they landed, when suddenly he heard Marcella cry out.

"Javier!" she exclaimed.

Zach's eyes darted toward the cockpit. Marcella unbuckled her restraint and was jumping up and reaching for Javier, who appeared slumped over and possibly unconscious. She started slapping him, then fist-beating his chest. "Javier!" she yelled again, "Stay alive!"

Javier was unresponsive and then suddenly spasmed erect, startling Marcella. She slapped him hard in response, followed by a harsh two-handed shake. "Can you land the plane?" she demanded to know.

Javier sadly gazed into her eyes, wondering what had just happened. Images of sun-drenched and white-sand beaches with expansive ocean horizons filled his thoughts. Thoughts that were suddenly fading. Then his eyes slowly narrowed into a quizzical squint that rolled down to his empty tumbler, then back up at Marcella. He suddenly knew, and she knew he knew. It would be poison again for Marcella. Meant to cause death after they had landed, this time the effects of the concoction were off by fifteen minutes. It had enacted too quickly.

"You…" he struggled to mumble, then forced out through bloodied spittle, "you fucking bitch!" Then in a final attempt to reach for her throat, his body went rigid, and his eyes rolled up as he let out a final raspy gasp, then slumped over the flying column. If the autopilot had not been engaged, the weight of his body would have sent the plane falling into a steep and deadly dive.

If she hadn't been already, Marcella certainly was in a frantic state now. She threw her eyes back to Zach. "Can you land this plane?!"

Realizing that they were in instant peril, Zach was in full anxiety mode. He remembered feeling the same way just before walking on stage with his High School debate team, which brought on the thought of puking.

"Only one way to find out!" he yelled back. "But you'd better hurry!"

Marcella rushed back to him and quickly loosened his chest bindings. While Zach attempted to shed the cord while his wrists were still bound, she went to her purse across the aisle and retrieved a knife and her gun. She pointed both aggressively at him and said, "Fifty-fifty? You go your way, and I'll go mine?"

"Agreed already!" he lied. "Hurry, or someone on the ground other than us is going to be rich!"

With no choice other than to attempt to land the plane herself, Marcella slipped the knife under his wrist binding, then applied back-and-forth pressure until the cord was sliced free. Zach surprised her by immediately grabbing both her wrists. Marcella had no time to react or give any resistance, and he easily took both her weapons.

"You sit there!" he said, forcing her down onto the adjacent seat and facing forward. Then, rushing forward, he called back to her. "If you have got another gun hidden back there somewhere and plan on using it, I'll crash this plane just to spite you! Then, reaching the cockpit, he unfastened the harness holding Javier and muscled him out and down the aisle, where he dumped him at Marcella's feet. The Spaniard's glazed eyes were still open and looking back at her as if asking, *why?* She held her own stare back at the man who, at one time, had been a lover. Then, reaching down, she pressed her fingers against his lids and closed them shut, then turned away to focus on not dying herself.

Zach had already leapt over the dead Spaniard, made his way back into the cockpit, and was plopping down behind the column and beginning to look over the instruments, trying to understand how they worked. Then just as he began to look up and out into the clear sky ahead, the radio crackled, followed by a voice in Spanish. "Aircraft 4427. Decrease altitude to one thousand feet."

With the engines droning on, the noise in the cockpit was near deafening, making it difficult to pick out the words. Zach gave a questioning look at Marcella. "He wants you to lower to one thousand feet," she said.

Zach took the radio mic in hand and replied while still scanning the instrument panel. "Uh, okay. And how does one do that, over?"

There were several seconds of silence. Then the crackle and voice returned, only this time in English. "You're kidding, right?"

"I wish I was," Zach responded. "We've had an issue with our pilot. He's not available at the moment."

"At the moment?"

"He won't be coming around anytime soon. Can you help, or not?" Zach said impatiently. "The runway is getting a whole lot bigger. I can see the tower ahead."

Another excruciating second passed, then the crackle. "Okay. Hold the steering column steady," the voice on the other side said.

"That part I've got down!" Zach said, frustrated. "But I think we are in autopilot."

"Flip the autopilot toggle down. You will feel pressure on the column, but hold steady."

Zach sighed, "Your English is pretty good," then he reached over and flipped the toggle.

"Thank you. It is required to be in the tower."

The next thirty seconds were a blur. The plane immediately lurched, nosing downward. He instinctively pulled back enough to gain control and level off. Then as he realized that he could handle the up and down, he pushed the column slightly forward and he was able to drive the plane down until the altimeter gauge arrow hit one thousand. "Okay. Now what?"

"Now you land," the voice on the other end started. "But you need to drop your speed to around sixty-knots."

"That's not helping."

"You need to drop your RPMs down to around eighteen hundred. To do this the throttle control should be on your right-hand side, but before you do this, set your flaps to fifteen degrees. Then as you drift lower, slightly raise the nose of the plane up. This will help in lowering your speed."

Zach was beside himself with all the instructions while trying to keep them in order. "Are you fucking kidding me?" he mumbled.

"Are we going to die?!" Marcella loudly called from behind.

"Probably!" Zach yelled back. "I'd assume the position!"

Zach forced a control of his breathing. The beads of sweat that had already been forming on his brow were now rolling down his face and into his now-stinging eyes. He quickly arm-swabbed the sweat away and rapidly blinked his clarity of sight back. Then forcing another deep inhale of calming air, he slowly exhaled and focused on the instrument panel ahead of him. First, he located the control of the flaps and set it to fifteen degrees as instructed; then he pulled back slightly on the column, and the nose came up. He could feel the plane slowing from the drag, but the runway was just a mile ahead and getting closer by the second. Then, reaching down to his right, he grabbed the handle that was conveniently marked "Throttle control" and pulled it slowly backward while keeping an eye on the speed and RPM gauges. He could feel the speed dropping, but he was still coming in hot.

Marcella gave up on the instruction to stay and was already back in the co-pilot chair next to him and strapping herself in snugly. Zach gave a quick glance over and registered that her usually beautifully smooth olive skin was as ashen as the sheets on his bed. "This is it," he cautioned, sounding almost too calm for the moment.

"Is there anything I can do?" Marcella asked while strapping her shoulder harness in then bracing both palms against the dash.

"Yeah," Zach said dryly. "If we survive, I won't be having a celebratory drink with you, so don't offer."

Marcella clenched harder while leaning over and closed her eyes tight. For Zach, the next few tense moments were quick snippets of noticing emergency vehicles and their lights spinning danger, rushing in pursuit. Large painted runway numbers and faces of standing control-tower personnel with their faces lined up against the windows as he passed. Then the lowering to twenty, fifteen, ten, and five feet and the first hard bump of wheels bouncing off the runway and taking air again. Then another softer bump and air, and then finally the landing. That brought a short-lived sense of relief and a loud laugh from Zach before it became instantly apparent that their speed was still too great, and the plane would soon barrel through the barriers at the end of the asphalt. Zach controlled a turn to an open field on the right while continuing to apply pressure on the braking system—it would be enough. The plane did rumble off the pad and into the field, the turn breaking one wheel bracket so that the right wing angled down and dragged the ground, forcing the plane to suddenly spin to the right. But by this time the speed had slowed to a point where the wing remained intact, and the plane came to rest just forty feet in front of another abutment.

"You did it!" Marcella exclaimed while attempting to quickly release herself from the harness. Caught up in the exhilaration of still being alive, she threw her arms around Zach, nearly squeezing the life from him. He almost didn't mind.

"We must go quickly!" she exclaimed.

Zach grabbed her arm. "Hold on!" he cautioned, while trying to catch the last few seconds of held breath. He was still processing what had just happened and also what he had actually accomplished. It had been a lot to think about between the mission, the papers, money, Tanner, Kalpakoff, Javier, and Marcella, but his mind kept wandering to his first image: Jenny Mathews. How he wished that the connection had not been lost. *Maybe I need to rethink that one when I get back to the States*, he thought.

"We need to go, now!" Marcella urged.

Her words finally resonated through, jostling Zach back to the current reality. "Okay!" he said while quickly unfastening his own harness. Then, pulling himself up from the awkward angle the plane had left them in, he reached over and helped her up through the tilted fuselage to the hatch on the angled downward side, only slowing briefly while negotiating past the lifeless Javier. As Zach struggled to open the hatch, he could see the blinking lights of the emergency vehicles just outside and the appropriate personnel running up and around the plane with all of their equipment to provide aid if necessary. The angle too great to stand, they both took turns sitting on the wing, then sliding down and off for a six-foot drop into the waiting arms of their willing rescuers.

Once settled on solid ground, Zach steadied himself. It had not gone unnoticed that once again, he had survived. As emergency crewmen fumbled around his body, assuming they would find an injury, a vehemently protesting Marcella was being escorted toward an ambulance, which at the time seemed totally unnecessary. She held the briefcase in one hand. Zach hadn't even noticed until then and wondered how she had managed it.

Zach rushed over and yanked the case from her. "Uh, I'll take that, thank you," he said, much to the chagrin of Marcella, "For safekeeping, of course."

Marcella's first reaction was to hold tight, but then she relinquished the case. "Will I see you at the hospital, Zachary Ransom?" she asked, while turning up her unrelenting charms and restoring her face back to its intended and God-given beauty. Zach just smiled and slowly backed away.

"Zachary?!" she continued, as a medic helped her into the ambulance, "I will see you again, won't I?"

Zach continued backing away, then grinned at Marcella while giving a two-finger brow salute as medics helped her inside the wagon, and the doors closed behind her. She sat and stared out the rear window at him, then mouthed his name one last time as the vehicle drove away. Zach clutched the briefcase with both hands while he watched her disappear from sight, then, on cue, he turned away and searched for the best way to disappear without being questioned. As he navigated through an inconspicuous gap in the maze of equipment and responders, he couldn't help but think about the woman in a more carnal way. She had been both stunningly beautiful and scary as hell at the same time. *What would it have been like?* he wondered. Just then loud voices and a commotion from behind the plane disrupted his thoughts.

"We have someone here!" one responder yelled in Spanish while having just opened the rear cargo hatch. Then others began calling for medical personnel.

Zach spun back just as two men were reaching into a small rear panel that led into a storage hold—they were pulling something out. Zach looked around while deciding whether to continue his disappearance or to see what was up. His curiosity gave way, and he moved between the growing crowds of personnel to see. First, there were feet, then a torso and head with a burlap sack over it—nothing moved. Then the body twitched abruptly as the sack was pulled from its head.

"Holy shit!" Tommy Postman yelled out. "Is it over? Where am I?"

A large grin came over Zach. His best friend in all the world had also survived. *"Posty!"* he yelled out over the throng of sirens and personnel while rushing over.

Tommy leaned forward and hopped up to see over the shoulder of an emergency worker to locate the voice. *"Zach?!"* he yelled back. The sea of personnel parted just enough, and the two found each other. Both excited for the unexpected reunion, they closed the gap and bear-hugged liked brothers that had been separated for longer than either could have imagined.

"Oh man!" Tommy yelped, "Are you a sight for sore eyes!"

"And you, my friend," Zach admitted. Then he threw his arm around Tommy's shoulder and started to escort him away. "I got this one," he told one concerned medic, "Not a scratch on him."

Tommy just had this big grin on his face. "Brother, you have no idea what I've been through!" he started. "I was thrown into that hold over yonder and when we were getting ready to land I heard all kinds of screaming, and then the plane just jerked down like we was gonna crash. Holy shit! I didn't know what was happening in there! Then suddenly we banged onto the ground and ran off the runway and tilted over. Hot damn! I thought for sure I was gonna die!"

"Must have been traumatic," Zach sympathized while finding it hard not to break out in laughter.

"Okay, I get it. Go ahead and laugh all you want. You weren't there man. I damn near soiled myself! Don't think the pilot knew what he was doing!"

"I think that would be a fair assessment, Posty." Zach commiserated while wondering when he would break the news of the truth. "I heard he was still in training. But let's talk about it later. I really want to hear the full story of your last three days."

"Well, it's a doozy, I'll tell you."

"But first, we need to get you out of here with as little fanfare as possible," Zach continued. "I have somewhere we can go and get a hot shower, clean clothes, then grub and a beer. How's that sound, little buddy?"

Tommy just leaned into his pal. "Boy, does that sound good! You lead the way, Zach," then he let out a loud sigh of relief. "And after I spin my little yarn, I want to hear what you've been up to the last few weeks. And I promise not to be bored."

CHAPTER TWENTY-FIVE

THE CORE

Savannah, Georgia—Two months later

THE TREE-LINED Street with its century-old magnolias and sycamores providing a canopy, reminded Zach of all that he had missed the past two years. Getting back home had been long-overdue and unnecessarily prolonged by those he had yet to meet. He had made it very clear from the beginning, though, that he was upset about not being allowed to go home the second he got back in from Spain, but he was given no choice. There were debriefings and documentation that had to be handled. Really, it had been an excruciating interrogation with just him sitting on a chair in an empty room and some unknown voice firing off questions one by one, and frustratingly repeated. It wasn't until he finally spoke with Jack to complain that he found out that he hadn't been the only one to endure the process.

Now, as the taxi brought him closer, he could think of nothing other than his return to family, a return to home. With early fall colors already manifested on the branches, summer was making every effort at being late in giving up the stale humidity that came with the Deep South, making him think that the cooling of autumn would just have to wait.

Zach rolled the window down and let in the warm and sticky air to flood his senses. He then closed his eyes and let his mind wander as he had always done in moments like these. One last time, he waded through all that had happened leading up to this, then once again, the question of what was to be going forward. It had always been too easy to drift to his dreams and nightmares, but it was everything that made him who he was. In rapid fire, the first vision is of a battered young boy stranded on a Pacific beach. His parents taken from him then a new and completely different life a few short months later. Six thousand miles from paradise, the south had been another animal and one that meant an entirely different existence for the next seven years. He would acknowledge, though, that the moments would ultimately be the ones to help move him forward in his growth as a human. The good and the bad. The safe and the dangerous. The encounters and the people that nurtured those passions. He had won and he had lost, but through all of it he had endured.

The next moment, he put his thoughts on pause as the taxi rolled into a right turn and they were on Sycamore Street. A few seconds more and after passing several homes, he placed his hand on the driver's shoulder, signaling he was home. The driver rolled through mounds of fallen leaves to a stop, and Zach took a moment to take in the little white house with the wraparound porch and the two-person swing and tea chairs. The hens still had their place to cluck away through the coldest of winters and the most sweltering and unbearable of summers. Nothing had changed but the passage of time.

The taxi driver was already out, popping the trunk, retrieving Zach's bag, then slamming the trunk lid back in place. He paid the driver who in turn thanked him and then climbed back into his carriage and drove off. Zach stood there and watched the black and yellow churn the dry leaves up in the air as it made its way to the corner, turned, and disappeared. He held his stare for additional pleasing seconds while his lungs were sated by the heavy air. Then he heard a screen door slam shut behind him, followed by his Aunt Emma's familiar drawl.

"Zachary Ransom! I do swear, will you not ever get on this porch!"

There she is, he thought to himself. Then he turned to her and gave a wide smile. *God, I missed her!* he thought. Then he bounding up onto the curb, crossed the lawn then leapt three at-a-time up the porch steps, then dropped his bag and threw his arms around the woman who didn't necessarily raise him through his early childhood years but definitely helped him navigate the most challenging years beyond.

"I've missed this place! And you, Auntie!" Zach admitted. "I've missed you so much!"

"Now you settle, my child," Emma said through her tears. "You only miss those that you love, and I will take that all day long."

The two of them held still, reveling in their moment of the warmth and love they shared for each other. The shadowy figure behind the screen door held silent. Feeling emotions that she too hadn't been sure she would still feel, Jenny Mathews placed a readied tissue to her eyes. Not wanting to intrude on a special moment, she held back a few more seconds before stepping out.

Zach heard the squeak of the rusted hinges and turned to see. "Jenny?" he managed through his own emotion. "You're here!"

"Hello, Zachary," she said, waiting to see if he would show any sign that they still had something.

There was no hesitation in Zachary, though. Releasing his aunt, he went to Jenny, and they embraced, receiving each other like no one could ever come between them. A few more precious moments passed, then he lifted her chin and kissed her long and hard on the lips. Surprised but willing, she received him and realized that she always would.

"I've been thinking of you endlessly, Jenny," he whispered to her. "You're my girl and always will be," then Zach pulled back just enough to let her know that it was real. "I never should have let you go. I should have followed and stayed in contact. I am so sorry for that."

Jenny had words forming but couldn't manage to vocalize so she just smiled back like she fully understood and just didn't care anymore. They are here now.

Then a sudden rush came over Zach and he gently released Jenny and turned to his aunt. "Where's Mama?"

Emma stepped forward and placed both of her hands over his. "She's here, Zachary. Just inside."

Zach quickly turned, but Emma held him back. "Wait!" she cautioned. "Things have changed for your mother, Zachary. She's not well."

"Not well?"

"She's been stricken with that insidious disease and is seldom herself."

"What?"

"Ever since you rescued her, your mother, my sister had been doing well and adjusting to her new life. But then, about six months ago, just a short time after you went away, she just got tired. By the time we realized, the doctors said that it's in her brain now and nothing can be done."

Stunned with the news, Zach held still for a moment while processing the unexpected and devastating news. Then he gently pulled away and went inside. His mother had endured so much. And now that he was finally home to build on the relationship that they both had missed those eight years she had been away, everyone thinking she was dead, it was not to be. They both thought they would have time to fill the blanks in—but they were wrong. He found her in the corner rocking back and forth, a knitted shawl over her lap for warmth, and her eyes glazed over as lifeless as Whistler's mother. He went to her, knelt down, and stared into her eyes. There was no expression of joy or excitement, only a vacuum of indifference.

"Mother. Your son is finally here," he said lovingly. Then he laid his head softly on her lap and began to weep. "I am so sorry," he managed through his tears.

Emma entered the room, followed by Jenny. They held hands while watching from a distance the man they knew crumbling for losing the chance to have connected one last time. Then what some would call a miracle happened. Abigail Ransom slowly looked down at her son's head, then a few seconds went by when unexpectantly she lifted and placed one hand upon it and began caressing his dark locks.

CHAPTER TWENTY-SIX

FROM THE ASHES

Four months later - Los Angeles, California

The late afternoon had turned balmy with the October warmth a welcome surprise. A rising Santa Ana's now blew through the open sash, billowing the shear curtain like an uncontrollable ocean shore break. Fredrick Simonson sat on the edge of the bed naked as he was born, having spent the last hour contemplating where he was and where he was going to be at the end of his next move. He would be in no hurry.

The tenth floor of the lavish Biltmore had been a good landing spot, and he could do no better than the Los Angeles scene to be his base of operations. He fit in perfectly with the pretentious, narcissistic, and gullible creatures of the Hollywood A-list community. To that effect, he had already had minor run-ins with the likes of Cary Grant, Audrey Hepburn, and the Duke, whom, he quickly had surmised, had not been a fan of his Germanic accent, but nevertheless had bought him a drink based on his simple charm and audacity to approach him. The man was a mountain and as large as the big screen made him out to be. Yes, he thought, Los Angeles is the place I can be seen yet not be found. A place to set a new plan in motion. A place where revenge could be contemplated and possibly achieved. Those that thought they would be able to thwart one plan, to achieve winning the one battle, would not see him coming.

"Freddy?" came a sultry voice from behind.

Simonson stood, walked to the window, and stared down at the street below. He hated being called Freddy, but he could handle it for just one night. "Yes, my love?" he said. "And I'm hoping you will get used to the name Bruno."

"I know, I know. Something about giving up the old life, but when are you coming back to bed? Surely there are no demons that would prevent you from keeping me company."

The fugitive Simonson turned back to his most recent conquest and took her in. She, a voluptuous blond actress who had just finished her first substantial role in a film called the asphalt something—he couldn't remember. But more importantly, she had just been offered a seven-year studio contract the past week and was out to party. Through their mutual admiration of several well-constructed martinis, he had gleaned that she had been floundering the past four years doing modeling gigs and bit parts under a different name. But she had requested he just call her Norma—he didn't ask why.

She had been celebrating when he found her earlier at the lobby bar. The intro of a casual bump from behind and flowery apology got it going, followed by a light and flirty conversation being easy and fluid. The fun fact of both being redheads had made it flow while causing occasional glances from the other patrons that eventually cluttered the Hollywood establishment. She had mentioned that the studio execs wanted her to bleach her hair, and she had asked him what he thought. He remembered saying that she would be stunning in any color.

It had been clear that there had been a mutual attraction from the jump. At one point, she had asked if he was an actor and pretended to have seen him somewhere when he had said that he was. Small parts and some off-Broadway work, but nothing substantial, he lied. Neither had asked the other as to how they had reached their current status, or if it even mattered, both only agreeing that the journey had, and continued to be, treacherous. Two hours later, she had been the one to request a visit to his room to freshen up before a dinner that they never made it to. It had been just too easy. Now she lay splendid while nude between half coverings of linen. A perfectly sculpted masterpiece that had given herself to him freely with no presumed strings attached. Everything had been truth or a perception of truth, as he believed she had wanted him to think, but he had known better. He really didn't even believe the name she had given was real, but like so many in this godforsaken town, one did what they felt they needed to in order to succeed. He would follow her lead and be no different.

Simonson came back to her and sat on the bed while resting a soft hand on an exposed thigh. She flinched.

"Fredrick, your hands are cold!"

"Bruno, please. It's what I want."

"Okay," Norma pouted. "You said Bruno. Mr Bruno Wagner."

"You see. Not so hard," he returned as if speaking to a child even though she was certainly not that. "I'm sorry, my darling. You have my full attention now," he softly offered and meaning every word.

"I was just curious what you were wondering about," she said with the slightest hint of a southern drawl. "I'm all alone over here and feeling quite neglected."

"I suppose I'm in question of this Miller fellow you mentioned, and if he would be a concern to me."

Norma frowned. "Oh him, Artie. He's just a passing line between point A and B. I'm here now, aren't I?"

She was beautiful, but he had been with many beautiful women. But there was something else, something she had those others did not. She was smart, as others had shown to be, but this one seemed to purposely hide her intelligence for her ulterior goals. He liked that. She was obviously bold enough to have sex with a perfect stranger and, he assumed, as well as whomever sat on the other side of a casting couch. Could that type of person be trusted with more? Bruno thought for a moment about what it would sound like to tell this bombshell what he was really on about. But the best burglar or assassin always worked alone. Confident on his decision, he slid his hand up her inner thigh and rested it on her plump bottom.

"Oh, Mr Wagner…" she moaned.

"How could anyone neglect you?" he started sincerely while enjoying the indulgence. "It's just that

I've been working on a screenplay, is all, and I've hit a bit of a snag."

"Is there a part for me?" she purred, as if honey dripped from her full lips. "Can't you tell me about it?"

"Tell you about it?" he questioned, but secretly relished the idea. "Okay, then. It's really about a young man who disrupted a very lucrative scheme by a gentleman, not so unlike myself."

"Ha!" she laughed, "Meaning what?"

"You know. Intelligent and handsome," he said with a sly grin.

"Well, I'll give you that," she admitted. "So? This man. Who is he, and will he be speaking with a German accent?"

"Oh, yes. The person I'm having in mind," Bruno stated while quickly forming a familiar scenario. "No accent, but, well, he is somewhat of an anti-hero, or at least that is how he perceives himself. Now he wants the money and revenge on the young man."

"It seems very diabolical."

"I suppose so."

"And how does it end?"

Bruno took a long pause while sliding his hand further up and over her full hips and up her stomach, finally resting on one of her perfect breasts.

"Fredrick?" she said while allowing him. "How does it end?"

His desire rising, this was no time to correct the young lady. "I'm not quite sure, my dear," he said as she closed her eyes and arched the small of her back up to him. "I haven't written the ending as yet. But what I can say is that at some point in the story, someone *will* die."

End

ABOUT THE AUTHOR

Born and raised in So. Cal., Cristopher Mann has endured all the awesome things that this area of the world brings. Beaches, mountains, unbelievable entertainment and perfect weather. A successful contractor for many decades, he has finally found time to unleash his written voice that has been held captive for most of that time by family and work. Life has finally been pushed back for him to attack his passion—the written word.